The Yankee Years
Books 1 – 3

The Shadow Ally
Acts of Sabotage
Keeping Her Pledge

Dianne Ascroft

Contents

Foreword 5

BOOK 1:
The Shadow Ally 7

BOOK 2:
Acts of Sabotage 125

BOOK 3:
Keeping Her Pledge 259

About the Author 329

Foreword

During the Second World War American, British and Canadian troops streamed into Northern Ireland. County Fermanagh, a quiet, mainly rural county in the west of the province, welcomed Air Force squadrons that hunted U-boats and defended shipping convoys in the Atlantic Ocean and Army battalions training and preparing to be deployed to the Western Front on D-Day and in the ensuing months of the war. These men and women had a profound effect on the county and, after their arrival, life in Fermanagh would never be the same again.

The Yankee Years novels and Short Reads strive to bring those heady, fleeting years to life again, in thrilling and romantic tales of the era.

Mullaghfad Church in rural Fermanagh

BOOK 1

The Shadow Ally

Corey's Hotel, Irvinestown, County Fermanagh, Northern Ireland
Friday, 20th June, 1941

Ruth Corey regarded the black-haired young man sitting alone at the table in the corner of the dining room. Frank Long probably wasn't much older than her, but his serious expression added several years to his age. She hadn't met many Yanks before. Well, only her uncle George when he came home for her grandmother's funeral two years ago. Once the funeral was over, he was all smiles, laughing and chatting with everyone. She thought everyone in America must be like him, but maybe not. This fellow certainly wasn't. She'd barely got two words out of him when she brought him his breakfast this morning and introduced herself. Her mother had told her that he had checked in late last night. They didn't often have such young guests staying at the hotel.

He must have come to work on the new aerodrome. If he intended to stay at her family's hotel for a while, he could at least be pleasant, she thought.

Ruth carried the pot of hot water to Frank's table. "Will I heat up your tea?"

The young man glanced up at her and smiled. "No, thanks. I don't suppose you have any coffee?"

She couldn't help noticing his deep blue eyes. He looked younger when he smiled, and his eyes twinkled. "No, but Mummy's getting what passes for it today. Do youse only drink coffee?"

"Who?"

"Yan – Americans."

The creases at the corners of his eyes deepened. "No, but my family drink lots of it. And they like it strong. My Nana makes the best coffee in our neighbourhood."

"Where's that, then?"

"In New York."

"My uncle George lives in New York. Maybe he lives near you."

"Uhh, I don't think so –"

"How do you know?"

"Where's your uncle live?"

"Manhattan."

"That's a big place."

"He's somewhere around 44th Street. Well, I've heard him tell the lads that it's a place called

8

Hell's Kitchen. Mummy doesn't like him saying it out loud – it doesn't sound very respectable, but he says the neighbourhood is alright. He works at Penn Station." She found it hard to imagine what a city with so many streets would be like.

"Oh, right." Frank nodded at her but didn't speak.

Goodness, it wasn't easy getting him to talk. She had told him about her uncle, but he hadn't told her much about himself in return. She would love to know more but it would be rude to ask directly.

Ruth lifted Frank's empty plate and turned to leave. Another thought struck her; she paused, turning back to face the guest. "I hope you get your goods in okay so you can get started."

"Goods?" Frank frowned at her.

"Aye, wood and iron and whatever else you need. There's that many shipping vessels in the Atlantic attacked by the U-boats. You wouldn't want to lose them. With all the Yanks in the town, you'll want to make a start at it."

"I, uhh, I don't know what you mean. I'm here on some business."

"Aye, I know. Building the aerodrome at Ely Lodge."

Frank's eyes widened and his mouth hung open. He opened and closed his mouth a couple times then spoke in a strangled tone. "How do you know that?"

"Know what?"

"About any building plans?"

"Oh, everyone's talking about it. We're right glad the Yanks are here to help win the war."

"The United States isn't at war. I'm a civilian. I'm not involved in the war."

"But you're building a camp for the flying boats."

Frank's expression hardened and he glared at her. "My reasons for being here are my business. Maybe you should think before you speak."

Ruth felt like she was a small child who had been slapped. The heat coursed into her cheeks. She opened her mouth to make a sharp reply, but she knew her mother would be annoyed if she was impertinent to a guest. She gripped the plate she was holding harder and threw a glance over her shoulder before she hurried away. "Sorry, I didn't mean to offend you."

Ely Lodge, near Irvinestown
Later the same morning

The sound of heavy footsteps approaching drew Frank's attention. He looked up from the list he was checking. "The timber isn't standard lengths, but I've calculated what we've received. It looks like we've got what we need initially, Mr Orchard."

A short, squat, slightly balding man stopped beside the young man. "Good. It's not going to be like working on a job at home. We'll have to make do with whatever we can get. I'm hiring extra men to help clear the land so the building can start."

"Local men, sir?" Frank frowned at his boss, the civil engineer overseeing the project.

"Of course. How else can we get them in a hurry? It'd take at least two weeks to get more men from home." Bill Orchard gave Frank an appraising look. "You don't sound happy about the idea."

"Well, security is so important. How do we know we can trust them?"

"Most of them were recommended by our contacts in the British military. They worked on the RAF base down the road so they've already been vetted."

Frank nodded, a frown still creasing his brow.

"You don't look convinced." Mr Orchard raised an eyebrow.

"This is just such a big project to keep quiet. It's a good location, outside the town on the lakeshore surrounded by woods. You can't see it from the road and it's not very obvious from the water either. And we're only clearing the area that we need for the airbase. But, if too many local men get in here, it'll really make security difficult. I'd say the fewer who know about it, the better."

"It's a risk we have to take to get the job done. This is the first big project you've assisted on. You'll learn as you go that you have to balance the risks against the needs of a project." Mr Orchard regarded him for a moment. "But I appreciate your conscientiousness. I expect you to tell me if you notice anything that concerns you – any aspect of the job."

"Yes, sir. I will."

Mr Orchard looked around them at the partly cleared wood they were standing in. Saws whined at the edge of the clearing and a bulldozer trundled across the open ground. Men strode back and forth through the clearing.

"Except for the rain, you could think you were at home – upstate New York, not Ireland, couldn't you?" Mr Orchard smiled.

"I guess so, sir. I'm more familiar with the city. Never really been upstate."

"You're from the Lower East Side, aren't you?"

"Yeah, Little Italy. Family's been there since my grandfather came over from Naples at the turn of the century."

"You're not using your proper name here, are you?"

"Longo? No sir, I signed in at the hotel as Frank Long."

"That's good. Likely wouldn't be a problem but there's no telling how the locals might react to an Italian name. Better not to find out."

Frank nodded agreement. It seemed strange to give his name as Long, but it wasn't so different. He would get used to it easily enough.

"How's your accommodation? You're staying at that small hotel in Irvinestown?"

"Yes, Corey's Hotel. Family-run one. It's not exactly what we have at home, but it's clean and the food's good. The family seem nice, though the daughter's a bit too nosy."

"Oh?"

"At breakfast this morning she was asking me how things were going here. I'd never even told her I was working on the project. But she seemed to know all about it." Frank remembered the young woman's lively green eyes calmly directed at him. She had an air of guileless confidence. But it had been quickly shattered by his sharp rebuke.

Mr Orchard chuckled. "This isn't New York. It's a small place where everyone knows everyone. If there's any news it'll travel like wildfire. We have to do our best to maintain confidentiality. We don't want information about the base to get into the wrong hands. But we won't be able to hide completely that we're here. When you talk to her, don't give her any specific information and don't confirm or deny any rumours she's heard. Just be vague. The same goes for any of the local people you talk to."

"Yes, sir. I'll do that."

Mr Orchard nodded his approval. He tapped Frank's shoulder then strode away across the clearing. Frank returned to his checklist, but Ruth's face floated across the page. He wondered whether she had a boyfriend. He shook his head and exhaled sharply. There was a lot to do to get this project rolling. He needed to put Ruth Corey out of his mind.

Main Street, Irvinestown
Later the same day

Ruth hurried along the street, puffing. "Sorry I'm late! There's more washing up now with the new guests."

"I left the office half an hour ago. I was beginning to think you'd stood me up." Harry Coalter glared at her reproachfully. "After working late and the day I'm after, that would be the last straw."

"You know I wouldn't do that." Ruth rested her hand on his forearm and smiled at him. "Don't you even feel a bit sorry for me, scrubbing the pots?"

"Hmmph. At least there's no one to annoy you. Your mother leaves you to get on with it. The assistant editor is on my back all the time. After all the time I spent on my story about the problems the evacuees who have come here from

14

Belfast are facing, he said it wouldn't grab readers' attention. He says they want the sensational. Where will I get that around here?" He spat out the last sentence.

"Ah, I'm sorry. Your day doesn't sound like it was very good." Ruth linked her arm through Harry's and leaned against his side. She was used to him griping about his job. Working for a newspaper was stressful. But she hoped she would be able to turn the conversation away from his frustration and improve his mood so they could enjoy the evening. Her mother couldn't spare her from the hotel every Friday evening and she wanted to make the most of it.

Harry glared at her. "It wasn't. There's damn all to write about to interest readers in a town like this. What chance've I got? Writing about the Council's shortage of horses and carts, a fire in a sweet shop and the Women's Institute's fundraising for the war effort won't get me noticed by The Newsletter or any other city paper. I should've gone to work in Belfast. I'd even be better off at home in Londonderry."

"Why would you want to go to the city anyway? It's nicer here and you've lived here long enough you know most everyone now."

"The pay's better and that's where I need to be if I want to make a name for myself as a journalist – a serious one."

"Well, there's not much you can do about it tonight. Why not let it lie and enjoy the evening?

There's a dance on in the hall." Ruth avoided looking at him. She hoped she hadn't been too bold suggesting they go to the dance. Harry had asked her to meet him after he finished work but he hadn't said what he had planned for the evening.

She glanced up at Harry's thin, angular face. Even glimpsed fleetingly, it was impossible to miss his intense eyes. It was no wonder that people answered his questions when he interviewed them. They were probably afraid not to. He could be charming, though, when he wasn't consumed with one of his ideas. But, once he set his sights on a goal, he clung on fiercely, as if he were drowning and must latch on to save himself. Harry's boss, the assistant editor, was a much more patient man and never pressed anyone who didn't want to talk to him. The difference in their personalities didn't make Harry popular with his boss, and the two men rowed often.

Whenever Harry had had a row with his boss, he threatened to go to the city. Ruth hated it when he started to talk like this; it made her very uneasy. She had first met him when he came to lodge at the hotel and she was glad he had made it his home. They had been walking out for a couple years now, so she thought his intentions must be serious. But, she was happy in

Irvinestown and didn't want to go anywhere else. She wasn't sure she could follow him if he left.

Ruth sighed. She must put these thoughts out of her head so she could enjoy the evening. If only she could get Harry into a better mood. Maybe she could make him laugh. "We've some right quare guests staying at the hotel. All those Americans over here to build the aerodrome. Sometimes you can barely understand a word they say. Have you noticed them at breakfast?"

Harry stared straight ahead and didn't seem to have heard her, so Ruth tried again.

"They don't much like tea."

"Who?" Harry turned toward her, his brows knitted together as he regarded at her.

"The Yanks staying at the hotel. They only seem to drink coffee. Mummy had a devil of a time trying to find any in the shop. She couldn't get real coffee, just a substitute. Haven't you noticed them?"

"There wasn't anyone in the dining room when I had breakfast any morning this week. I didn't even see you." Harry gave her a reproachful look.

"Oh, I wasn't thinking. They start work early so I've their dishes cleared away before you come in. I've been washing the delph every morning after they leave then I start the rooms. Mummy's serving the later breakfasts."

"Americans, you said. Staying at Corey's?"

17

Ruth gave Harry an incredulous look and laughed. "You're a reporter. Don't you know what's happening in the place you live?"

Harry scowled at her, and she realised that was the wrong thing to say. She wouldn't help his mood by taunting him, especially about something like that. He was sensitive about his prowess for finding information and news.

"I didn't mean anything by it." Ruth smiled and squeezed Harry's arm. "It's just that there's been so much talk about them. When you go into any of the shops, the women are full of it. All these Yanks coming over here to build an aerodrome for themselves. And some of them are staying in our hotel." Ruth tried to keep the excitement out of her voice. It wouldn't do to make Harry think he had any reason to be jealous on top of everything else.

"I knew there were new guests in this week, but I hadn't paid much attention to them as I was on a deadline for a couple stories."

"Ah, well, I know you're busy. The work's never done at a newspaper. Some of the Yanks are rare ones. They'd make good stories in themselves with their odd ways. They like loads of milk and sugar on their porridge and have to have toast too. They're not careful with the jam either. We'll have a job feeding them, I'd say. Especially the size of them – some of them are huge." She raised one hand above her head to indicate their height.

"Hmmm."

Harry looked at Ruth but she could tell he wasn't really seeing her. She had better get him to the dance. Once he was inside the hall, hopefully, the music would make him forget his worries. She gripped his elbow and gently pulled him until he started walking in the direction of the hall. They were only about five minutes' walk from it.

"Most of the Yanks are friendly and chatty. But, there was one this morning that must have got out of the wrong side of the bed. When I asked him if they were getting in everything they need for the building, he just about jumped on me. He wanted to know how I knew about the aerodrome. Sure, everyone knows they're here to build it. And everyone knows how many goods are lost by attacks on the convoys coming across the ocean."

Harry turned to look at Ruth and, for the first time since they had met this evening, she thought he was actually paying attention to her.

"And, are they getting everything they need?" he asked.

"I don't know. He didn't say."

"What else did he say - about the aerodrome?"

She noticed that Harry was watching her face intently. He was finally listening to something she said. It was a shame that she had nothing interesting to tell him. The American hadn't told her anything. "He never answered my question.

19

And after the look he gave me, I didn't dare say aught more on the subject."

"Never mind him, then. It's a good thing the other lads aren't as bad. You said they were friendly. You might have more chat from them."

"Aye, they always seem in right good spirits and chat through their breakfast. Dinner too." Ruth was puzzled that Harry seemed happy for her to chat with the Americans. He didn't seem to mind at all. Since they had walked out together for so long now, he must be very confident that he could trust her. Maybe that meant he would soon ask her to marry him. At least his mood had improved. As they approached the hall and she heard music coming from inside the building, her spirits lifted. She would salvage this evening.

Corey's Hotel, Irvinestown
Early August 1941

As Ruth lifted the waste bin to empty it, a half-crumpled sheet of paper lying in it caught her eye. Harry's tight, hurried script filled the page. She set the bin on the floor, lifted the piece of paper and placed it on the dressing table before she tipped the contents of the waste bin into the bag she was holding and set it back beside the dressing table.

As she straightened up, she glanced at the piece of paper. Harry would have torn it up if he meant to discard it. He must have dropped it in the bin accidentally. It might be important. She would have to remember to mention it to him tonight. She anchored the paper with one hand while she smoothed the creases out with her other hand. As she glanced at it, phrases stood out and grabbed her attention: *American troops, aerodrome, operating capacity*. She knew she shouldn't nose through guests' personal belongings, but it was Harry's. She was walking out with him. Surely there was nothing he would hide from her. She scanned the sheet of paper more carefully. It seemed to be notes about the aerodrome that the Americans were building.

Why would Harry be making notes about that? And where did he get the information? He didn't seem particularly friendly with the American guests staying in the hotel. He hadn't even noticed them when they first arrived. She pursed her lips. Something didn't feel right about this.

Ruth turned away from the dressing table and began moving around the room, throwing the curtains open wide to let in the light, making the bed, hanging up the clothes draped across the chair and dusting the windowsill. Since the blackout began, curtains must always be closed before dusk each evening. Most people could barely wait to let the light in again each morning, but Harry didn't seem to mind the darkness. She stopped to glance around the room, checking everything was in order before she went on to the next room.

She followed the same routine in each room on the corridor, taking little notice of the details of individual rooms. She wasn't one to be nosy. It was just that one piece of paper that had caught her attention. When she was finished, she climbed the stairs to the second floor, carrying the broom, dustpan and the bag to empty the waste bins, and walked down the hall to the first room. She unlocked the door and stepped inside.

The room was well-ordered. The blankets on the bed were pulled up and tucked under the pillow. No clothes lay on the chair or the floor. The curtains were open wide, letting a shaft of light illuminate the middle of the room like a stage. She smoothed the bedclothes, emptied the waste basket and fastened the curtains to hooks in the wall to pull them away from the window. Although it didn't look as if it needed to be done, she brushed the bare floor.

She stopped and looked around her, checking whether there was anything she had missed. The room was neat as a pin. As she turned to leave her gaze fell on the dressing table. Two thick books with drawings of buildings on their covers were stacked on the left-hand corner. Sharpened pencils and a block of paper lay beside them. A pocketsize rectangular card with a neat crease down the middle of it lay in the middle of the surface.

Ruth leaned over to look at the card more closely. A photograph of Frank, the American builder, was glued on the front of it. It must be his identification card for his job. Maybe he had forgotten to take it with him this morning. She hoped he didn't need it today. She lifted the card and set it beside the paper and pencils. As she let go of it she noticed the name under the photograph. Frank Longo. That wasn't right. He had signed the hotel guest register as Frank Long. Longo sounded like an Italian name. But the Italians were fighting on Mr Hitler's side. It must be a mistake. Why hadn't he got it corrected? Maybe she should mention it to him. He might not have noticed. But then he didn't seem to like her to pry, so it might be best to say nothing.

Ruth straightened up and lifted her broom, dustpan and bag. She locked the room and moved on to the next one, hoping that there wasn't too much tidying needed in the last few rooms. She would love a cup of tea, even the substitute stuff. If she hurried, she might get down to the kitchen in time to catch her mother taking the bread out of the oven. Mummy was careful with the rations but she might let her have one slice with her tea.

***

"Thanks." Frank looked up and smiled at the young woman refilling his cup with coffee, or what passed for it. He had enjoyed his meal. Although it wasn't the best cut of beef, it had obviously been roasted slowly; it was tender and tasty. There was a pile of potatoes on the plate to go with it. His grandmother would approve of the meals he was getting here.

The young woman straightened up, gripping the handle of the coffee pot firmly. "Goodness, you Yanks like your coffee. It's not real, of course, but it's the best Mummy could get in the shop."

"I know. I guess I'll have to get used to it."

"Mummy tried but that's all she could get."

Frank held the young woman's gaze. He had learned that her name was Ruth. She was chatty, but now that he had known her for several weeks, he knew she meant no harm, so he was making an effort to curb his impatience with her. He needed to be pleasant to his landlady and her family since he would be here for a while yet. He had enough to occupy his mind without upsetting them.

"Don't worry. I know that there's lots that isn't easily available." Frank gave her a placating smile. He didn't want her to think that he was implying that they weren't providing well for their guests. He had only been here a little more than a month but it was obvious that, despite the availability of black-market goods at a price, rationing and shortages were having an impact on people's lives. He drew his eyebrows together as he considered an idea. "I might be able to get a tin of real coffee from –" He paused, staring at her. "Well, it doesn't matter where it's from. But I'll see what I can do. If I can, I'll give it to your mother for the hotel."

"That would be grand. We'd appreciate it. And you'd make several Yanks very happy." She glanced around at the other tables in the dining room and giggled.

Frank studied Ruth as she talked. She was an attractive young woman. Her hair was tied back tightly with a black ribbon. Behind the ribbon, it spilled down her back in brown waves. Her bubbly personality added to her attractiveness. She seemed to bounce when she walked as if she were riding waves spilling out from her unruly hair. But he had a feeling that there was more to her than just a sunny nature. He would bet that she could do anything that she set her mind to. She wasn't indestructible though. He ruefully remembered her mortified expression when he snapped at her for enquiring about his work the first morning he met her. After that first meeting, he had rarely spoken to her. It was obvious now, though, that he had overreacted. He would need to make an effort to be nicer to her from now on.

He wondered whether she had a boyfriend. He had noticed that she chatted with all the guests, and there was one local man that she seemed very friendly with. Oh well, it didn't matter, as he didn't really have time to think about girls while he was here. This was the biggest project he had worked on and it would be the making of his career if he did well. That's what he needed to focus on.

Frank started as he realised that Ruth must have been speaking. Her facial expression indicated that she was waiting for a response from him. He smiled apologetically and raised one eyebrow.

She didn't seem annoyed when she spoke again. "I guess you're flat out at work? I think half the lads in the county are on that job."

Frank hesitated and considered how to reply. The security of the project was paramount. He must be careful not to give away any important details, but he had realised weeks ago that hiding the existence of the aerodrome was completely impossible. It seemed that nearly everyone for miles around knew that it was being built. And a large number of the local men were working as labourers and delivery drivers on the job. He could safely chat with her about it as long as he didn't say too much. "Yes, there are a lot of the local men working on it. Do you know any of them?"

"I've heard a few of the lads from the town were hired. The Beacom brothers – there's three of them – are labouring."

Frank nodded but didn't comment.

"There's a right few of youse Yanks staying at the hotel. They all seem to be working out there. Are you the gaffer?"

"The what?"

"The gaffer – are you in charge? Only I hardly ever see you sitting with the others. You don't seem to be one of the lads."

Frank paused, deliberating what he should tell her. It probably didn't matter if she knew a little about him, without any details about his actual work.

"No, I'm not the boss. More like an assistant to the engineer in charge of the job. I keep an eye and make sure everything is going as it should."

Ruth nodded. "I guess everyone knows you, then."

"Yeah, I guess they do," he agreed. He had noticed that the people here always talked about who they knew in common and seemed to be trying to find connections between them whenever they met someone new.

"Then it wouldn't have mattered that you didn't have your ID card with you today."

Frank was surprised by the direction the conversation had taken. He had expected to be quizzed about the local men they had hired until she found men they knew in common. He drew his eyebrows together. "How would you know that?"

He noticed a pink blush spreading up her neck and into her cheeks.

"I was cleaning your room this morning and it was lying on the table. I saw it when I emptied the bin." She looked at him and glanced away again. "I don't nosy when I'm in guests' rooms. It was lying there."

"That's fine. I didn't mean to imply you were snooping."

Frank smiled at Ruth. She gave him a tight smile and headed to the next table to pour more coffee for its occupants. As he watched her walk away, he thought about her comment. She had noticed his ID card on the table. Had she looked at it closely? She didn't mention the discrepancy in his name. Had she seen it? His real name wouldn't matter to the American workers, but it might cause him problems with the British. He didn't want to deal with any hassles on that score. He had to focus on the job. Hopefully she hadn't noticed it.

He took another sip of his coffee and grimaced. It sure wasn't real coffee. He would make a point of bringing a tin of the real stuff back from the construction site tomorrow evening.

***

Ruth noticed that Frank was watching her as she stopped at the next table. She hoped he wasn't annoyed that she had mentioned his ID card. She didn't want him to think she would nose through his things. She wasn't like that. At least she didn't need to worry that Harry would be upset. No doubt he would be glad that she noticed he had almost thrown away notes that he probably needed. But why was he writing about the aerodrome? It was a puzzle that was niggling at her. Although everyone knew about it, it was supposed to be hush-hush. She had never seen any mention of it in the newspapers. To satisfy her curiosity she would ask Harry when she met him this evening.

Ruth glanced at the clock on the oak mantelpiece that surrounded the large open fireplace. Even without a fire burning in the hearth, the gleaming mantelpiece gave the room a homely and inviting air. It was past seven o'clock. She had better hurry to clear the dining room as the diners left.

For the next half hour she bustled back and forth from the dining room to the kitchen, lifting dirty dishes and carrying them to the kitchen sink where the extra girl her mother had hired to help in the hotel was washing up. As she moved around the dining room, she was aware of Frank still sitting at the table. Sometimes he glanced over at her. He was sipping the coffee she had poured for him and seemed lost in thought. Except for being a bit touchy about some questions, he was a nice fella and he had lovely eyes. She'd like to ask him more about himself but was never sure what might annoy him. Best not to say too much, as she didn't want to cause a row.

When she had cleared the last dishes away, wiped the tables and set them again for breakfast, Ruth hurried into the kitchen, untying her pinafore. She hung it on the back of the kitchen door.

"I'm away out now, Myrtle," she called to the girl at the sink.

"I'll be away myself by the time you get home. See you in the morning," Myrtle replied.

Ruth clipped up the stairs to her room. She quickly washed at the small sink in the corner and put on her good yellow blouse. Her brown A-line skirt was decent enough to go out in; she had been careful not to get it dirty while she worked. Bending down to peer into the mirror on the dressing table, she brushed her hair then dropped the brush onto the table with a loud clatter. She lifted her brown cardigan and purse and rushed out the door and down the stairs.

Although they hadn't arranged where to meet, she knew she would find Harry in the residents' lounge. He looked up from the newspaper he was reading and smiled at her as she entered the room. Unusually they were the only two in the room.

"It took ages getting cleared up tonight. I thought I'd never get away." Ruth bounced into the middle of the room and stopped. "Will I wait for you to finish reading the paper before we go?"

"No, I've seen most of it already. I've been stuck at my desk most of the day working on the last couple pieces for this week's edition. I'll be glad to get out and stretch my legs."

As Harry spoke, one of the American guests came into the room. Ruth gave him a big smile. She noticed that Harry's expression didn't change. He merely nodded at the other man.

"Lovely summer evening, isn't it?" Ruth said to the American.

"It's not bad. But, is this summer?" The American raised his eyebrows. "Where I come from, it ain't summer 'til it's 90 degrees outside and the horizon is swaying in the heat haze."

Ruth laughed. "Goodness, we don't often have temperatures like that! And I don't think I've ever seen a heat haze – only autumn fog."

"Golly, if that's all I can hope for I might be on the next boat home." The American laughed.

Harry gave him a tight smile then turned to Ruth. "We'd best be off."

Ruth nodded to the American as she followed Harry out of the room. She didn't speak until they were halfway down the street. "He was just trying to be friendly."

"They're irritating if you have to spend any time with them." Harry grimaced. "How do you stick their chatter?"

Ruth regarded Harry earnestly. "I have to be nice to the guests. We never had so much custom until the troops started arriving. Mummy and Daddy are much less worried now we have money coming in every week."

"Mmmm." Harry quickened his pace.

Ruth skipped to catch up with him. "You said you had a busy day at the paper today." She hoped the topic wouldn't worsen Harry's mood. "Did you get all your articles finished?"

"Aye. Just got the last one done in time for the proofreader to check before it went to the typesetters."

"It must be hard work being a reporter. You always have deadlines to meet. I don't think I'd like that at all."

"It's not the sort of work that would suit a woman. Too much pressure. You're best here with your family in the hotel." Harry smiled at her. Ruth met his gaze briefly then turned her head to look into the windows of the shops they were passing.

She wasn't afraid of hard work and she liked meeting the guests. She always did her best to make them feel welcome. She knew her family needed her in the hotel, but sometimes she thought she could do more to help the war effort. She knitted socks, rolled bandages and did fundraising with the Red Cross, but she still thought she could do more. So many service men and women had come to the county from England and overseas. Billets for the British troops and the American contractors were in short supply, and she knew their hotel was providing an important service housing them, but she wanted to do more. Doing something for the war effort outside the hotel would feel more like a real contribution than what she was doing. But she was sure Harry didn't want to hear about her frustration. He had enough to worry about at his own job.

She remembered Harry's messy room. He obviously was in a rush when he went to the office each morning. He was always under pressure. Thinking about this reminded her of the piece of paper she had retrieved from the waste basket this morning. Had he noticed it?

"Did you see the piece of paper I left on your table?"

Harry gave her a quizzical look.

"The one that had notes about the aerodrome written on it."

Harry glanced at her quickly then looked away. "Ahhh, oh yes, thank you. It must have fallen off the table." His gaze darted around the wide street as if he were looking for something. Keeping his gaze fixed ahead of him, he took a deep breath. "The evening's clear. Will we walk out of town a little way? Let's take the road to Necarne Castle."

"That's a grand idea."

It was one of Ruth's favourite walks. They continued briskly along the main street and headed out of the town, walking in silence for several minutes with Harry setting the pace. As they walked, Ruth's thoughts kept returning to that piece of paper. Why had he written those notes?

"That sheet of paper I put on your table –" Ruth turned to look at Harry as she spoke and was surprised to see him look away from her hurriedly. "Why were you making notes about the new aerodrome?"

"It was just a bit of scribbling I was doing while I was thinking about an article I'm working on." Harry still didn't meet her gaze.

Ruth had to skip again to keep up with him as he increased his pace. "That was a lot of detail for a bit of scribbling. Isn't it an odd thing to be thinking about?"

Harry snorted. "Never you mind. I don't expect you to nose around my room but, if you must know, it's for an article I'm thinking about writing. I'd be the first to cover the building of the new base."

"But, the papers don't report on that sort of thing. 'Careless Talk Costs Lives,' as the posters say. Surely they wouldn't run a story about the aerodrome? Frank doesn't even like me to ask him about how it's going." Ruth drew her eyebrows together. It just didn't make sense. Harry didn't usually put such effort into stories that weren't likely to be accepted by his editor.

"Well, I don't answer to Frank. And these small-town papers are behind the times. In the cities they want real news."

Ruth gave him a doubtful look but kept quiet. He knew much more about newspapers than she did, and he didn't like being corrected about anything. While she doubted that the big city papers would print stories that revealed secret war activity either, Harry wouldn't like her saying so. She couldn't see that it would help his career as he seemed to think it would. She stifled a sigh. Something else was bothering her too. Where was Harry getting information about the aerodrome from? Frank never mentioned any details of his work to her and none of the other American guests talked about it either. It was a mystery how Harry knew so much about it.

Ruth took a deep breath. There was no sense pursuing these thoughts. Harry didn't seem keen to talk about it and from experience she knew that if she continued to pester him, he would end up in a horrible mood and their evening would be ruined. It wasn't really her business anyway. She had best change the topic.

"What's Mervyn at?" she asked.

"Mervyn?" The corner of Harry's eye twitched.

"Aye. Mervyn Gormley. You were chatting with him outside Reihill's pub this morning when I passed you on my way to the butcher's."

"Oh, aye, he's grand. Never better." Harry seemed to be staring at something in the distance and Ruth squinted to see what he was looking at. She could see nothing of particular interest.

"I guess he's right glad to get work at the aerodrome. What's he think of it?"

"How would I know? I'd not be speaking to him about that."

Ruth thought his answer was rather sharp, but she knew better than to pursue a topic if it annoyed him. Best to change the subject.

"Can you believe we're into August? I don't know where this summer's going at all." Ruth smiled brightly at Harry, determined to make the most of their time together. "We'd best enjoy the evening while we can. The long nights will soon be here, and we'll be back to blackout curtains and stumbling around in the dark."

Harry nodded but his thoughts seemed to be elsewhere. At least he had slowed his pace. Ruth wrapped her hand around his arm and leaned in against him as they walked.

Ely Lodge, near Irvinestown
Tuesday, 9th September, 1941

Frank signed the delivery note and handed it back to the labourer. "Thanks."

"Everything okay with it, sir?" the man asked.

"Yeah. Everything's arrived, for once."

"You certainly need a lot of goods to build a place like this, sure you do." The man turned his head to look around him. "How much timber do you reckon it'll take?"

Frank frowned but kept his tone of voice neutral. "We should have what we need now the trees have been cut."

"That was a right big job clearing them out. It'll take a good measure of concrete to surface all that space. How much do you reckon you'll use? Will it suit any type of airplane?"

Frank scrutinised the man's face. Mervyn Gormley. The general labourer seemed to appear just about every time Frank turned around. He was always eager and helpful and chatty. Much too chatty. Frank was used to loud, boisterous family and friends. Little Italy, where he came from, was like that, and he'd found that the Irish were very sociable too. But there was something he didn't like about this man and his inquisitiveness. He didn't trust him but he couldn't say why. One thing was for sure, he had no intention of answering his question about what aircraft would be housed here and there was certainly no need for the man to know that the concrete area was intended as parking space for seaplanes when they were out of the water for repair.

"Well, it won't be much use to any plane if we don't get it built." Frank held the man's gaze until

Mervyn shuffled his feet and looked down at the ground. "Get some of the guys to help you shift this delivery over beside the rest of the supplies so it'll be out of the way."

"Right, boss. We'll have it done in no time." Mervyn raised his head and grinned before he walked back to the construction site.

Frank glanced at the delivery note again. It seemed in order, and he had checked himself that they had received everything on the list. He took a deep breath and huffed it out. He wished everything was so straightforward.

"Everything okay, Frank? Did we get the whole order?" Mr Orchard stopped beside him.

"Yeah, it's all there, sir. We're lucky after all the problems we've had with shortages. This load is fine."

Mr Orchard studied his face. "What is it, then? You look like something's on your mind."

"I don't know. Probably nothing. It's Mervyn Gormley."

Mr Orchard raised his eyebrows, waiting.

"That guy who just left me." Frank nodded his head to indicate whom he meant. Mervyn was sauntering through the construction site, casually glancing around as he went.

"There's just something about him that I don't like. He's always asking questions," Frank continued.

"It's good to have workers that are keen."

"But it's not about the job he's doing. He always wants to know details about the whole project. Something doesn't feel right about it."

"He's probably just curious. All the locals are."

"Maybe. But I have a feeling it's more than that. I just don't trust him."

"Well, if that's the case, tell him only what he needs to know, same as everyone else, and keep an eye on him."

Frank nodded.

"Once they have the delivery put away, come and find me, and we'll inspect the site. Check how the work's going."

"Will do, sir."

Frank watched his boss walk away. Mr Orchard was even-tempered and fair with all the men. He wasn't unduly suspicious but he wasn't stupid either. He wouldn't take any unnecessary risks with the security of the project. If he told Frank to keep an eye on Gormley, then he meant it. Frank made a mental note to keep tabs on the labourer from now on.

Frank turned his attention back to the construction area. Nonchalantly resting his weight on his left leg, Gormley was standing in the centre, talking to one of the men. His manner suggested that he was chatting rather than recruiting men for the task he had been assigned. Frank stared at Gormley for a full minute until the man seemed to feel his supervisor's eyes on him. The labourer glanced over his shoulder at Frank then hurriedly finished his conversation. As Frank watched, Gormley shouted to three men nearby to follow him; then he strode across the site to where the order was stacked.

Frank watched for several minutes while the men began shifting the materials to the supply area. Once he was satisfied that they were working, he went to the office to file the delivery note. He would check on them again in half an hour to see how they were getting on. He shoved his hands into his trouser pockets as he left the office. Pausing on the step, he looked left and right as he debated where his boss might have gone. He decided that Mr Orchard would likely be checking progress on the area at the water's edge that was being concreted. It needed to join seamlessly with the underwater slipway so that the seaplanes could be easily manoeuvred in and out of the water. He walked down the steps of the building and headed toward the lough.

"Mr Long –"

Frank heard the name called a second time before it registered that the man was talking to him. It still seemed strange to have workers calling him Mister, and Long wasn't quite Longo. He looked at the young American technician. "Yes?"

"Some of the guys asked me to speak to you." The young man seemed nervous.

"Okay." Frank tried to keep his expression neutral. Mr Orchard was always approachable, and he wanted to establish the same rapport with the workers.

"When we came over we didn't think it would be like this."

"Like what?"

The man waved his hand around him. "This – nothing here. Nothing to do after we knock off for the day."

"You can go into Irvinestown to the theatre, and there's movies at the RAF base at Castle Archdale. Don't they have dancing both places too? There's always transport to them."

"Yeah, but I'm from Chicago. It's not the same thing."

"I'm from New York so I know what you mean. It sure isn't the city, but it's not all that bad. Give it a chance. And if you guys keep up the pace we're going the job'll be finished before Christmas. You'll be back to the city lights before you know it. It'll be a swell Christmas at home. Tell the guys to keep meeting the targets and it'll get them outta here faster."

The technician looked glum. "Maybe it wouldn't be so bad if it didn't rain all the time. We're sick of being cold and wet."

"Remember – it's not for long. You'll soon be finished with the job and back Stateside. Aim for that."

The worker gave him a reluctant nod before he walked away. By the way the young man slouched, Frank knew that he hadn't really been motivated by the pep talk. What was Mr Orchard's secret for inspiring the workers? He would need to watch and figure it out. As Frank stood thinking about this, his boss walked toward him from the lough. Frank turned to check that Gormley and the other men were still unloading the delivery then hurried to meet the older man.

"I was just coming to find you, sir. That order will be completely stowed away soon."

"Good. What did he want?" Mr Orchard nodded toward the worker who was walking away from them.

Frank followed his gaze. "Some of the guys sent him. They're bored here."

"Did they expect it to be New York?"

"Maybe. I guess some of them have never been anywhere so small before. I reminded him there's stuff to do in Irvinestown and they are welcome at the RAF base."

"We'll have to keep an eye on the mood among the men. If they're unhappy, they'll get into trouble. I won't tolerate rowdy crews that fight among themselves or annoy the locals. We're here to do a job, not give America a bad name. Talk with the men every day and get a feel for their mood."

"I will, sir." Frank stifled a groan. The job was enough responsibility. He hoped that he wouldn't have to babysit the American technicians too.

Town Hall, Irvinestown
Friday, 12th September, 1941

Ruth tapped her foot in time to the music. She didn't know why Harry was in such a good mood tonight, but she was happy he had suggested they come to the dance. They had had a fantastic evening. Harry seemed almost carefree for once. He had hardly talked about his work at all.

"Shall we?" Harry held his hand out and led Ruth onto the dance floor for the last set of waltzes.

She leaned against his shoulder as "A Nightingale Sang in Berkeley Square" began. She loved the song. It was so romantic. Maybe one day after the war was over she might visit London and see where the square was. Hopefully it wasn't one of the places that had been ravaged by bombing. She was so lucky to live here away from the worst bits of the war. Often, as she went about her daily routine, it was possible not to think about the really horrible things that were happening; they seemed so far away.

"We don't do this often enough." Harry pulled her closer to him.

Ruth nodded against his shoulder but refrained from pointing out that they rarely went dancing because he always seemed to be working lately. Most evenings they went for a walk after dinner, and then he either went to his room to write notes for an article or went to the pub. He said it was important to make contacts in his line of work. And it seemed the only place you could find these contacts was in the pub. He spent more of his time with Mr Rehill, the publican, and his customers than he did with her. But she didn't want to complain and spoil their upbeat mood.

"I love the new songs the bands have been learning since the war started. All these places far away that they sing about." Ruth sighed.

"Aye, the new songs – there've been lots of changes in the last couple years. All those soldiers and airmen over from England and now all the Yanks working at Ely Lodge. You must have some interesting conversations with the ones staying at the hotel."

"I don't get too much chance to talk to them. I mostly see them when I'm serving breakfast and tea." Ruth laughed. "But, it is a change from talking about the harvest and the price of cattle at the market."

Harry laughed. "What do you know about the price of cattle?"

"Not much, but yon farmers talk about it without stopping for breath when they call in for their dinner on mart days."

As the last waltz in the set ended, Harry spun her around and gave her a squeeze before he released her. "We'll waltz home tonight."

Ruth giggled. "Mind you don't waltz us into a wall in the dark!"

As they left the hall, she was still smiling to herself, imagining the two of them waltzing along the street to the hotel. Several other young women she knew called goodnight to her as they passed. Ruth raised her eyebrows as Harry draped his arm across her shoulders and pulled her to his side. He was very bold tonight. Of course, everyone knew they were walking out together, but he wasn't usually so forward on the main street.

"I hope that Yank, Frank –"

Ruth giggled at the rhyme. Harry looked at her quizzically then laughed too.

"Maybe I didn't put that well. How's he been with you? No more rudeness?"

"No, he's grand. I shouldn't have asked him prying questions when I first met him."

Harry squeezed her shoulder. "You were just chatting. There was no need for him to be huffy about it."

"Well, he's grand now. He even makes an effort to chat sometimes." Ruth remembered Frank's polite smile and warm blue eyes. He was a nice lad and very handsome.

"The least he can do is be civil." Harry paused and looked at her out of the corner of his eye. "I imagine he's right busy in his job."

"I don't know – I guess so. He does seem to be deep in thought over breakfast. Then he hurries out when he's finished eating."

"Wonder how the work's going?" Harry looked intently at her for a moment before he slid his arm down to her waist and pulled her closer.

Ruth shivered. She didn't like the look he had given her. He was making her feel uncomfortable, but she wasn't sure why. Other than putting his arm around her, he hadn't done anything that could be seen as too forward. She had noticed Mrs Beacom behind her net curtains as they passed her house. The older woman stepped back from the window as they passed but not before Ruth spotted her. Ruth's mother always said that it was a great advantage to Mrs Beacom to live in a house with a front door that opened directly onto the footpath on the main street. Her house was flanked by a medical hall and one of the new eating houses that had appeared since the troops arrived. Most of the town passed her door and she rarely left her vantage point by the window so she wouldn't miss a thing that happened. But Harry hadn't done anything that would scandalise her. She wouldn't be telling Ruth's mother what she didn't already know: Ruth had been out dancing with Harry tonight. She decided to put the woman out of her mind and turned her attention to Harry's question.

"I don't know. He doesn't talk about it."

"Not even the odd comment?" Harry watched her carefully.

Maybe it was the way he was looking at her that was bothering her, rather than his actions. But what did the look mean? Was he worried that she might be getting too friendly with Frank? He should know she would never do that.

"No doubt the other lads there aren't as standoffish as he is," Harry continued.

"They chat and laugh all the time. Mostly about their nights out. They like the dances and the pubs. Some of them go to the pictures too."

"And they talk about work as well?" He was still looking at her.

"Not really. They seem more interested in going to dances and meeting the cutties." Oh dear, why did she say that? Now he would think that one of the workers might have an eye for her. She stifled a sigh.

"Well, if you hear any chat about the aerodrome, let me know. After all the research I've been doing for my article, I'd like to know how it's going." Harry smiled at her and kissed her on the cheek.

Ruth hesitated. "Umm, alright. It looked like you had lots of information for your article on that piece of paper. Are you still researching it?"

"It's always best to have up-to-date information."

"When do you think it'll be printed?" She tried to push aside the uneasy feeling she had. Harry must know what he was doing, but she still couldn't understand why the *Fermanagh Times* would publish an article that likely contained information that shouldn't be released.

Harry waved his hand in the air. "It's always difficult to say with these things. That's up to the editor."

No matter how she tried to rationalise it, this article he was writing made her uneasy. After all the government warnings she had heard about protecting military secrets, Harry planned to write about one. It just didn't seem right. She pursed her lips and hesitated a moment before she spoke. "But I thought the *Times* didn't write about the military camps. You know, like it says on the posters, 'The Enemy Is Listening'."

"They don't have a clue about what's safe to print. Besides, they aren't the only ones who might be interested in my information – uhh, story."

Ruth's chest tightened and she had to force herself to breathe normally. Harry would think she was a hysterical female if she started ranting at him. But she didn't like his attitude at all. She whipped her head around and stared at her fella. Harry returned her gaze but his expression was inscrutable. Was he annoyed that she was questioning his decision to write the article?

As they passed the second medical hall on the main street, separated from the first chemist by a commercial hotel, Harry tightened his grip on her shoulder and steered her to the left, into an entry to a yard behind the main street. Ruth stiffened. What would anyone think if they noticed the couple turn off the street? She didn't want staff in shop doorways and women in the houses along the street to stare at her as she passed them tomorrow morning on her way to the butcher's shop. It wouldn't take much to get a bad reputation. Once they were out of sight, folk would imagine all sorts of things.

"Harry – where are we going?" Ruth pushed back against his arm to stop him going any further. "Mrs Beacom was at the window when we passed."

"Never mind that old biddy. I just want a few minutes alone with you. The hotel's so crowded these days. We'd have more time alone in the train station." He reached down and kissed her gently on the lips.

Ruth let him do so but didn't return the kiss. The image of Mrs Beacom at the window niggled at her. It shouldn't really matter, as Harry was sure to propose to her soon, but, still, she didn't want any talk about her.

Harry wrapped both arms around her and kissed her again. Ruth tried to relax, but she couldn't shake off her unease about who might have been watching them and the conversation they had just had. Too many thoughts were going through her mind. She needed time to sort them out. She tightened her arms around Harry's waist briefly then let go.

"I'd best get back and help Mummy bank the fires for the night. No doubt she's been darning and knitting all evening and she'll be tired." Ruth stepped away from Harry and turned toward the main street. She heard him huff but ignored it, hoping that he would shake off his annoyance before they returned to the hotel.

In the darkness she was surprised to see the silhouette of Harry's head nodding agreeably before he wrapped his arm around her waist again and steered her to the street. "Aye, you're right. You'll need your sleep too. You don't want to be tired and grumpy in the morning. Those Yanks will want to chat with a friendly girl."

Ruth let Harry lead her back to the main street. Before they emerged from the entry, she looked in both directions to check whether anyone would notice them reappear. Several servicemen were walking arm in arm with their girls along the street, but she didn't recognise any of the couples. Two men were standing outside Rehill's pub, but they didn't take any notice of her and Harry. It was likely too dark for them to identify the couple anyway. At least her reputation wasn't in danger. Nevertheless, the evening had turned sour for her. If only Harry would drop the daft idea of writing about the new American airbase. And she didn't like him pressing her to get the Yanks to talk about their work. She would just ignore his pleas and hope he wouldn't ask again.

Main Street, Irvinestown
Thursday, 18th September

"Morning, Ruth. I thought you might be in town this morning."

Ruth turned her head to find out who was speaking and drew in her breath when she saw the black hair and smiling face. His eyes seemed to shine as he looked at her. But what was Frank doing on the main street at this time of the morning? He had left for the construction site as soon as he finished his breakfast.

"Out on your errands?" he continued.

Ruth drew her eyebrows together as she regarded him. The Yanks had some quare expressions. What was he talking about?

Frank seemed to notice her confusion. "Are you doing some shopping?"

"Uhh, oh yes. With the rationing, I need to get to the butcher's early as there's bound to be a

51

queue. And Thursday's half day as well. I need to get all my messages done before the shops close at dinnertime."

Why was he in town? Once he left for Ely Lodge each morning she didn't usually see him until tea time. She opened her mouth to ask him then stopped herself. Harry's entreaty to find out what she could about the work at the aerodrome flashed through her mind, and she tensed. What she didn't know she couldn't tell Harry. She wasn't sure why she felt so strongly about this, but she did.

She pulled her basket in against her waist, grasping the handle tightly. "I must get on." She moved to step around him but he stopped her.

"Can I help you?"

"Oh no, don't worry. I'm grand." She wanted to end this conversation before she learned anything that she might have to hide from Harry. She stepped to the left in order to walk around Frank, but he rested his fingertips on her arm. Her heart beat faster as he smiled at her.

"Where's the butcher's?" he asked.

She pointed to the end of the street. Although there was another butcher closer to the hotel, she always bought their meat from Mr Thomas's shop. He was generous with portions and, since the hotel was a steady customer, he always kept decent cuts of meat for them.

"I'm heading that way too. I asked at the grocery store across the street and they said I might find Andy Noble out that way. I stopped by his farm but he wasn't there."

"Aye, his brother's not far out the road. Just at the edge of the town. He's often there." She wondered why he was looking for the farmer. Andy Noble owned a small farm not far from the town. The land wasn't very good, and he did whatever odd jobs he could find to supplement his income in order to make a living. Maybe Frank wanted to hire him to work on the aerodrome? But many of the local men were looking for work there. Why would he seek out Andy? She forced herself not to ask. It was better not to know things that Harry could pry out of her.

Frank lifted the basket from her grip and, dangling it at his side, he nodded toward the end of the street. "Let's go, then."

With a quick glance at Frank, Ruth fell into step beside him, her head down and shoulders hunched.

"I really hope I haven't done anything to offend you. I thought we've been getting along well the past few weeks, but you seem very uneasy this morning."

"No, I'm grand. I –" Ruth wished she could tell him about Harry's quest for information about the aerodrome but that would be disloyal to the man who was almost her fiancé.

53

As they passed a greengrocer's shop, two women standing in front of a barrel of apples greeted them. The pair returned their greeting. Ruth was aware that the women were watching them as they continued along the street. From the corner of her eye, Ruth saw Frank glance back at the women before he turned toward her. A pink flush deepened on his cheeks.

"Oh gosh, I never thought about the gossips in town. Will I cause you trouble with your boyfriend?"

Ruth could feel the heat rising in her cheeks as she met his concerned gaze. He really was a nice lad. Although it would be best to avoid spending too much time with him, she was enjoying his company. She slowed her pace and hoped Frank wouldn't notice her deliberate action.

"I wouldn't mind the gossips. They'll always latch onto something." Ruth avoided answering his question about Harry. What harm was there in chatting with Frank in full view of everyone on the main street? "Does your Nana live with you in America?" She saw his eyes widen in surprise. He probably didn't expect her to remember a small detail which he had mentioned to her two months ago. Oh dear, she hoped he didn't think she was keeping note of things he said. He had been so suspicious when he first arrived.

The smile settled back onto Frank's face as he answered her. "No, she and Nonno, my grandfather, live just down the street from us. My whole family lives within a couple blocks of each other. I'm one of the youngest, so I was at home with my parents."

"Have you many brothers and sisters?" Ruth felt encouraged by his openness.

"There's seven of us. Two of my sisters, who aren't married, and I were living with my parents. My sisters are still at home. I always worked in New York before this."

"A town like this will not be what you're used to, then."

"You can say that again! Golly, it's nothing like New York. I'd never really spent much time in the country before."

Ruth wanted to ask him what New York was like, but she didn't want him to think she was too inquisitive. They walked a few yards in silence.

"I guess you know Andy Noble?" Frank asked.

"Aye, everyone knows everyone about here."

Frank gave her a keen look. "What's he like?"

Ruth wasn't sure how to reply. She had known Andy Noble all her life, but what was there to tell? "He's a decent sort. Lives on his own at the farm and keeps to himself most of the time. Quiet, like."

"Sounds okay for a contractor."

Ruth had the impression that he was talking to himself, but she replied anyway. "He's just a small farmer and handy if you need a job done.

Do you want him to do a job for you?" She wished she could take back her last question as soon as she said it. To her ears, she sounded very forward.

"Do a job?" Frank looked puzzled.

"He's a good man for odd jobs." Why did she say that? Surely, they didn't need someone to do odd jobs at the aerodrome site. Ruth wished he would just forget her question.

"Is he honest and a man to keep his word? Not someone with a loose mouth?"

"Aye, I'd say he is. I've never heard a word spoken against him."

"That's the kind of man I need."

What did he need Andy Noble for? She really wanted to ask him. She drew in her breath as a terrible thought occurred to her. Did he want the farmer to do something that he wanted to hide? He wasn't telling the truth about his real name. She'd seen it on his ID card. Was he up to some badness?

"What's his farm like?"

Ruth raised her eyebrows. What a strange question. How could she describe the farm? It was just an average small farm. Nothing remarkable about it. "It's just a wee farm. A few fields. He keeps some cows and a couple pigs. Not the best ground for grazing, though. Too rocky."

"That sounds good."

She tried to hide her surprise. "It's a shame for him that he doesn't have better land."

"Well, that'll be to his advantage now." Frank looked at her for a moment. "Keep it to yourself, but I don't think it'll hurt to tell you that I'm going to see him about buying stone from him. He's got limestone there that can be quarried. We're looking everywhere for any rock we can get."

Ruth didn't realise that she had been holding her breath until she exhaled. She was relieved that there was a good reason that Frank was asking about the Noble farm. She drew her eyebrows together as she thought about this. Why should it matter to her what he did? Frank was only a guest in the hotel. It was nothing to do with her. But he was so nice. She felt warm when he smiled at her. She didn't want him to be involved in anything dishonest. Maybe one day she would mention the name on his ID card and ask him about it.

"Don't worry. I won't say a word about it."

"Thanks. It's not easy to keep anything quiet around here. Sometimes I think the residents of Irvinestown know about most things at the base before I do." Frank turned to her and smiled.

"Aye, they may well do." Ruth returned his smile, hoping the heat she felt in her face wasn't obvious to him.

"They don't miss much, anyway."

"And if they do, they ask."

Ruth noticed Frank's eyes narrow and his gaze suddenly seemed intent.

"Who's been asking?" he said.

"Well, you know how people talk. Even Harry's asked me a few questions." Ruth felt her face get hotter. She hadn't meant to say that. It had just slipped out.

"What sort of questions?" Frank's gaze never left her face.

"Nothing really – just about how the building's coming along." She wished she hadn't raised the topic. Harry would be annoyed if he found out she had told Frank about his interest in the aerodrome. And she didn't want Frank to think badly of Harry. "He was getting facts together for a newspaper article he's going to write."

Frank's eyes widened and his mouth dropped open as he stared at her. "Newspaper article? He can't write about the base! Do you have any idea what that could do? The States isn't at war. If Germany finds out we're preparing for war, that will be our neutrality finished. We'll enter the war on our own terms, when we're ready. Not because they push us into it."

Ruth shrank away from the ferocity of his words. If only she had been more careful with what she had said. Now Harry and Frank would both be upset with her. Her chest felt tight as Frank's words sunk in. She had always known that Harry shouldn't write about the aerodrome and she had reminded him about the government posters, 'Careless Talk Costs Lives'. But the enormity of the damage that he might do hadn't fully occurred to her. Her stomach rolled as she thought about it.

"I'm sure he wouldn't give away secrets. He's not like that. And the paper he works for wouldn't print anything they shouldn't. Maybe he's getting the information so he can write about it later – if America joins the war. I'm sure that's it." She decided that she had better not tell Frank about Harry's assertion that he would take his story to a larger paper in the city. That would only make things worse. She would have to talk to Harry and convince him not to pursue the story about the aerodrome. And even if he didn't heed her, surely no newspaper would print a story that would endanger the Allies' cause?

"I'll have a word with him and see that he doesn't write it." Frank's jaw was set in a determined line as he stared at her.

Ruth sucked in her breath and hunched her shoulders inwards under his gaze. "Oh, that's not necessary. I'll speak to him."

Frank paused and seemed to be thinking. He exhaled slowly. "Okay but I'll have a word with my boss. I think we may have to go through official channels and remind the newspapers where their duty lies during wartime."

"That might be best." She barely raised her voice above a whisper. She was relieved that Frank wouldn't confront Harry. Hopefully, if Harry heard that the newspaper had received an official warning, he would have no idea what had sparked it. She would avert a row with Harry and the *Times* would be dissuaded from printing any stories about the new airbase. And she might still have a chance to convince Harry to abandon the idea of selling the story to the city papers. Everything would work out in the end. Meanwhile, she had better be vigilant. As much as she might hate prying, she would have to keep an eye on any notes Harry left in his room to be sure he wasn't still pursuing the story. Maybe she could even think of some other topics he might write about. He would be pleased she was taking such an interest in his work.

Ruth stopped in front of Mr Thomas's shop and extended her hand, pointing to the end of the street. "If you carry on to the end of the street and turn right, Andy Noble's brother lives about six doors from the end of the road. The one with the red door. Thanks for carrying the basket for me."

She retrieved the basket and gave Frank a wide smile before she stepped into the butcher's shop, hoping that she had allayed his worries. She would watch Harry's mood during the next day or two and would soon know whether Frank had spoken to him or not.

***

"Yon road. That's it." Andy Noble pointed to the right.

Frank gripped the steering wheel tightly as he turned off the main road onto the one Mr Noble indicated. The Morris van bumped along the uneven surface.

This is hardly a road! It's barely a track. There's enough rocks on it to get the gravel we need without quarrying for them. It was certainly nothing like any road Frank had ever driven on in New York, but it wasn't the first one that he had seen here. He clenched his jaw and continued until he reached a small cottage set in front of a farmyard.

Andy Noble leaned back in his seat and looked around the interior of the van. His lips curved slightly into an appreciative smile. "Beats walking out the road, son. Ta for the lift."

Frank cringed at the familiar form of address. The farmer might be old enough to be his grandfather, but this was a business transaction. He wouldn't let the man patronise him.

"That's okay, Mr Noble. I hope we'll be able to do business. But first I need to have a look at the stone you've got here."

The older man nodded and climbed out of the van. "Would you like a cup of tea, son, afore we go up there?"

Frank stepped out of the van and leaned his hand on the roof. The country was at war so you'd think this farmer would understand the urgency of the work. But, you just couldn't get some of these people to move quickly. He'd already learned to his detriment that, except at the construction site, you couldn't compel them to hurry up. As they would say here, much like a donkey, the harder you pushed, the slower they moved.

"Thanks but maybe after we take a look at the stone. Will you show me where it is?" Frank lifted his hand off the roof of the van and straightened up as he spoke.

"Right, then." Mr Noble pulled a package of tobacco out of the pocket of his threadbare wool jacket, tore off a piece and put it in his mouth. He began to chew in a slow, regular motion as he walked into the farmyard.

Frank followed the older man through the farmyard and out to a field where several cows were grazing, unconcerned about their presence. They passed through two more fields, rising in a gentle slope, before they came to one that ended in a steep bank at the far end. When he got close enough to get a good look at it, Frank noted that there were loose rocks lying at the foot of the slope and the grass and earth had been dug away from a section of the bank to reveal limestone beneath the surface. He inspected the exposed area. The stone looked to be of sufficient quality to make concrete. They couldn't be too picky, as they needed as much stone and sand as they could get.

"Yeah, that looks okay. We could use it," Frank said. "When can you get it quarried and deliver it?"

"Well now, I'm a farmer, not a miner. And I wouldn't be fit to dig it out at my age. I'm on my own here." The old man shrugged his shoulders.

Frank frowned. It would save him time and effort if the farmer could do the work, but materials were in short supply and they needed all the gravel they could get so he couldn't turn it down. By the look of it, it wasn't a large piece of rock. He could send a bulldozer, a truck and several men out to the farm and they should be able to dig out the rock in a day or two.

Frank nodded slowly. "Okay. I'll see if I can spare some men and I'll get them over here to quarry it. We'll pay you by the truck load we cart away."

"That'll do grand. You're welcome to it."

The old farmer spit into his palm and extended his hand to Frank. The younger man stared at the farmer's outstretched hand, surprised until he remembered that this was how local people sealed a deal. He spit into his own palm and clasped Mr Noble's hand.

"It's a deal, then, Mr Noble. Thank you."

"My wee brother fought in the Great War and our Roy's away fighting now. So I want to do what I can to help."

"Your son?"

"No, he's my brother's coddy. Good, steady lad. God keep him."

Frank couldn't help liking the man. He was sure the farmer could use the money he would earn from selling the rock, but it wasn't his only reason for agreeing to the deal. Frank had quickly learned that you had to be on your toes to determine who welcomed the American contractors for the money they could make from them and who had more honest, patriotic motives. He knew the arrival of the Americans was helping the local economy, but he didn't like dealing with those who only saw the money they could make. That was just profiteering. He preferred honest, decent people.

"We appreciate your help, Mr Noble. Your country and mine need people like you. As I said, I'll send some men over early next week. They should be able to quarry it in a couple days at most."

The old man nodded. "That'll do grand."

Frank stared into the distance as he thought for a minute. He would send one of the American bulldozer drivers with several local men to do the job. He needed to keep as many skilled men on the main construction site as possible. "I'll send one of my bulldozer drivers with Mervyn Gormley and a couple others."

Mr Noble made a grunting noise deep in his throat and looked at the ground.

"Is there any problem with that?"

The old man frowned as he shook his head. He chewed hard on the tobacco. "I suppose not."

"You don't seem happy about something." Frank watched the older man carefully. He had found that local people often didn't say what they were thinking directly and he was left trying to guess what they meant or what the problem might be.

"You've Mervyn Gormley working for you?" Mr Noble lifted his head to look at Frank.

"Yes, he's a labourer in charge of a small work crew."

"Hmmph."

"Is that a problem?"

"It's not for me to say, but I wouldn't let him mind my hens. He'd probably be working with the fox."

Frank's chest tightened as he considered what the older man had said. He had wondered whether he was being too suspicious about Gormley's motives when the man constantly asked questions, but maybe his suspicions weren't unfounded; it seemed that Mr Noble might have some knowledge of the man's character.

"You don't trust him, then?"

"It's not for me to say but he's one to watch. Never had anything but wanted as much as he can get."

"Money's what drives him?"

"It's not a sin to want to earn a decent living, but some would do anything for a few bob."

"And Gormley's one of them?"

"I don't know that for a fact. I just wouldn't turn my back on him. You want sharp eyes with him about."

Frank made a mental note to keep an eye on the stores. They were having enough trouble getting materials with cargo ships crossing the Atlantic Ocean being sunk by the U-boats. He didn't need supplies to go missing once they did get them. The black market was a thriving business. No doubt someone like Gormley could make good money trading on it. Was that why he was always asking questions about the job? It would explain a lot. If he knew a bit about the building plans, he might be able to figure out what supplies were expected and he could make deals before they even arrived.

"Thanks for the heads-up, Mr Noble. I appreciate it. I'll send the bulldozer and men over to you early next week."

"Right-o. I'll be about."

Corey's Hotel, Irvinestown
Wednesday, 15th October, 1941

During the past few weeks Harry had been his usual self, complaining about his lack of recognition at the newspaper and searching for an article to write that would draw attention to his talent. He didn't seem to have found an idea to replace the aerodrome project story, but he didn't seem unduly worried about it. At least he was in a good-natured, though rather preoccupied, mood.

Ruth hadn't noticed anything out of the ordinary in Harry's room when she tidied it each day. She felt rather disloyal poking through his personal possessions, especially as she couldn't say there was a good reason for it. But she had a strong suspicion that Harry might do something foolish if she didn't keep an eye on him. He worked so hard. She didn't want him to do something that could get him in serious trouble and ruin everything he had achieved.

She bent down and emptied the contents of the waste bin into the bag she held then stood up and straightened the papers on the table. She glanced quickly through them. There were some notes for a couple articles he had mentioned to her and receipts for expenses. But nothing that she should worry about. After she had mentioned the notes about the aerodrome to him, that piece of paper had disappeared from the table. She hoped that he had disposed of it.

She lifted a shirt that was lying on the chair beside the bed. It could be worn at least once more before it would need to be washed. She slipped it onto an empty hanger and hung it on the rail in the wardrobe. As she did so, the jacket hanging next to it fell to the floor. With a sigh, she lifted the jacket then reached for the hanger it had fallen from. As she slid the wire hanger into the garment, a piece of paper brushed her hand. She lifted it from the inside jacket pocket and unfolded it.

Quickly scanning the page, she realised that it was a letter Harry had started to write. Why had he stuck it in his pocket? He usually left draft correspondence on the table with his notes and other papers. Why would he fold the paper before he even finished writing the letter?

Ruth stepped over to the window to see it better in the light. It was written in pencil and wasn't Harry's usual firm hand. He had scratched out and replaced several words, and the script was jerky and small, as if he had been gripping the pencil tightly. There was no salutation. She began to read the body of the letter.

I'm afraid I haven't had the pleasure to make your acquaintance and I'm not a fellow Galway man, if I may refer to you thus. We do have an esteemed mutual colleague, who you may remember from your days at St Ignatius. He will be pleased to bridge our communication.

Ruth noticed that *who you may remember from your days at St Ignatius* had been scored out. Why would Harry not want to remind the person he was writing to how he knew their mutual contact? She frowned as she resumed reading.

I believe you share my enthusiasm for gathering news and like to keep abreast of recent developments. Sometimes you seem to know about events before the instigators do, an ability I find admirable. I take a keen interest in my locality and have spotted something I believe may be of particular interest. A new flock of the creation that is neither a bird nor a fish will soon come to roost with us, a brood from a new location that will be of interest to you.

Harry had stopped writing at this point. Ruth squinted at the word that had been squeezed into the last line above 'interest': *significant.* What on earth was he writing about? A creation that is neither a bird nor a fish? Ruth raised her head and stared out the window, not seeing a horse pulling a cart loaded with coal passing the hotel on the street below. Oh, goodness! Was he talking about the flying boats? A brood from a new location – surely, he wouldn't be writing about the American flying-boat base that was being built? She had hoped that he had given up on writing that story, especially after Frank had told her that the local newspapers had been warned off printing anything on the topic.

She had hoped that would be the end of Harry's obsession with the project. But he must have contacted someone who had connections with an Irish newspaper. Since that country was neutral, she imagined that they could print whatever they wished in their newspapers. But what good would this do him? It might get his name known at the big newspapers in Ireland, but he could be charged with treason in Northern Ireland for making public confidential military information.

Ruth sucked in her breath. What was he thinking of? He would be arrested if his name was linked with an article like that. In wartime he could even be shot. She had to make him see how foolish he was and stop him from pursuing this dangerous path. She pressed her lips together until she felt her teeth digging into her bottom lip as she pondered the problem. She hadn't meant to tell Frank about Harry's questions that day he walked with her to the butcher's shop but when he heard about it, he was able to block Harry's attempt to publish the story in the local papers. Maybe he could help her if she asked him about this. She pursed her mouth as she thought about it. She didn't like being a tattletale, but this was serious.

She put the partially written letter back into Harry's jacket pocket and hung the garment in the wardrobe. She would speak to Frank this evening.

Corey's Hotel, Irvinestown
Later the same day

Ruth hurried from the dining room into the hallway and peered through the large window set in the top half of the heavy wooden door. Frank should arrive back from the aerodrome any moment and she didn't want to miss him. She said a silent prayer that Harry would stay late at his office as it would be very awkward if both men arrived at the same time. The street in front of the hotel was empty. Disappointed, she returned to the dining room.

She rearranged a couple place settings on the table nearest the door leading into the hallway as she strained to listen for the front door opening. Their handyman was a diligent worker; the door hinges were always well oiled. She forced herself not to race out to check the hallway again. Earlier she had startled a commercial traveller who was staying in the hotel when she popped her head through the doorway and peered past him as he entered the building.

As she lifted a knife and set it back on the table in the exact place where it had been, she heard the whoosh of the front door closing. Her gaze darted to the doorway in time to see Frank breeze past and bounce up the stairs. She dropped the knife and hurried after him.

By the time she reached the second floor she was out of breath. She let her hand fall onto the large knob at the top of the banister and hauled herself up the last step. Taking a deep breath, she straightened up and hurried along the hall. Frank stood at his door, coins jingling as he rummaged

71

in his trouser pocket. He withdrew his key and pushed it into the lock.

"Hiya," Ruth gasped.

Frank turned toward her, his eyebrows raised as he watched her approach. "Hi."

"I'm glad I caught you." She stopped beside him, puffing as she tried to get the words out.

"What's up?" He waited, still grasping the key in the lock.

Ruth looked into his eyes and felt reassured by his calm, steady gaze. Surely, he would be able to help her. Suddenly she was conscious of how close she was standing to him. Warmth emanated from his body in the chilly hallway. She had never been this close to him and alone before. The hairs on her neck prickled; she wanted to reach up and scratch them. At the same time, she didn't want to move and break the connection she felt with him.

She took a deep breath, rubbed the back of her neck and tried to concentrate on the reason she had raced up two flights of stairs after him. "I need to ask you a favour."

"If I can help," Frank said slowly. His tone of voice was distracted. She noticed that his gaze had strayed to her figure. Colouring, he looked up at her face again as he spoke. "What do you need?"

"Umm, well, remember when I mentioned that Harry was thinking about writing a story about the aerodrome for the paper?"

Frank nodded.

Ruth continued, "You must have had a word with someone, 'cause he's never written it."

"My boss and I discussed it. He took care of it."

Ruth's heart started to pound. She didn't like to hear that his boss knew about Harry's ambition. The fewer people who knew about it the better, especially anyone in authority. But she couldn't worry about that right now. She needed to discuss Harry's latest action with Frank.

Ruth licked her lips and paused, holding her breath. She was aware of how blue Frank's eyes were as he watched her. She exhaled. "Oh, that's good. I hadn't realised how serious it was until I spoke to you."

"Does the favour have something to do with that?"

"Kind of. I guess it does."

The way Frank held her gaze indicated that he was listening. She tried to ignore how hard her heart was pounding. "Harry might be thinking about writing the article for another newspaper. I think so anyway."

"What one?"

"Umm, I don't know. But one in Ireland."

"What makes you think that?"

"He was writing a letter to a Galway man."

"He showed you the letter?"

Ruth felt her face flush and lowered her gaze to the floor. Frank would think she was terrible, rummaging through her fella's room. "No, I found it when I was tidying his room." She decided not to say that it was in his jacket pocket.

"And he talked about writing an article in it?"

"Not exactly. He said to the person he was writing to that they were both interested in news and he mentioned the aerodrome. I can't recollect exactly how he put it but I know that's what he meant."

Frank shifted his gaze away from her and stared over her shoulder for several seconds. What was he thinking? Was he annoyed with her for searching Harry's belongings? Maybe she shouldn't have mentioned this to him.

Frank turned his gaze back to her. "I don't like invading another man's privacy, but this is a security issue. Information about the base is classified. I've already told you the huge amount of damage it would do if an article is printed. I'd like to see the letter."

"I could get it later tonight, I think. Harry usually goes to Reihill's on a Wednesday evening. Once he's away I'll go up."

"Okay. I'll sit in the residents' lounge after dinner and you can find me there."

"Ta. I don't like nosying but I want to stop Harry doing anything that'll get him into trouble." Ruth smiled gratefully at Frank then turned and walked away. She heard Frank's key turning in the lock as she reached the staircase.

Ruth was clearing dishes away from the tables when Harry left the dining room after tea. On his way out, as she had expected, he stopped and told her he was going to the pub. She finished clearing the tables and re-set them for breakfast the next morning then took a box of cutlery from the Welsh dresser and began polishing the knives. Sitting at a table near the doorway leading into the hall she could see anyone walking through the hallway. It was eight o'clock, later than usual, before Harry left, calling cheerio as he passed. When she heard the front door close, she lifted a torch from the dresser drawer and went into the hallway. Watching through the window in the door, she saw Harry's dark form walking along the street. Once he entered the pub, she turned and hurried up the wide staircase.

There was no one in the first floor hallway. She quietly turned the key in the lock and slipped inside Harry's room. Once she had closed the door behind her, she turned on the torch and went straight to the wardrobe. It opened soundlessly. She gently tugged the jacket toward her and reached into the pocket. Frowning, she dug her hand deeper into the pocket but she felt only the silky lining. She ran her fingers around the seams of the pocket, checking that the letter hadn't slipped through a broken seam, but they were in good order. She patted the other pockets in the garment then searched them carefully but the letter wasn't in any of them. Where had it gone?

She searched the pockets of the other garments hanging in the wardrobe, but there was no sign of the letter. Turning the torch to her wrist, she checked the time. Twenty minutes past eight o'clock. Harry might be at the pub for ages yet, or he might be back within the hour. There wasn't time to search the whole room thoroughly on her own, not with only a torch, and she wouldn't dare to turn on the light as Harry's room faced the street. Even with the blackout curtains tightly closed, she wouldn't take the risk that even a glimmer of light would be visible outside. Harry was very observant and might notice it if he was returning from the pub.

Her chest tightened and she felt panic starting to grip her. She had to find that letter. Who knew when Harry might finish writing it and post it? She would have to get Frank to help her. She closed the wardrobe, locked the room and hurried downstairs.

Glancing into the residents' lounge, she spotted Frank sitting on a sofa near the door. Two or three other men sat in armchairs, reading newspapers and chatting. Frank looked up at the sound of her footsteps. Her gaze met his for a second then she turned and walked down the hall. She heard Frank's footsteps behind her as she entered the dining room. Without turning on the light, she took several steps into the room then turned to face him.

"I can't find it," she whispered as soon as he was close enough to hear her.

"Where did you look?"

"Where it was this morning – in a jacket in the wardrobe. I searched the rest of the wardrobe too but it's not there."

Frank drew his eyebrows together in concentration. "Where else might it be?"

"I don't know. Will you come and help me look?"

In the light from the hallway, she saw Frank nod his head. She walked past him and whispered, "Come upstairs a minute or so after me."

"Have you got two flashlights?"

Ruth stopped and stared at him, perplexed. "What?"

Frank made a motion like someone shining a torch.

Ruth shook her head. "Oh, a torch. I've only got mine."

"I'll go up first then and get mine from my room. Then you go up and meet me at his door. What's his room number?"

"Eight. On the front of the house. First floor."

Ruth waited in the dining room for several minutes before she climbed the stairs. When she reached the first floor, she glanced anxiously up and down the hall but it was deserted. She walked to the far end of the hall. If she heard any of the guests returning to their rooms, she would walk along the hall as if she were coming from a room. She listened intently for any sound on the stairs.

A couple minutes passed before she heard footsteps descending from the floor above. She held her breath and prayed that it was Frank. She began to walk slowly along the hall and let out her breath in a rush of relief when his black-haired head appeared. She half-ran up the hall toward him and stopped abruptly at Room 8. After glancing left and right, she turned the key in the lock. Motioning for him to follow her, she stepped inside.

Once she had closed the door, she was surprised by how dark the room was. She heard breathing nearby and realised that Frank was standing very close to her. She could reach out and touch him. What would it be like if he wrapped his arms around her and kissed her? His body would be comfortingly warm against her. She shook her head. How could she think such a thing? She was here to help Harry. The man she would marry one day.

She switched on her torch. Frank did the same, shining his around the room, scanning the floor and the walls.

"How long until Harry comes back?" he asked.

"I couldn't rightly say. He might be back around nine or he could stay on longer."

"Okay, I'll take a look inside that cupboard in case you missed anything. You check the table and the garbage pail. Check the bed too – under the pillow and the mattress."

Ruth nodded and began inspecting the contents of the table, being careful to put everything back in the same order she had lifted it. There were several sheets of paper covered in notes and a couple books, but no letter. The waste bin was empty and Harry had not set anything on the chair beside the window. She pulled back the bedclothes and felt under the pillow but found nothing. As she lifted the edge of the mattress, Frank appeared beside her. He lifted it high so she could duck underneath. Again, she found nothing. She re-made the bed as Frank grabbed the chair, carried it to the wardrobe and began searching the top shelf and the top of the wardrobe. She was glad she always dusted thoroughly; she wouldn't want him to think she was slovenly. She sighed to herself. Why was she worrying about what Frank thought of her?

After she had straightened the bedclothes, Ruth shone the torch on her watch again. Ten minutes to nine o'clock. Surely, Harry wouldn't be back so early. She went to the window and pulled back the edge of the curtain so that she could look up the street toward Reihill's. It wasn't easy to see much in the dark, but she would know Harry's determined stride.

A glint of light shone from the pub as the door opened and closed. Ruth held her breath until she spotted a stooped figure shuffling away from the pub. That certainly wasn't Harry. She was about to turn away from the window when the door opened again. In the dim light, she saw a figure the same height and build as Harry step out and push the door closed behind him. Even in the darkness that descended, she recognised Harry's manner as he shrugged his shoulders, darting glances left and right. She drew back from the window, sucking in her breath. If Harry came straight back to the hotel and upstairs, they would have no more than three or four minutes to get away from the room.

"He's outside the pub," Ruth hissed.

Standing on the chair in front of the wardrobe, Frank turned and looked down at her. She motioned toward the door. Frank jumped down with a thud. Swinging the chair in one hand, he crossed the room in a couple steps and set it back where it belonged then returned to the wardrobe and closed its doors. As he did so, Ruth scanned the room to be sure everything was in its place. Harry was sure to notice if it wasn't. Then she went to the window and peered around the edge of the curtain. A figure silhouetted in the moonlight was halfway between the pub and the hotel. She was sure it was Harry.

Switching off her torch as she moved, she rushed to the door. Frank's torch also winked out. Without waiting to find out where Frank was, she opened the door and stepped into the hallway. She glanced back and found his solid presence right behind her. Her hands were trembling as she fumbled for the key in her pocket. Where was it? Had she left it in the room? For a sickening moment she feared she had then her fingers found the cool metal. She yanked it out of her pocket. Her hand shaking, she thrust the key in front of her, on a wobbly course toward the lock, as if the door were her adversary. Without a word, Frank closed his hand around hers, took the key from her and locked the door. He grasped her elbow and steered her toward the stairs.

"I'll go up to my room. Maybe you should go downstairs to the kitchen until you've had a chance to catch your breath."

Ruth nodded, her knuckles white on the banister. Frank patted her shoulder then started to climb the stairs. He leaned over the banister and whispered, "We can talk about this tomorrow."

Ruth took a deep breath and started down the stairs, trying not to show her agitation. She peeked into the residents' lounge as she passed. Two of the gentlemen who had been there earlier were still sitting in the same chairs. They didn't appear to notice her pass by. She ducked into the dining room and through to the kitchen, feeling her muscles relax as she reached its safety. Maybe she would make herself a cup of tea; she would use only a few tea leaves, a tiny portion of the weekly ration. Once she felt up to it, she would go to the residents' lounge to chat with Harry, if he was there, like she usually did. As she set the kettle on the range to boil, she wondered how she could find out what happened to the letter.

Ely Lodge, near Irvinestown
The next morning

As Frank approached the shore, he knew by their facial expressions and gestures that Mr Orchard and the worker he was talking with were having a heated discussion. He paused for a second, not sure whether or not to intrude, then strode toward them. As Mr Orchard's assistant, he should know what was happening.

"Winter'll be here in a few weeks and it'll get worse," the worker said. "We came over here expecting this job would be finished long before Christmas, but there's still tons of work to do. And you want us to stay on to build another site at Killadeas and maybe more too. The men miss their families and they're bored. They couldn't stick a whole winter here. Some are talking about going home."

"How many are complaining?" Mr Orchard asked.

"Hard to say. There's lots of grumbling."

"Find out for me whether some of the men really do want to go home. If they do, I want to know how many."

The worker nodded then turned away from the boss, glancing at Frank as he walked past him to the construction site.

Frank joined Mr Orchard and the two men stood silently side by side, looking at the shoreline and the half-finished jetties jutting into the lough. Beyond the end of the jetties, where the seaplanes would be moored, rhythmic, choppy waves bounced on the normally calm surface of the lough, shoved by the sharp autumn breeze. In comparison to the discontent among the workers, the lough looked peaceful and unperturbed.

"The men are still complaining about being here?" Frank said.

"The frequent rain and gray skies get them down. And they didn't get a summer like in the States. You can't blame them for missing their families either."

"What're we going to do about it?"

Mr Orchard shoved his hands into his trouser pockets. "Let's see how much of a problem we have first. If some of them want to stir up trouble, it'll be best if they go back. We need this job to progress as quickly as possible. Those who dishearten the other men should go home. We don't have time to waste on problems like that."

Silence stretched between them as they continued to gaze out at the water. Surrounded by such majestic scenery it would be easy to dismiss the seriousness of the problem. What could be wrong here? But, Frank was attuned to the tension in the site behind him. He could hear the normal sounds of a building site, hammering, heavy machinery, men shouting, but beneath that, he was sure he could sense an undercurrent of dissatisfaction brewing.

Frank turned to look at his boss. "Do you think the States will enter the war soon?"

"I can't see how it won't happen. It's only a matter of time. So we have to be ready. This contract has to be fulfilled on time."

He looked at Mr Orchard's tired face. His boss had a lot on his mind. Should he mention the letter? The one that he and Ruth couldn't find last night. He hadn't even seen it and Ruth wasn't sure whom it was intended for. So how did he know if there was anything to worry about? Frank shook his head slowly. He just had a bad feeling about this. There *was* something to worry about. He was sure of it. He looked back at his boss.

"Mr Orchard, there was something I wanted to discuss with you. I'm not sure it's important, but I thought you should know."

"Okay, shoot."

"The daughter from the family that owns the hotel where I'm staying told me yesterday that she had found a letter one of the guests was writing. In it he was talking about the construction of this base."

"Who was he writing to?"

"There wasn't any name or address on it. Apparently it was a draft that wasn't finished."

"Apparently?"

Frank felt his cheeks warm. "That's the thing – I didn't see it. She told me about it and took me to see the letter but it wasn't there."

"Took you to see it? Where?" Mr Orchard was staring hard at him.

"Umm, we went up to his room." Frank couldn't meet his boss's gaze.

"And the man who wrote the letter didn't know you were there? Or give you permission?"

"No, sir." Frank felt like he had been chastised although his boss hadn't actually rebuked him.

Mr Orchard exhaled loudly, shaking his head. "You have to be very careful. You can't just search someone's room without permission. Even though we're guest workers in this country, we're not above their laws. You know I've been in the courts in Enniskillen and Brookeborough, guaranteeing good conduct for a couple of our men who were convicted of speeding and drunk-and-disorderly violations. This would be more serious if that man found out that you had effectively broken into his room."

"I'm sorry, sir. I don't want to do anything that would get the company into trouble. But I think this may be important."

"Even though you never saw the letter and don't know who he's writing to?"

"Ruth – that's the daughter – thinks he might be trying to get an article published in an Irish newspaper. He's the same man I talked to you about before. British censorship wouldn't have any influence on an Irish newspaper since the country's neutral. If it gets in their newspapers, it wouldn't just be the people around here that would know the States are preparing for war."

"Yes, I see." Mr Orchard rubbed his chin and turned to stare out at the lough. He didn't speak for several minutes. Finally, he said, "Without any concrete evidence there's not much we can do. But, since it could be serious, I'll report it to an RAF commander I liaise with and they can decide what to do about it. At the least, they can put him on their list of people to watch. What's his name?"

"Harry Coalter. He works for the *Fermanagh Times* – the local paper."

Frank felt the tension leave his shoulders. It was a relief to share his concern with his boss. If he hadn't said anything and that reporter published an article that revealed the preparations America was making for the eventuality of war, he would be responsible. He wouldn't let someone like that betray the Allies.

In his mind, Frank saw Ruth's intent green eyes last night as she told him about the letter. If she hadn't been so worried, he could have stared into her eyes for a long time without any other thought in his head except how beautiful they were. He wondered if he should tell her that his boss planned to alert the RAF to Coalter's activities. He knew she wanted to help her boyfriend without getting him into trouble. If Harry did end up in hot water over this, he hoped Ruth wouldn't blame him. He didn't want her anger directed at him.

Frank shook himself. He really shouldn't daydream about her like this. She had a boyfriend and she was obviously very sweet on him since she was trying so hard to keep him out of trouble. Besides, he didn't have time for girls. He had to keep his mind on the job.

Corey's Hotel, Irvinestown
Evening the same day

Ruth could scarcely believe that she and Frank had had the nerve to search Harry's room last night and barely escaped being caught. She remembered how she had jumped at every noise afterwards and had been unable to settle the rest of the evening. She hadn't slept well either, but she felt a little more relaxed this morning after a quick chat with Frank in the hallway before he left for work. He had assured her that he would have a quiet word with his boss to see if there was a way to stop Harry from publishing anything in an Irish newspaper that would land him in trouble with the British authorities. She hoped they could find a way to discreetly exert some influence over the newspapers.

She had avoided Harry last night and crept up to bed while he was in the residents' lounge. This morning she had told him she was very tired the previous evening and went to bed early. Harry didn't seem to mind and had been in good spirits at breakfast. He made her promise she would meet him tonight.

She lifted her brush from the dresser and flipped it through her thick hair to give it a bit more curl then swept several stray hairs from her shoulder with her hand. She had decided not to change her clothes. Her everyday skirt and blouse would be fine. Harry hadn't said they were doing anything special. They would likely go to Stuart's Cinema. They hadn't been there for a couple weeks and a new film had just started.

Ruth closed her bedroom door and walked through her family's quarters. "I'm away out, Mummy."

"Where are the pair of you going?"

"Harry didn't say. We might go to the pictures."

"Oh, that's grand. Mind yourself, dear, you never know who you'd meet out there in the dark. Though you'll be safe enough with Harry."

Ruth quietly shut the door to the family's quarters and went down the hall to the residents' lounge. She was surprised to find Harry waiting in the doorway to meet her.

He held out his arm and took a couple steps toward the front door. "Let's be off, shall we? Do you fancy seeing the new film?"

Ruth nodded and took his arm as they left the hotel. *Major Barbara* sounded like a great film, and she loved Rex Harrison. He was such a splendid actor. Harry walked briskly, and she had to lengthen her stride to keep up with him. It was as well that she hadn't worn heels, as she couldn't walk this fast in them. She wondered why he was in such a hurry. They only had a short walk to the cinema and the film didn't start for a quarter of an hour yet. Since rationing started, you couldn't buy a twist of sweets in the cinema foyer, so there wouldn't be any queuing except to purchase the tickets.

"We're grand for time," Ruth said. "There's no panic."

"Am I going too fast for you?" Harry smiled at her, without slowing down.

"I'm alright. Only there's loads of time."

"We'll get the best seats if we're first in."

They had almost reached the cinema by this time, and Ruth realised that there was no point continuing the discussion. She grinned when she saw the large placard planted on the footpath. The poster showed a man in a Salvation Army uniform leaning over a bass drum, facing a determined-looking young woman on the other side of it. The text above the photograph proclaimed the title of the film: *Major Barbara*. Ruth slowed down to take a closer look at the poster, but Harry didn't let her stop. He steered her past the placard and into the foyer, where she waited while he queued at the ticket booth to purchase their tickets, then he led her to the centre of the high-ceilinged room. The electric chandeliers cast shadowy light around the large open space.

Her friend Jenny Mollan waved at her across the room. She was standing beside a uniformed man; Ruth wondered who he was. Harry followed Ruth's gaze, spotted Jenny and steered Ruth over to her friend. Before Jenny could introduce her escort, Ruth felt Harry let go of her arm.

"I just need a word with someone. I'll be right back." Harry gave her a tight smile before he strode to the door.

Ruth tried to concentrate as Jenny introduced her companion. The young man was a bombardier from the RAF seaplane base at Castle Archdale, a few miles from the town. Jenny said she had met him at a dance the previous week.

"Hello," Ruth said, shaking hands with the young man. "I'll introduce you to Harry in a minute. I don't know where he went in such a hurry. You'd think the hounds were after him."

As she spoke, Ruth glanced toward the door. People were streaming in allowing the door to remain open longer than usual under blackout precautions. She caught a glimpse of Harry outside, talking to another man. As the two men moved toward the door, she could see that the other man was Mervyn Gormley. She had never realised they were friendly until she had seen them outside Reihill's pub during the summer. Harry seemed to have a lot to chat with him about lately. But what was so urgent that he had to rush out and meet him right now? Harry would likely see him in Reihill's next week if not before. As she watched, her fella clapped Mervyn on the back in farewell and entered the foyer. She turned back to Jenny and her airman friend so that he wouldn't catch her watching him.

As an usher rang the bell and called loudly for patrons to take their seats in the cinema, Harry swept up behind her and wrapped his arm around her shoulder, drawing her toward the door leading into the cinema before she could ask him anything about Mervyn. Jenny and her new beau followed them.

In the cinema Ruth pressed her lips tightly together as she watched the newsreels. She would never get used to the sight of whole areas of London and other cities in England devastated by bombs. It was terrible to try to imagine what those people had to endure while she was warm and safe in her home only miles across the Irish Sea. So, every time the newsreel about the sinking of the *Bismarck* last spring was shown, she felt justified in rejoicing about this victory. The RAF's aircraft and the Royal Navy battleships had done a fabulous job of hunting it down.

When the film began Ruth quickly put everything else out of her mind and lost herself in the story. She laughed at the absurdity of some scenes and rooted for Major Barbara to triumph on the side of patriotism and morality.

The film was still playing in her mind as Harry walked her home. She tucked her hand into his elbow and pressed against his side. As they walked, Harry pulled his arm free and put it around her shoulders.

"Wasn't Major Barbara wonderful? She never wavered from what was right." Ruth bounced as she spoke.

"Films are always black and white," Harry replied.

"Of course they are." Ruth drew her eyebrows together, puzzled.

"I mean, everything isn't always that simple."

"Yes, it is." She didn't know what he was trying to say. Didn't he enjoy the film?

"No, life isn't."

"Of course there's right and wrong, and you have to know the difference. Like fighting Hitler. That's right. We have to stop him."

"Maybe there's two sides to it. Maybe he isn't all bad. He did a lot to improve his country's economic situation before the war. He was looking out for them."

Ruth sucked in her breath. "How can you say that! He's attacked innocent countries. He has to be stopped. There's no doubt about it." She turned and stared at Harry. "Anyone knows that."

"Not at all. It's not that simple. You have to look at things objectively."

Her heart beat faster. "I don't like to hear you talk like this, Harry. It's not loyal and it's dangerous." She lowered her voice to a whisper. "Like the story about the new aerodrome. Things like that'll get you into trouble."

Harry squeezed her shoulder. "Now, don't be annoying yourself. I won't do anything that'll get me into trouble. I'm a journalist. We have to question and examine everything. You have to get to the heart of the story. Look at it from every angle."

Ruth blew her breath out in an emphatic sigh. "When it comes to the war there's only one way to look at it. We're fighting for what's right. Like Major Barbara standing up to her father for using his business to make money from the war and putting money before anything else. She stood up for what's right."

Harry shook his head. "War or no war, I have to think about my career. I must do what it takes to advance it, no matter that there's a war on. What sort of future will we have if I don't? I have to look for opportunities wherever I can find them."

"You have a decent, steady job at the newspaper. What else do you need?"

"I can do better than that and I will. Just trust me. I'll make a name for myself throughout Britain and Ireland."

"It worries me when you talk like that, Harry. Something bad will come of too much ambition."

"That's what's wrong here. Nothing ever changes. No one will take a chance. I'm not going to live my life like that."

"What are you going to do?"

Harry put his finger up to his nose and tapped it. "All in good time. I've set some ideas in motion."

"Nothing that will get you into trouble?" Ruth felt her chest tighten and her voice squeaked as she spoke.

"Why do you keep thinking I'll get into trouble! Can't you trust me?"

Ruth pursed her lips. Now she had annoyed him after they had had such a lovely evening. Maybe she was worrying unnecessarily. Maybe he wouldn't do anything that he shouldn't. She would like to ask him about the letter and who he was writing to, but it wasn't as if it had been lying in plain view and she had stumbled across it. No, she couldn't say anything about it. But, she hoped it wasn't part of his plan to advance his career. It seemed that she would need to continue to keep an eye on what he was doing. She prayed that she could keep him from getting into serious trouble and make him see sense.

"I had better only take you to comedies after this. You're much too serious after that film." Harry laughed as he squeezed her shoulder. "Now come and say goodnight to me properly before we go back to the hotel."

He steered her into the entry a few doors from the hotel and pulled her to him, wrapping his arms around her as soon as they were out of sight of the main street. She still didn't like him doing this. What if anyone saw them come into the entry and got the wrong idea? She wasn't that kind of girl. But she didn't want the evening to end on a sour note after their conversation. She would spend a while courting with him before they went home.

Corey's Hotel, Irvinestown
Thursday, 23rd October, 1941

During the past week, Ruth hadn't noticed anything unusual in Harry's room. There was still no sign of the letter he had been writing. She tidied the room as usual each day, always allowing herself some extra time to sift through the papers on his table and have a look in the wardrobe. But, no matter where she looked, she hadn't seen the letter. She wasn't as uncomfortable doing this now. Men could be so rash at times. Harry had to be protected from making a terrible mistake. If she couldn't reason with him, she would save him from his own foolishness.

As the days wore on she began to relax and allow herself to believe that maybe the conversation she had had with Harry on the way home from the cinema might have hit home with him. She would be so relieved if he had re-thought his plans and decided that he should put his loyalty to their country before anything else. She knew his career was important to him, as it was to any man. But, if only he would give up the idea of being the first to write a headline-grabbing story about the coming of the American aerodrome to their county. There had to be another way to further his career.

She straightened the papers on the table, picked up the bag she had emptied the contents of the waste bin into, and turned around to grasp the door handle. As she turned, her gaze swept the room. On top of the wardrobe, the corner of a piece of paper stuck out over the edge. She didn't know why she hadn't noticed it earlier. She set the rubbish bag on the floor and lugged the wooden chair from its place beside the window to the wardrobe. The paper was near the front of the wardrobe and easy to reach.

Standing on the chair, she lifted the rectangular sheet and examined it. It was an envelope addressed to the German Academic Exchange Service, Trinity College, Dublin. She didn't recognise the name of the man it was addressed to. She turned it over and found it was unsealed. There was a single sheet of paper in it, written in a neater hand than the previous letter she had found. This one was written in Harry's distinctive composed script. She scanned the page.

The beginning of the letter was very similar to the draft she had read the previous week, but without words scratched out or ones added between others in sentences. This was obviously a cleaner draft. After reading the first two paragraphs, her eyes widened. The next sentence left her in no doubt that Harry was writing about the aerodrome. There were measurements and distances recorded, and an account of the progress of the building work. He had even drawn a rough diagram of the airbase. What on earth was he doing? This didn't sound like an enquiry to a newspaper about writing an article for them.

Ruth's heart pounded and she swallowed hard. Couldn't Harry see the terrible consequences his actions would cause? He said he was loyal to his country, so how could he even think of sending this information to someone at Trinity College who obviously had some connection to Germany? What on earth was he thinking!

Ruth could barely focus her attention as she looked back at the letter and read the last paragraph.

I am indebted to you for your help, relaying my news. I hope you will find your old school chum in good health and pleased to receive my communication. When I have anything else of interest I will be sure to contact you.

Ruth drew her eyebrows together. This wasn't an enquiry to a newspaper; she feared it was much worse. She didn't know who this information meant for, but she had a feeling that Harry would get himself into serious trouble if she didn't do something to stop him sending it. She would have to speak to Frank as soon as possible.

She looked at her watch. It was only ten thirty and it was half-day closing in the town this afternoon. She must get through her chores quickly and persuade Mummy to allow her a couple hours free this afternoon. Mr Thomas, the butcher, filled the orders for the aerodrome's camp kitchen and she knew that he did his deliveries when the shop was closed half day. She hoped that he would have deliveries for RAF Castle Archdale and the American aerodrome today. She would ask him for a lift. She had to find Frank before Harry got home from work tonight.

Ely Lodge, near Irvinestown
Early afternoon

"Will I call back for you on my way home from Castle Archdale?" Mr Thomas asked.

Ruth held the Morris van's door open. "I'm not sure how long I'll be, so you go on ahead. I'll get home okay. Thanks for the lift, Mr Thomas." She didn't know how she would get home but she would worry about that later.

"Just be careful with the Yanks. Some of those lads don't know their manners at all."

"I'll be fine, thanks. I just have to deliver a message."

Ruth closed the door of the van and waved as Mr Thomas drove away. When the van disappeared around the bend in the road, she turned toward the entrance to the aerodrome where two burly men were checking vehicles coming and going from the enclosure. The men weren't local; they must be Yanks. At home it had seemed a very simple idea to come out here and find Frank. But now that she was here, she realised that she had no idea where to look. Where exactly did he work? And how would she get into the airbase?

She took a deep breath and let it out slowly. There was a stout fence around the perimeter of the camp so her only option was to approach those men checking the vehicles. She walked up to the entrance and spoke to the guard closest to her. "Not a bad day, sure, it's not."

He gave her a quizzical look then smiled. "Well, it hasn't rained today – not like most days since I got here, ma'am."

"I wonder if you could help me? I'd like to speak to someone who works here – Frank Longo." She thought it was best to use his proper name, the one on his ID card.

"Longo?" The man frowned. "Don't have any Longo here that I know of." He spoke to the other guard. "Don, you know any Longo working here? Frank Longo?"

"There's a Frank Long. Works with Mr Orchard."

"Oh yeah, right. I know who you mean." The guard turned back to Ruth.

Before he could speak she said, "Can I talk to him?"

"I'm afraid I can't let you go wandering around on your own. I'll get one of the guys to send him up here." The guard flagged down a passing labourer and Ruth's eyes widened. It was Mervyn Gormley. Of all the bad luck! She didn't trust the man and didn't like the furtive conversations that she had seen between him and Harry. She had to make him think that her visit today had nothing to do with her fella.

Mervyn noticed her and nodded a greeting.

She smiled in reply. "Thanks, Mr Gormley. I don't want to bother anyone only there's an urgent letter that came from America for him this morning."

"Do you want me to give it to him?" Mervyn asked.

"Ach, I'd rather give it to him myself, if you don't mind."

The labourer nodded then went off to find Frank. She hoped that her ruse had fooled him and he wouldn't deduce that Harry was actually the reason for her visit.

She waited at the gate for ten minutes, exchanging pleasantries with the guards, before she saw Frank striding across the open space between a row of Nissan huts and the main entrance. Even hurrying, with his face creased into a frown, he had a commanding presence; he seemed to belong here.

Ruth raised her voice and called to him, "Hi, Frank."

As he got nearer, she could see that his eyes were clouded under his bunched brow. Mervyn must have told him what she had said about the letter. She hadn't meant to make him think there was bad news from home. Before Frank could speak, she stepped away from the guards and gave him a look that she hoped he would interpret as a request to follow her.

They stopped several yards away from the guards and, when she turned to face him, she was again aware of the intensity of his blue eyes.

"You had word from my folks?"

"No, sorry, it's not your family. I didn't mean to worry you. I had to speak to you, and I didn't want Mervyn Gormley to wonder why."

Frank's face relaxed and his shoulders slumped. "Nonno, my grandfather, is getting on and I thought something might have happened to him."

"I'm really sorry if I worried you. But, it is about a letter. I found a good copy of the letter

Harry was writing – the full letter and envelope. And I'm so worried."

Her voice trembled as she finished the last sentence. Suddenly the enormity of the situation hit her. Her eyes filled with tears and she pressed her lips closed to keep herself from crying. Harry would be in so much trouble if he posted that letter. He could be jailed. Maybe even executed. And now that she had come here, he would still be in trouble, but hopefully not as much as he would be if she didn't stop him.

Frank reached out and gently cupped her shoulder in his hand, looking down into her eyes. She wondered how such blue eyes could be warm and intense all at once.

"Okay, tell me about the letter."

Ruth told him about the part of the letter that had been added since she had seen the earlier draft, including the fact that it contained detailed measurements of the camp and other information about the aerodrome.

"And you said there's an envelope with it? Who is it addressed to?"

Ruth gulped and nodded. "A man at Trinity College – in the German Academic Exchange Service."

She shrunk away from Frank as he dug his fingers into her shoulder. He noticed her expression and loosened his grip. "Sorry."

Ruth shrugged her shoulder to relax the muscles after his tight grip, keeping her gaze on his face. What was he thinking?

"Where's Harry right now?" Frank asked.

"He'll be at the newspaper office. Or maybe out on a story."

"I'll need to see that letter. Will you wait here for a few minutes? I'll have to speak to my boss; then I can give you a ride back to town."

"I will, surely."

Ruth followed Frank back to where the guards stood at the entrance to the camp and watched him half-run across the grounds. Somehow, she managed to make small talk with the guards while she waited. After several minutes, she lifted her arm and glanced at her watch.

"I'm sure he won't be long, ma'am," the guard named Don said.

As he spoke, she gazed past him at an empty lorry that was leaving the airbase. Mervyn Gormley was the driver.

"Where's that lorry going?" she asked the guard. She tried to keep her voice from trembling.

"He's going to collect supplies for the camp."

"Where?"

"Sorry, ma'am. I can't tell you that."

Ruth nodded, peering anxiously in the direction that Frank had gone. It was probably just coincidence. There was no reason for Mervyn to suspect anything about her visit to the camp, but she still felt uneasy. She wished Frank would hurry.

Several minutes later, a black Morris van approached the inspection point from within the airbase. Ruth wanted to cheer when she saw Frank behind the wheel. An older man sat beside him. Frank stopped the van at the entrance and motioned for Ruth to get in. She opened the passenger door and slid in beside the older man.

"Ruth, this is Mr Orchard, the head engineer on this project. I thought it was best that he see this too. Sir, this is Ruth Corey, the daughter of the owners of the hotel where I'm staying."

"Pleased to meet you, Ruth." Mr Orchard was quiet with kindly eyes and she felt comfortable in his presence.

"Hello, Mr Orchard."

Ruth looked across the older man to Frank. "While I was waiting for you, I saw Mervyn Gormley drive out in a lorry."

Mr Orchard looked from one to the other.

Frank answered his unspoken question. "He's been seen hanging around with Harry Coalter, and you know he's been asking questions on the site." He turned to Ruth. "Do you know where he was headed?"

"The guard wouldn't tell me."

Mr Orchard motioned for Frank to roll down the window. The younger man reversed the vehicle back to the inspection point.

"Where was Gormley headed?" the boss asked the guard.

"He was picking up a load of gravel at a farm outside Irvinestown."

Mr Orchard nodded his thanks and turned to Frank. "He's not too far ahead of us anyway."

"Will we go find Harry Coalter before Gormley does?" the younger man asked.

"No, let's see the letter first and find out if we have grounds for concern," his boss replied.

Frank put the vehicle into gear and drove toward Irvinestown. He increased his speed quickly, and the trio were jostled against each other as the vehicle jolted over bumps and potholes in the road. Ruth squinted, straining to see any sign of Mervyn Gormley's lorry, but he had disappeared. She hoped that he was really going on a journey related to his job and wasn't going to tip off Harry.

Corey's Hotel, Irvinestown
The same afternoon

There were no vehicles parked in front of Corey's Hotel when Frank stopped the Morris van outside the building. He wondered whether Gormley had found Harry Coalter yet, if he was actually looking for him. They would know soon enough.

Ruth had already hopped out of the passenger door and was hurrying into the hotel. Frank followed her with Mr Orchard close behind him. As the men entered the hallway, Ruth emerged from the dining room, a set of keys clutched in her hand, and began climbing the stairs. Frank moved to follow her, but Mr Orchard laid a hand on his arm.

"Best to let her go herself. We have no legal right to go in there," the older man said.

Frank tensed, trying to control his impatience. "But what if Coalter's there? She shouldn't go alone."

Mr Orchard pursed his lips then inclined his head in an almost imperceptible nod. "Okay, go with her."

Frank took the steps two at a time. He didn't trust Coalter and would never forgive himself if that little girl got hurt. She didn't have to tell him about the letter; she could have protected her boyfriend. As he stepped into the first floor hallway, Ruth inserted the key in the lock. He heard her gasp as she opened the door.

"Ach, Harry, I didn't expect you back yet," she said.

Frank reached the door before the journalist could reply and flattened himself against the wall, out of sight of the doorway, listening.

"I forgot some notes I need for an interview. Just popped back to collect them," Coalter said. "Were you looking for me? Looks like you've got the room tidied already."

Ruth didn't reply to his question. "Oh, is that a letter you have there? Will I post it for you in the morning? It's half day closing today, remember?"

Her voice was higher pitched than normal but steady. Frank admired her spirit. This whole thing couldn't be easy for her.

"No, it's grand. It's for Dublin and I've to see a man in the Free State later so I'll post it there and save a few pence."

Frank stepped into the doorway and faced Coalter. "It'll also avoid anyone in the Royal Mail office seeing the address it's going to. I'd like to see that letter."

"What the – What gives you the right to make such a preposterous demand?" Coalter's face turned bright red. "How dare you! Do you have no respect for privacy?"

"That letter is a threat to the security of your country and mine. And your country is at war. Give me the letter."

"Of all the nerve! What's going on here? Tell me this instant, Ruth!" Coalter demanded.

Ruth looked from one man to the other, her lips parted and brow creased. She took a deep breath.

"You'd best show him the letter, Harry. I don't want you to get into serious trouble." She stared at him pleadingly, her voice cracking as she finished speaking.

"Get into trouble? What nonsense. As I've said, I've an appointment, so I'll not stay for whatever foolishness is going on." Coalter put the envelope into the inside pocket of his suit jacket and strode to the door.

Frank didn't move from the doorway. "Give me the letter."

The young American's voice was firm and determined, but Coalter ignored his command, staring past him. Frank grabbed the journalist's arm as the man stepped to one side to pass him. He had hoped that he could get the letter without force, but it seemed that if Coalter couldn't bluster his way out of here, he planned to barrel through. Frank wouldn't let that happen.

"Let go of me. What are you doing?" Coalter tried to pull his arm free but Frank held him firmly.

"This is the last time I'll say this: Give me the letter or I'll take it from you." Frank spoke calmly and quietly, but there was no doubt he meant it.

"I will not put up with this." Coalter glared at him. "That's a business letter. Journalists must protect their contacts. I will not let you see it."

Frank was ready when Coalter tried to push past him; he hung on tightly. The one shove quickly turned into a wrestling match between the two men. Frank was surprised by the strength of the thin journalist. When Harry aimed a wild swing at Frank, the American ducked then hit back, landing a hard blow on the journalist's jaw. Frank heard Ruth's cry in the background but forced himself to ignore it. The two men shoved back and forth, fists flailing, for several minutes, until Frank thought he finally had Coalter. He wrapped his leg around the back of the journalist's knee, confident that he would bring him down, but the other man pulled free from him and ran to the door.

Frank heard Coalter's receding footsteps in the hallway as he raced out of the room in pursuit. At the top of the stairs, he shouted to Mr Orchard below. "Don't let him get past!"

The young American was surprised by the speed of his boss's reaction. When Coalter reached the bottom of the stairs Mr Orchard shoved him sideways, knocking the journalist off balance. Coalter smashed into the hall table and a vase flew off, landing on the wooden floor with a loud crack. Frank raced down the stairs and grabbed Coalter before he could straighten up. Mr Orchard grabbed the man's other arm and after a brief struggle, they managed to subdue him. The two men marched Coalter into the residents' lounge, closed the door, and stationed themselves between the journalist and the door. Frank heard the door open behind him and glanced over his shoulder; in the corner of his vision, he saw Ruth enter the room.

"Now let's see that letter," Frank growled at Coalter. "And no more nonsense."

Coalter reached into his pocket and slowly withdrew the envelope. Scowling, he handed it to

Frank. "You Yanks have no respect for a journalist's duty to his sources."

Frank examined the envelope. As Ruth had said, it was addressed to someone at the German Academic Exchange Service. He removed a sheet of paper from the envelope, scanned the letter briefly then handed it to his boss. He didn't doubt for a minute that this man was trying to pass on classified information to the Germans. And he didn't believe that this communication was work-related, not when the man had fought so hard to avoid giving them the letter. Mr Orchard read it then looked up at Frank.

"I think we'll let the authorities deal with him," the older man said. He looked at Ruth. "Where's the nearest police station, Miss?"

Ruth gulped, looked wide-eyed at Harry then turned back to Frank's boss. "Just down the street, sir."

"Would you get an officer here straight away, please?"

As she nodded in response to the older man's request, Frank could see her eyes brimming with tears. The poor girl. He would gladly volunteer to go in her place, but he didn't want to leave his boss to guard Coalter on his own. As Ruth left the room, Frank motioned the journalist to one of the armchairs at the far end of the room. "I think you had better sit there where we can see you."

Frank perched on the edge of an armchair beside the door. Mr Orchard stood beside him.

The minutes stretched in silence as they waited for Ruth to return. Eventually they heard the hall door open and the sound of a light set of footsteps mixed with heavy lumbering ones. The door to the lounge opened and a constable entered, followed by Ruth and a second officer.

"Good day, gentlemen. I'm Constable Dowler and this is Constable Barry. What's the problem here?" the first officer said.

"Constable Dowler, I've been assaulted by these uncouth Yanks. I demand you arrest them." The journalist spat out the words. "I'm Harry Coalter and I work for the *Fermanagh Times*. They are interfering with my work."

"Have a look at this letter, officer." Mr Orchard handed the envelope to the police constable.

The police officer read the letter, passed it to his colleague and looked up at the two Americans. "We'll take Mr Coalter to the station and contact the District Inspector. We'll soon establish whether this is work-related. Come with us, Mr Coalter."

Frank watched Ruth's face as Coalter stood up and walked across the room to stand beside the police officers. *Stricken* was the only way he could describe it. He wanted to comfort her and take the hurt away, but he didn't know how he could do it. So he stood motionless, looking on as her boyfriend was handcuffed to Constable Barry. Before the journalist was led away, he turned to Ruth.

"What on earth have you done? You know how important my work is to me. This could be the story that will make my name. And here you are, rummaging through my things and jumping to ridiculous conclusions. It will soon come out that this is all a mistake, but you've ruined our future. I wouldn't walk out with a girl who doesn't trust me."

Tears pooled in the girl's eyes as she stared at Coalter. "I was trying to keep you from getting into serious trouble – jail, even."

"Well, you certainly made a bad job of it when you got these Yanks involved."

"We've talked about how important it is not to reveal anything that could hurt the war effort. You just don't seem to see the harm you'd do." She glanced nervously at the other men in the room then dropped her gaze to the ground. Her cheeks were a warm pink and her eyes glistened with tears. She was so pretty even when she was distressed. Frank wished he could ease her suffering. She was struggling to do what was right, and Coalter was trying to make her feel guilty.

"You're a silly girl. You'll soon see what a terrible mistake you've made setting the Bobbies on me."

"That's enough now. Don't be annoying that slip of a cutty. Come with us." Constable Dowler grasped Coalter's arm firmly and led him to the door. The journalist left without looking back.

Frank and Mr Orchard followed the police officers into the hallway with Ruth trailing behind them. The two men stopped inside the front door and watched through the glass in the door as the constables marched Coalter down the street between them and into the police station.

Frank took a step back and laid his hand on Ruth's shoulder. "If we're wrong about the letter, the police will get to the bottom of it. But it has to be investigated."

He didn't believe that Coalter would be found innocent, but it might be easier for her to cling to that hope until they knew the full truth. He vowed to make an effort to be especially nice to her in the coming weeks. She had such a lovely smile. He didn't want it to disappear with that scoundrel of a boyfriend of hers.

"You did the right thing, young lady. Remember that," Mr Orchard said gently.

Frank wondered if his boss expected him to return to work this afternoon. He didn't like the idea of leaving Ruth alone here. She looked so forlorn. If only he could put his arm around her and soothe her.

At a loss as to what to do next, the three of them stood silently in the hallway. The whoosh of the front door opening intruded on the stillness, startling Frank. "Hello, Mrs Corey," he said.

114

"Mummy –" Ruth began. Her eyes widened and Frank was sure she would cry but she just stood and stared at her mother.

"Youse look like you've seen a ghost. Whatever's the matter?" Mrs Corey asked.

"We came to get – And Constable Dowler took Harry." Glancing around the hall, Ruth's mouth dropped open when she noticed the small flower vase lying in two pieces under the hall table. "Oh, and he must have broke your vase."

Mrs Corey looked at the two men and then her daughter. "Will we go through to the dining room and get a cuppa. Then you can tell me what's been happening. Dear me, I was only down the road to take some broth to Mrs Preston. She's bad with her chest. I've only been gone this past hour."

Mrs Corey led the trio through to the dining room. Frank walked behind Ruth, his gaze resting on her silky brown hair and soft curves.

Town Hall, Enniskillen
Saturday, 22nd November, 1941

Ruth studied her image in the mirror as she ran the brush through her hair. She wasn't sure she should have come to a dance barely a month after Harry was arrested. She wasn't really comfortable about it and she was sure that folk would talk. But

Frank had been trying to persuade her to accept his invitation ever since the American contractors announced that they were hosting a dance in the county town to thank the people of Fermanagh for their hospitality. He said that since her family were billeting contractors in the hotel, they were among the people who the dance was for. She hadn't been able to find a rebuttal to that.

And he had been so nice since Harry was arrested. His smile when she entered the dining room each morning lifted her spirits. He also sought her out during the evenings to chat. She was so lonely and worried, and she could sense people talking behind her back as she left the butcher's and the greengrocer's shops. They probably thought she had known all along what Harry was up to. She found herself deliberately walking past the residents' lounge in the evenings to see if Frank was there. He rarely sat in the lounge before Harry was arrested but he was a regular now. On Sunday afternoons, he had taken to inviting her to go for a walk with him. She enjoyed his company, and it gave her a chance to talk about what Harry had done with someone who understood. He was the only person she felt she could really talk to about it. She was certain others would judge her harshly; some would criticise her for reporting Harry and others for not standing by him, no matter what he had done.

She wished she could go and talk to Harry. But it was a long way to Belfast, especially with petrol rationing, and Constable Dowler said it might be best if she didn't go since he was being investigated for treason; it was better to distance herself from that. Her initial pain after he broke up with her was past and she didn't want to walk out with him again. She could never trust him after his traitorous actions, but she just wanted to understand why he did it. Supplying information to Germany wouldn't further his career in Northern Ireland. Although no date had been set for a trial, he was being detained in Crumlin Road Gaol in Belfast. Because of the charges against him, there was no hope that he would be granted bail.

For tonight she must try to put it out of her mind. Ruth straightened her dress and went back to join Frank.

"There you are. Will I get us sodas?" he asked. She noticed that his glance took in her figure as well as her face but not in a way that made her uncomfortable.

"A mineral? Yes, please."

She waited while he went to the refreshments table and returned with two lemonades. He handed one to her.

"Will we go out into the lobby for a bit? It's like the Bronx in summer in here," Frank said.

Ruth let him lead her into the ornate, high-ceilinged foyer. She had always loved the majestic, gleaming banister on the central staircase and the intricate design in the cornices overhead. Glancing around, she remembered one day before the war started when she was waiting in this foyer while Harry spoke to one of the councillors. It was during the Irvinestown half-day closing on a Thursday afternoon. Harry only had the one appointment that afternoon, so he had called at the hotel to invite her to join him for tea in Enniskillen after he met the councillor. While she waited for Harry, she had stared absently at the wooden banister, twisting her head back and forth to watch beams of light darting across its surface. She sighed. Harry had his good, kind side; he wasn't only driven by ambition and strange political ideas.

"Are you okay?" Frank regarded her with concern. "I hope you're enjoying the dance."

"Oh, yes, it's lovely. Thank you for inviting me. I was just thinking about something."

"What's that?"

"One time I was here with Harry."

"I'm sorry – I didn't realise the place has memories you probably want to forget."

"It's not that. I just get confused sometimes when I think about him. He desperately wanted to make a career for himself no matter the cost, even to our country, but he was also good to me. Maybe I judged him too harshly. Maybe I was wrong to report him." Ruth drew her lips together tightly.

Frank reached out and gently rubbed her arm. "I hate to see you upset. But you've got to believe you did the right thing. You know what that policeman said – after Coalter's room was searched by those guys in trench coats." Frank lowered his voice. "You know he told us they had found that the man Coalter had been writing to had links to Lord Haw Haw in Germany. That guy who broadcasts *Germany Calling*. If that's the mutual friend that Coalter wanted the information sent to, then there's no doubt America's neutrality would have been destroyed if he had succeeded. We can't let it be known that we're building military bases when we haven't declared war. That's exactly the sort of thing Lord Haw Haw would shout across Germany. You definitely did the right thing."

He gently cupped her chin in his hand and drew her to look at him. "I'm sorry this has made such a mess of your life. Caused you a lot of pain. I guess all you can hold on to is that you did the right thing. I admire your strength."

Even feeling as low as she did, she couldn't help but feel a warm glow as she looked into his gentle but intense eyes. She felt her mouth begin to curve into a tentative smile.

"I don't know how he thought it would further his career or if that's what his reasons were. I doubt we'll hear the whole story, not with a war on, but we know enough to know that you did the only thing you could. Try to put it out of your mind." Frank stood and listened, his head cocked toward the hall. "Are they playing Glenn Miller? Will we go back in?"

Ruth nodded and followed him into the hall.

"Do they jitterbug here?" Frank asked.

"What kind of bug?"

Frank laughed. "It's a dance. It's all the rage in the States."

"I've never heard of it."

"When the band takes a break, I'll ask them if they know any songs that you can jitterbug to – I'll teach you."

The band struck up a waltz and Frank held his hand out to her. She felt her cheeks heating up as he led her onto the dance floor. He was broader and more solid than Harry; she could feel the heat from his body even though he held her at a respectable distance. Suddenly she felt shy. She had seen other girls admiring Frank when they walked into the hall, but he hadn't seemed to notice anyone else. Every time she looked at him, he was watching her. She shouldn't be feeling this way so soon after Harry had broken up with her, but, now that Frank was holding her, she wanted to stay in his arms all evening.

"It'll be Christmas soon. Do you have a big celebration here? The lights and window in Macy's in New York used to amaze me when I was a kid. I still like it," Frank said.

"Not as much since the war started. But Mummy manages to get a roast for us and we have a lovely day with the family. Maybe Daddy will get home from the building site in England for it. Did I tell you he drives lorries over there?"

"No, you didn't. That would be swell for you, if he gets home. I bet you're a daddy's girl!" Frank laughed.

"I'm not spoiled!" she protested. "I do my share in the hotel."

"I know you do. I'm only kidding you."

"I guess you might be home with your family for Christmas?" Ruth felt her chest tighten at the thought. She would miss him when he left.

"Not this Christmas."

"But I thought the work was nearly done. That's why there's this thank you dance. Will you not be going home soon?"

Frank looked into her eyes. "Well, I can't say too much – even though I suspect half of this county already knows, but we have other work here once the airbase is completed. I can't tell you too much, but we're converting a mansion not far from here into a hospital. I'll be here until the spring, at least."

"I'm sorry you won't get home to your family at Christmas." Ruth looked away then back at him, hesitating before she spoke. "But I'll miss you when you leave, so I'm glad you're here for a wee while yet."

"I'll really miss you too." Frank gave her a gentle squeeze, smiling.

Reluctantly Ruth drew her gaze away from his. She didn't want him to think she was too forward. He had been a good friend to her during the past month and she didn't want to spoil it.

"A hospital? Will it be at the castle? Necarne?"

"You figured that out quickly. But keep it to yourself, okay?"

"Of course I will. You can trust me. I've never told anyone about your name after you explained about that to me."

Frank looked serious. "I know that. Sorry."

"I wonder will they need folks around here to work in the hospital?"

"I don't know what the plans are. Why? Do you want to be a nurse?"

"I'd never set myself for that, but I want to help with the war effort. I'll not sign up for any of the services because I might be posted somewhere else – Mummy needs my help at the hotel while Daddy's away. But I'm in the Red Cross, I might be able to help at the hospital and work in the hotel too."

"I'll let you know if I hear they're looking for staff locally – it won't be for a few months yet."

Ruth smiled. It would be good to have him here for a few more months. And he would be here at Christmas. An idea suddenly popped into her head.

"Since you won't be home for Christmas, you'll have to join my family."

"Thank you. I'd love that." He held her gaze and the blue in his eyes seemed to deepen as he looked at her.

"Ask your boss too – if you don't mind him spending the holiday with you."

"Sure thing. I don't mind asking him."

"Even though there's a war on, we'll make it special. After all, America isn't at war. That's something you can be thankful for."

"Oh, I've got lots to be thankful for this year, war or not."

Ruth let herself enjoy Frank's warm gaze as he twirled her around the dance floor, dreaming of the Christmas they would spend together.

View of Lough Erne from the shore near Blaney

BOOK 2

Acts of Sabotage

Residents' Lounge, Corey's Hotel, Irvinestown, County Fermanagh, Northern Ireland
Monday, 8th December, 1941

"Ruth, clear off the top of the dresser. Frank, would you set the radio there, please." Mrs Corey indicated the tall mahogany dresser that stood between two large windows covered with blackout curtains. "Quick, daughter. It's ten to nine. We don't want to miss the news tonight."

"Don't worry, ma'am. We won't miss it." Frank flashed an assured smile at Mrs Corey as he set the radio down in the space Ruth had cleared. He turned it on and fiddled with the dial until the background static lessened and the sounds of a BBC Home Service music programme emerged from the noise. He turned to Ruth and grinned conspiratorially.

Most of the hotel guests were gathered in the room: American technicians hired to build

American military installations in the county. As the music flowed from the radio, the men quietened and classical music filled the ensuing silence. Ruth glanced at the serious faces surrounding her. Her mother's brow was furrowed in deep ridges as she perched on a chair near the radio, leaning toward it. Frank stood beside her mother, within reach of the radio, his hands in his pockets, one ear cocked toward the instrument. The other men sat in the armchairs and sofas clustered in groups around the room. Two of them rose and moved closer to the radio.

"You're sure of what you heard, Mummy?" Ruth raised an eyebrow questioningly as she regarded her mother. Her mother sometimes confused information that she relayed.

"Of course I'm sure! The presenter said Mr Churchill has announced that Britain *and* America have declared war on Japan."

"My boss was listening to the news this afternoon and he heard it too," Frank said.

As several of the men discussed the reports and rumours that had been flying around the town during the day, the static noise emanating from the radio increased, drowning out the music. Frank reached over and fiddled with the dial until the sound became clear once more. As he removed his hand from the dial, three sharp raps on a drum, followed by a pause and a final, decisive rap caused everyone to lean toward the radio. The British Broadcasting Corporation's call sign, the opening notes of Beethoven's Fifth Symphony, representing Morse Code's V for Victory, preceded news bulletins. Complete silence descended on the room.

Ruth glanced at Frank as he stood beside the radio. His intensely blue eyes were striking despite his heavy black brows drawn down tightly over them. She wondered what he was thinking. America's declaration of war on Japan would have repercussions for him and the other American technicians staying at her family's hotel. Ever since the Americans arrived last June, they had worked tirelessly in secret to build a flying-boat base for American military seaplanes, in preparation for their country's entry into the war. If the Axis powers had discovered America was actively preparing for war, it would have ended their neutrality before they were ready to join the conflict. In the end their country's hand had been forced by Japan's attack on Pearl Harbour. The pressure on the technicians would be even greater now to finish their work as quickly as possible.

Ruth had rarely seen Frank look so serious. Not since the first morning after he arrived when she had innocently enquired as she served his breakfast about the progress of the top-secret project he had come to work on. His sharp response had made her think he was a cold, arrogant man, but she had learned during the intervening months that that was not the case. Tonight she wanted to go to him and give his hand a reassuring squeeze to lessen his worry, but that wouldn't be seemly in a roomful of men, especially as he was their supervisor.

She restrained herself for other reasons too. It wasn't even two months since Harry had been jailed. She had spent a great deal of her free time with Frank since then. They often went for walks in the countryside and spent hours chatting in the evenings. He had even taken her to a dance a couple of weeks ago. Although a penetrating look from his blue eyes could make her blush, as she got to know him, she felt more and more relaxed and comfortable with him. She knew he liked her, but was it only friendship or more? She often felt that she shouldn't even be thinking like this, but she was coming to realise that the feelings she had had for Harry had been crushed beyond repair when he revealed himself to be a traitor to their country and she knew that she was right to forget him and make a fresh start. From the moment she had first met Frank she had been aware of his good looks, and, as she got to know him, she discovered that his personality was appealing too. He really was lovely.

Ruth's reverie was interrupted by the rousing tone of Mr Churchill's voice. Somehow, the Prime Minister managed to sound sombre yet impassioned at the same time. She heard her mother mutter 'such evil men' when he referred to Japan's surprise attack on Pearl Harbour; several of the men pounded the arms of their chairs, supporting the Prime Minister's condemnation of the attack.

As she concentrated on the voice emanating from the radio, Ruth heard the Prime Minister say, "One thing is certain: The need for greater effort in munitions production." Her heart beat faster and she wanted to bounce up and down on her chair. For several months now, she had longed to do more for the war effort than merely provide accommodation for others engaged in war work. So when the waste paper collection drive started, she had eagerly volunteered to help. Nothing daunted her enthusiasm and she had soon been put in charge of the team collecting from the homes and businesses in Irvinestown. The paper they collected would supply materials to make the cartons that bullets and shells were shipped in, as well as so many other things. Even pilots' seats in fighter planes. It was hard to get people to take the waste paper collection seriously but she knew it was important. Now she would be able to quote what Mr Churchill had said and tell them how the collectors were helping the war effort.

The voice on the radio continued, "In the past we had a light which flickered, in the present we have a light which flames", and the men in the room burst out cheering and pounding their fists on the armchairs, drowning out the remainder of the sentence.

"So, this is it, guys, we're at war!" one of the men shouted from the far end of the room. "Wonder where we can sign up over here?"

"Hang on, who said we had to sign up? I ain't doing nothin' 'till I know a heck of a lot more," another voice responded.

Frank reached across to turn down the volume on the radio then looked at the assembled men. "Wait a minute, guys. No one's signing up yet. We have a contract to fulfil before anyone is free to even think about enlisting. In the morning everyone reports to the construction site as usual. Mr Orchard will tell us more about what's happening. But remember, we have a job to complete, so don't think even about going anywhere yet."

Frank turned the volume up on the radio again and smiled at Ruth. "At least we know for certain now the rumours we've heard since yesterday are true."

Ruth nodded. Her head was spinning after everything the Prime Minister had said. It was terrible that Japan had attacked Pearl Harbour the way they had. It was bad enough Germany attacked ships as they crossed the Atlantic, but those poor American sailors weren't expecting it at all. And now America had entered the war. Everything was changing so fast.

But those weren't the thoughts that jumped to the forefront in her mind. Frank had just told the other technicians that they weren't going anywhere yet. That meant *he* wouldn't be going anywhere until the job was finished. What a relief! She tensed her lips to stop a smile forming. She couldn't let on how happy she was when everyone was so upset about the attack on Pearl Harbour. She had secretly worried that Frank might leave as soon as it was official that America was at war.

Another thought occurred to her: the work Frank and the rest of the men were doing wouldn't be quite as hush-hush now as it had been. She couldn't help feeling relieved that, although the details would still be classified, it wouldn't matter if people knew the base was being built. During the past six months she had had so much worry and such a battle with Harry to keep him from revealing information about the airbase to the wrong people. In the end, she and Frank had had no choice but to turn him in to the police when they discovered that he was intent on gathering information about the base to pass to the Germans.

The level of noise quickly rose in the large room as the men talked excitedly about the news report. Ruth caught snatches of their conversation but she wasn't really listening. She tried to keep herself from staring at Frank. She wanted to just drink him in and enjoy the knowledge that he would be around for a while yet.

"I'm away back to our sitting room." Ruth's mother stood up, speaking as she passed her daughter. "I've some knitting to finish."

"Right, Mum. I'll be in soon." Ruth felt her conscience prickle that she wasn't joining her mother. The Red Cross needed as many socks, mittens and other knitted garments as womenfolk could produce. She should be helping as she often did in the evenings after the chores were done. But she wanted a chance to talk to Frank before she went back to the family's quarters.

Ruth glanced around her. It felt strange to be the only woman in the room but at the same time, she had known all of these men for several months and she was in the hotel's Residents' Lounge, not a pub. It wasn't an unseemly place for her to be. They didn't even serve alcohol in it, and the American men always treated her with respect.

She became aware of someone standing beside her and turned her head to see Frank watching her.

"That Mr Churchill knows how to fire up his audience." He shook his head ruefully. "I might have a job keeping some of the guys from running off to join the Army."

"It was quite a speech," Ruth agreed.

"I'm glad we know where we stand now. It was a strange situation preparing for a war we weren't actually fighting. But now we're in the thick of it." Frank ran his hand through his abundant black hair. "Hey, why don't we get out of here for a while? I can't sit still after listening to that speech."

Ruth wasn't sure she liked the enthusiasm in his voice. Maybe his men weren't the only ones eager to finish the building project so they could get away to fight.

Frank ushered her in front of him into the hallway and waited while she ran up to her room to get her coat. As they left the hotel, he held open the heavy front door for her and stood aside to let her pass. She snuggled her neck into the collar of her coat as the cold air hit her. Slipping her hand under Frank's elbow, she let him lead her along the street. Her eyes quickly adjusted to the absence of street lamps and she could see the buildings they passed clearly outlined in the darkness.

"We'll not have any trouble finding our way about tonight," she said.

"You're right. It's some moon. You could almost do a night's work by it."

"Surely you won't have to work at night to get the aerodrome finished?" She wanted as much time with him as she could get.

Frank laughed. "No, I didn't mean that. We'll be working the men hard and long hours, but not nightshift too. They'd collapse."

"I guess you'll be glad to get it done and be away?" Ruth tried to keep the anxiety and sadness out of her voice.

"The pressure sure is on to get the airbase completed now, but I won't be glad to leave. I kind of like it around here."

She heard the warmth and the smile in his voice and it lifted her spirits. At least he wanted to be here, even if it wouldn't be for as long as she would like. She was only beginning to realise how very fond she had become of him. It had crept up on her as she got to know him.

"That's good." She didn't know what else she could say without betraying her feelings. While they got on well, he had never declared any feelings for her other than friendship. They walked for a short while in silence. Ruth sighed.

"What is it?"

"I was so looking forward to Christmas this year. At least your country wasn't at war. That would have been something to be glad about."

"It'll still be good. For one day we'll forget about the war."

Frank's upbeat attitude made her want to believe this could be true.

"Will you still be here?"

Frank chuckled. "Christmas is barely two weeks away. There's no way we'll be finished before then."

Ruth tightened her grip on his arm and leaned closer. "I'm glad we'll still be able to celebrate like we've talked about. We'll make it a proper Christmas! Maybe Da will get home from England too."

"Sounds good to me. You and your mother have made me feel so welcome. It'll be the next best thing to being at home." He paused. "It's probably just as well that we get along so well, as I'll be here for a while yet."

Ruth drew away from his side slightly, still holding his arm. She was sure he would feel her heart pounding if she didn't put the distance between them. "You've lots more to do on the aerodrome then? If you don't mind me asking?"

"Well, I still have to watch what I say. You know how it is. But, the aerodrome isn't our only building project here. I've already mentioned one of the others to you."

"Oh yes, that's right." Ruth had completely forgotten it in her anxiety about America's declaration of war and what that might mean to Frank. A fortnight ago he had mentioned that they would be converting a country house into an American field hospital.

"At the rate things are going, I may not be going anywhere for a very long time." Frank seemed to be speaking to himself.

"Why's that? Are you having problems with the job? Oh dear, I'm asking more questions. Sorry."

"It's not the job itself. Sometimes we get slowed down because we're short of materials or even tools."

"The attacks on the merchant ships are terrible, aren't they?"

"Yeah." Frank let the word trail off. He sounded as if he were thinking about something.

Ruth waited, silently, until he began to speak again.

"But it's not just that. We do get shortages we have to deal with. But sometimes things go missing after they're delivered."

"Ohhh!" Ruth sucked in her breath. "That's shocking. Who would take things meant for war work?"

"I don't know yet but I'm gonna find out. Don't say anything about this, of course."

"Oh no, you know I wouldn't." She was glad he trusted her enough to confide in her.

They slipped into silence again until they neared the far end of the main street. Frank slowed down and placed his free hand over hers where it rested on his arm. "Let's not think about that tonight."

They turned and slowly retraced their steps to the hotel. Ruth's mind was still racing after the news bulletin, but she pushed it to the back of her mind. She would enjoy these precious moments with Frank.

Ely Lodge, near Irvinestown
Tuesday, 9th December, 1941

Frank was relieved that despite the men's high spirits and displays of patriotism after the announcement of America's declaration of war yesterday evening, when Mr Orchard finished speaking to them this morning they settled to work. Walking through the construction site, he saw a renewed enthusiasm and energy among the American workers. The flying-boat base they were building would house American airmen and ground crew and their fellow countrymen wanted to have it ready when the troops arrived. He didn't think his boss's speech had done anything to rouse the local workers' enthusiasm or dedication, though. But then, the declaration of war changed nothing for them; their country had been at war for a couple of years already.

As Frank approached a partially completed Nissan hut, he noticed several workers gathered around the open space where the door would be hung. A couple of the men turned to look at him.

"How's it goin'?" Frank directed his comment to Larry, an American carpenter in the work crew.

The sturdy young American frowned. "I thought we'd have this finished today but we've hit a snag. We're out of boards for the flooring."

Frank checked his stock sheet, suppressing a groan. "You requisitioned enough material yesterday for this job. We can't afford to waste lumber."

"We didn't. It was here last night but it's gone this morning."

"Gone?"

Even as Frank questioned the carpenter, he knew the man was telling the truth. It wasn't the first time that lumber had gone missing. It seemed to be an increasing problem on this job. And it wasn't the only thing that was disappearing: bolts, nails, electrical cable, and a few of the metal rings for tying up flying boats at their moorings had all vanished too. What use would the metal rings be to anyone? Was some farmer using them to tether his bull? Even bricks and some of the metal sheeting seemed to vanish between the time it was collected from the central store and when it was used. Hammers, saws and drills also mysteriously vanished.

"We left everything piled inside the hut last night, ready to start this morning. But some of the stuff's gone. And to top it off, my ruddy hammer's gone too. That was a good one I brought from home. I left it in here this morning when we went to listen to the boss." Larry glared at Frank then dropped his gaze to the ground.

Frank frowned. This was happening too often. Equipment and materials were too valuable to lose, especially when the base had to be operational soon. Every second counted. And items such as lumber and metal were scarce. They would be difficult and costly to replace. He had no intention of running out of materials or letting costs spiral on this job.

Frank straightened his shoulders and took a deep breath. "Right. Go to the storeman and replace what's gone, then get to work."

"Will I get back the cost of my hammer? It was a good'un – a Stanley."

"Yeah, I'll make a note of it. Meanwhile, get another one from the storeman."

Frank wrote a few notes on his clipboard and then walked away from the hut. He had several other jobs to check before he reported to Mr Orchard.

Half an hour later Frank bounded up the single step into the Nissan hut that served as the site office. Mr Orchard, the civil engineer in charge of the project, looked up from behind a battered wooden desk.

"There's coffee just made." Mr Orchard inclined his head toward the Primus stove on the bench in the corner of the room.

Frank lifted the coffee pot and poured the black liquid into his cup, inhaling the aroma as he did so. Without bothering to add milk to it, he took a sip of the steaming brew and crossed the room to his boss's desk. He drew up a metal chair and sat down across from the older man, leaning back and resting one ankle on the opposite knee.

Mr Orchard scribbled on the sheet of paper in front of him until his pen reached the edge of the page then looked up. "What's the mood like now?"

"Our guys are all fired up to get the job done after you spoke to them. Can't do enough. I'm not sure anything would move some of the locals any faster, though." Frank shook his head then took another sip of his coffee.

"We just have to work with what we have. We've had some setbacks, but we're on target to get this job in on time."

"Yeah, I hope so." Frank exhaled loudly.

"What's the matter?"

"We won't keep making our deadlines if we don't have the materials – or the tools."

"We haven't been short in any of the supply shipments recently."

"I know, sir. The stuff gets here okay but it doesn't seem to hang around."

Mr Orchard raised his eyebrows.

Frank continued. "I just spoke to Larry Milton. His crew had lumber go missing overnight. And Larry's hammer disappeared this morning while you were talking to the men. I had to okay more material for them to finish the hut they're putting up. And it's not just them. This keeps happening."

"You're keeping a record of what's been taken?"

"Of course, sir. I know there's some theft on any job but this is getting way out of hand. If it isn't already nailed down, it's in danger of walking." Frank shook his head. "And sometimes I think that it still might vanish even when it is nailed down. What on earth does anyone around here want mooring rings for!"

"Right. The first thing we need to do is find out who's doing it."

"I've been keeping my eye on a couple of troublemakers, but I can't pin anything on either of them."

"Well now, we won't be collaring anyone. We'll watch for possible suspects and quietly report them to the local police for investigation."

"Shouldn't we be doing more than that, sir? It's our responsibility to maintain discipline and keep up morale. The men are getting fed up with it too. How can we seem to do nothing if we suspect someone's involved? We'll look like complete suckers and easy marks."

"We aren't going to let discipline slip and we'll make sure that the men know we aren't taking the thefts lightly, but there's other factors to consider."

Frank swallowed the last of his coffee and lowered the cup, waiting.

Mr Orchard lifted the papers on his desk, shuffled them, then set them down again in a neat pile. "It's likely more than just a couple of crooks doing this. It could be much bigger."

"How? There's no Mob here."

"They're not the only thing bigger than two-bit crooks."

Frank's eyes widened and he lowered his voice. "You mean, like fifth columnists? Have Nazi sympathisers got in here? You don't think any of our guys are traitors, do you?"

"No, I think our men are sound."

"The local men, then? I never liked having to hire so many of them. Look at what happened with that reporter, Coalter. And we were never able to get Mervyn Gormley on that." Frank thrust his hand into his hair and gripped the longish strands brushed back on the top of his head.

Mr Orchard shook his head. "No, not what you're thinking. I've been in contact with the CO at RAF Castle Archdale further along the lake. They don't think Nazi collaborators are the biggest worry in these parts. There's another, closer threat."

Frank drew his eyebrows together. "Not fifth columnists then?"

"Not the ones you're thinking of. A different kind. The IRA and their supporters. We're so close to the border with Ireland here, it's an easy place for them to operate. The local authorities are always on the lookout for them."

"Why do they want to interfere with our work?"

"They don't. They're more interested in their own cause, getting a united Ireland. Remember, this island was only partitioned twenty years ago. There's some radicals who want to undo that."

"So why target us?"

"Not us - our supplies. The RAF officer I was speaking to told me that the British have to keep a tight eye on the weapons and ammunition at their base. The IRA would love to get their hands on them to use in attacks against the British. But our building materials could be useful to them too. They need to build hiding places, ammunition dumps and who knows what else."

"Jeez, this is one hard country to understand. I came over to help us prepare for the war. And now it's like we're in a war within another war." Frank stared at his boss. "Do we have to suspect all the locals working on the site as possible terrorists?"

"Not quite." Mr Orchard cleared his throat and avoided Frank's gaze. "It's the Roman Catholics that wanted to be part of Ireland. The Protestants wanted to stay with England."

"But I'm Catholic! Do I have to watch everyone I go to Mass with?" Frank's eyebrows shot up his forehead.

"Not everyone would sympathise with terrorists. But pay attention. Use the same observation and discretion you always do around the site. At least it just narrows it down a bit to know who you need to keep an eye on."

Frank shook his head. He didn't like to think that he would have to distrust his fellow Catholics from now on. If it weren't for the fact that he really enjoyed the time he spent with Ruth, he would be tempted to just chuck in the job and get out of here, despite what he'd said to the men last night.

"Remember, we'll report anything suspicious to the authorities so they can check the men involved. We aren't going to tackle them ourselves. They're dangerous. We won't be wrestling them down like Coalter. Understood?" Mr Orchard watched Frank closely.

"Yes, sir."

"Good. Report anything suspicious to me and I'll pass it on."

"I will." Frank stood up and set his cup back on the bench. He needed to get out and think about what he had just heard. With a nod to his boss, he turned and left the hut.

Corey's Hotel, Irvinestown
Christmas Eve, 1941

"It's quiet in here tonight." Ruth surveyed the Residents' Lounge, surprised to find only two of the American technicians in the room.

Sitting beside the open fireplace, Frank turned his gaze from the dancing flames to her. "Most of the guys were invited to visit families they've met here. Just about every one of them's dating a local girl."

Ruth felt the heat creep up her neck to her face. She wondered what Frank thought about his workmen dating local girls. And what he wanted himself. Did he want to date her? Or were they just friends?

Frank turned his gaze back to the fire, then lifted his head to look at the mantelpiece, decorated with holly, as Ruth seated herself in the chair opposite him.

"It looks festive in here. We don't have real holly back home."

Ruth's eyebrows rose in surprise. "Don't you?"

Frank laughed. "It doesn't exactly grow on the street in the middle of New York."

"Well, I guess it doesn't. You do have paper chains though?" Ruth looked up at the chains that criss-crossed the high-ceilinged room. "We usually have more colourful ones, but we have to make do with what we can get this year."

"They're real pretty. You did a good job."

"I spent ages gluing each link in the chains." Ruth's expression became serious. "We're not just being frivolous and wasting paper, though. After Christmas I'll put all the chains in the waste paper drive. We need every scrap we can get."

Frank smiled at her. "That's a good idea."

Ruth felt the heat flood her face again and looked away from him. She was silly to be so flustered by him tonight. She tried to distract herself by concentrating on the fire. For a couple minutes, the only sounds in the room were the fire crackling and the rustling of the newspaper that Matt Harper, the American technician seated at the other end of the room, was reading.

"We usually have a tree too, but with Da away we didn't go to get one." Ruth sighed as she thought of her father. She had really hoped he would be able to get home from England for the holidays, but he had said in his last letter that they were working long hours and he doubted he would get leave from his work.

"You should have said something. I'd have helped you get a tree." Frank paused, seeming deep in thought. His eyes lost some of their intensity and seemed a softer blue in the light from the fire. "You know, it's the lights I really miss. At home they're everywhere – on trees, windows. Just everywhere and every colour. Every shop is gleaming and so are lots of houses. New York is always bright but it seems even brighter at Christmas."

"Gosh. It must be so beautiful. We usually have candles in the windows but not since the blackout started. They're on the dresser and the hall table instead." She folded her hands and gazed down at her lap. "Everything's different since the war started."

Frank reached across to her side of the fireplace and set his hand on top of Ruth's. "One day the blackout will be over and you'll do it just like you used to. Everything will be back to normal."

Ruth tried not to shiver as the heat of his skin warmed her hands. She raised her head and gave him a tremulous smile, even though she knew that what he had said wasn't true. Life would not go back to the way it was before the war. Nothing could change the fact that the fella she had walked out with for more than two years had been arrested for suspected espionage. Her dreams of marriage to him had already been smashed and the course of her life altered. "Of course it will," she said.

Frank released her hand and gazed into the fire for a moment then back at Ruth. "After Midnight Mass on Christmas Eve we all go to Nonno's, my grandfather's, apartment. My grandparents live just down the street from us. My grandmother makes this great fish dish. We eat a cake called pannettone after the fish. The youngest puts the baby Jesus into the big Nativity Set in the living room. My grandparents never had a Christmas tree but they always had a manger. Where they come from in Naples, it's famous for its Nativity Sets and everyone tries to have a magnificent one.

Nonno repaints the figures in theirs every year. He's always so proud of it."

Ruth watched Frank's face. His eyes had a faraway look as he talked about his grandfather. "You're right fond of him."

"Yeah, I sure am. I spent every minute I could with him when I was a kid. He's getting older now and I worry about him. He hasn't been very well."

Ruth's eyes clouded. "Oh, I'm sorry."

"But I got a letter from my mother yesterday. She said Nonno is determined and won't lie in bed. He says he's never been better. He's a fighter. When I go to Mass I always light a candle for him and say a prayer."

Ruth's eyes widened. Even though Frank went to Sacred Heart Church each Sunday, she hadn't really thought very much about him being a Roman Catholic. Each week he walked her to the Church of Ireland church, St Tighernach's, and then continued along the road to his church. What would her parents think if they knew about her growing feelings for him? She tried to push that thought out of her mind. "It must be hard being so far away from them all, especially now your country's at war too."

"Yeah, it is, but I'm sure you miss your dad just as much even though England's only across the sea."

"Aye, that's true enough."

"And if I hadn't come over here to work I'd never have met you and your mom. I got lucky when I was billeted here." Frank's eyes twinkled as he smiled at her.

Ruth felt the blush spreading to her face again and hoped it wasn't too obvious. She wanted to tell him how glad she was she had met him too, but it seemed very bold to put it into words. Instead, she held his gaze as she returned his smile.

As they sat there in silence, the newspaper rustling at the other end of the room seemed almost as loud as the fire crackling. She turned to gaze into the flames and let her mind drift. It was lovely to sit here like this with Frank. Christmas Eve always seemed to her a magical time, one of quiet expectation. She loved the joyful peace as she anticipated the festivities that would follow the next day.

The world outside seemed to have disappeared. There were no sounds of footsteps passing the window or shouts as men called to each other outside O'Reilly's or either of the other two pubs on the street. The pubs had shut early and folk must have rushed home to sit in front of their own hearths. In the distance, she could faintly hear a soft whirring noise. It must be an airplane engine. Since RAF Castle Archdale had been built on the lough shore, several miles from the town, she had become accustomed to hearing

British aircraft flying overhead at all hours of the day and night. Often, when she was busy working in the hotel, she didn't even notice them. Maybe it was the stillness tonight that made the sound stand out.

"Aw, the poor lads. They aren't even getting a night off and it's Christmas Eve." Ruth sighed.

"Yeah, what a shame." Frank cocked his head to listen to the approaching aircraft and frowned.

Noticing his expression, Ruth bent her head, concentrating on the sound. She wasn't sure what she was listening for. "What is it?"

"Something doesn't seem right."

As Ruth strained to listen, she heard it. The engine sound wasn't steady. "Oh, no, it doesn't."

Frank stood up and strode to the window. He pulled back the edge of the blackout curtain a couple of inches to peer out.

"Mind. I may be friendly with Robbie Hetherington, but he'll be spitting tacks if he sees any light spilling into the street," Ruth said.

Frank turned to look at her, raising one eyebrow enquiringly.

"Robbie's in the Home Guard and he takes it very serious. They're always checking the blackout curtains. He never misses a thing and he gets very stroppy if he catches you breaking the rules."

Frank let the curtain fall into its proper position. "Sorry. I don't want to get you in trouble. I can't see anything from here anyway. I think I'll have a look outside."

The other technician glanced up then returned to reading his newspaper without speaking. Ruth followed Frank out of the room.

Wrapping her arms around her waist and hunching over against the cold night air, Ruth stepped out of the front door and stood on the pavement beside Frank. She followed his gaze as he squinted at the sky, looking for the airplane. The new moon revealed only the glittering dots of stars. "Can you see anything?"

"Not yet. And in the dark it'll be hard to tell if it's one of ours."

The realisation that it might not be made Ruth shiver. Last Easter Belfast had suffered horrific attacks as Germany tried to destroy its shipbuilding and aircraft industries. What if they were now targeting military bases in Fermanagh? There had been rumours that the airbases would be targets. Lord Haw-Haw had even mentioned them in his radio broadcasts from Germany. Did the Nazis know that the American airbase was almost finished? Did they want to destroy it before it was ever used?

"I still can't spot it." Frank craned his neck as he continued to study the sky.

The uneven sound of the airplane's engines was getting louder, but Ruth couldn't see the aircraft either. Several doors opened along the street. Neighbours came out of their houses and stood on the pavement in front of their own premises, their voices raised as they discussed the disturbance. She noticed that Mrs Beacom was among the residents who had ventured outside. Although the woman rarely missed anything that happened on the street, for once she didn't know any more about what was happening than anyone else.

"There it is!" Frank was stabbing his finger at the sky.

Norman Booth, the chemist from the Medical Hall a couple of doors down the street, squinted at the sky for a moment before he spoke. "Indeed it is."

Mr Harte, an elderly neighbour who lived several doors away from the hotel, shouted, "Like as not, that queer-sounding engine is the Boche."

There was a loud murmuring of agreement from the other residents of the street as their neighbour voiced what everyone suspected and feared. It was likely a German aircraft. Ruth realised that Mr Harte was probably right. A couple from Belfast, who were visiting their relations in the town, had stayed at the hotel several months ago and had talked about how they could recognise the sound of the German bombers over the city, as their planes made a funny sort of noise, not the steady roar of the RAF aircraft.

Without realising she was doing it, Ruth pressed against Frank's side. He took off his suit jacket and draped it over her shoulders then clasped her hand and tucked it under his elbow. Although she knew it was silly, she immediately felt safer.

"Where's the rest of them?" Mr Booth said.

Like everyone else, Ruth scanned the sky, looking for more aircraft, but the sky was black behind the new moon. So far, only the one aircraft had been spotted and it could be heard more clearly than seen. But it was obvious that the single, dark silhouette against the black sky was on a course toward the town.

"They might not be far behind," Frank said.

"Maybe this one got lost." Ruth felt her neighbours' eyes on her. "Maybe they're heading to Londonderry."

Her speculation received a murmur of agreement. Someone said that one aircraft wouldn't do much harm, but another agitated voice reminded them of the damage the bombers had done in Belfast the previous spring. One bomber could devastate a street.

Frank raised his voice. "Everyone should take cover." He squeezed Ruth's hand. "Can we let them shelter in the hotel's cellar?"

"Aye, of course."

She felt Frank's rib cage expand as he took a deep breath. Before he could issue the instruction, the sound of the engine changed, becoming higher and missing the odd beat.

"Yon boyo's not right at all," Mr Harte muttered.

Suddenly the aircraft was clearly visible over the far end of the town, flying parallel to the main street. There was a collective intake of breath from the residents standing on the street as the airplane dipped; several tensed to run, though it would have been futile, as they would not have had time to escape its path. Before anyone could move, the aircraft's nose lifted and it levelled off, at a lower than normal cruising height. The engine continued its high-pitched whine, interspersed with moments of silence. But the aircraft maintained the height it had gained and, as it neared the clock tower at the near end of the street, it veered away toward the lough. Everyone stood motionless, watching it. Although only a few seconds had passed, Ruth felt as if it were hours.

Frank continued to gaze in the direction the aircraft had gone. "I'm sure I saw floats on the wings."

"One of our flying-boats in trouble," Mrs Beacom said. "God keep them."

Ruth heard sighs and prayers for the safety of the crew from neighbours standing near her. Mr Booth, the chemist, and the young lad who lived next door to him rushed into the entry beside the chemist's shop. They emerged on bicycles and pedalled off along the road that led to the lough shore.

"Should we go and help them? There's bicycles 'round the back of the hotel," Ruth said.

"There'll likely not be much they can do. They'll never catch up with the plane. If it doesn't make the lough, someone near where it goes down will be there first."

Ruth felt the tension in Frank's arm and side. She was sure that despite his sensible words, he also wished he could help.

The residents of the street stood in their doorways or milled around aimlessly, listening. The noise of the engine faded quickly but there was no sound of an explosion and no flames were seen in the direction it had headed. After a few minutes, Mr Harte muttered about the cold, called goodnight to his neighbours then disappeared into his house. The rest of the neighbours remained outside, wandering up and down the street, chatting with each other. Ruth stayed close to Frank as neighbours stopped to speak to them.

Mrs Beacom approached Ruth, shaking her head. "Aww, the poor lads. I hope they land safely. What a terrible business, altogether."

Frank smiled at the older woman. "They have a good chance. We haven't heard or seen anything."

Ruth noticed Mrs Beacom carefully observing the young man standing beside her. She wondered what the older woman was thinking. Was she remembering the evenings she had watched Ruth and Harry walk past her window on the way home from the cinema? No doubt she would love to ask about him. But, even if Ruth was inclined to talk about it, she had no information about her former beau. As far as she could glean from the police officer who had arrested him, he was still being held in Crumlin Road Gaol in Belfast. There had been no word that a trial date had been set. No doubt, Mrs Beacom also wondered about her relationship with Frank. Ruth resisted the urge to step away from his side. She had no reason to be uncomfortable. She wasn't doing anything wrong.

As Mrs Beacom turned and headed back to her house, the older woman shook her head and spoke as if she had not heard Frank's last comment. "A terrible business, indeed."

A quarter of an hour passed without any news about the aircraft, and neighbours began to drift into their homes. Half a dozen people remained outside. Ruth pulled Frank's suit jacket tighter around her shoulders and hunched forward to suppress a shiver as cold air slipped beneath it and enveloped her.

Frank turned to Ruth. "There's not much we can do out here. Why don't we go back inside before you turn into a popsicle?"

Ruth straightened her shoulders and tightened her grip on his arm. "I'm alright. But you must be foundered without even a jacket on you!"

"I found what?"

"No - foundered – freezing."

"Oh. You'd be surprised how cold New York winters are. I'm a tough city boy."

Frank put his hand on top of hers where it rested on his arm and squeezed it. "Let's go." He opened the hotel's door and ushered her inside in front of him.

As Ruth stepped into the hall, something soft brushed her leg. "Oh, what's that!" She stopped and leaned over to peer at the floor.

As she bent down, she felt herself propelled forward and put out her hands to stop her fall. But the impact she expected didn't happen. Instead, she felt strong but gentle hands grasp her waist and hold on to her until she regained her balance.

"Easy there! Sorry, I didn't realise you'd stopped," Frank said.

Heat flooded Ruth's face as she straightened up. "I shouldn't have stopped like that. Thanks!"

Something caressed her leg again and she heard a humming noise near her feet. She looked down and laughed. "Where did you come from?"

A thin tortoiseshell cat wrapped itself around her leg, purring happily. Ruth bent down to stroke it. "You're lovely!" She glanced up at Frank. "After ours died last year Mummy didn't want to get another cat. She said it was on account of the rationing and we had enough to feed. But this one's beautiful. And it's cold out there tonight. I'll bring it in beside the fire and get a sup of milk for it. When she sees it, Mummy won't be able to resist it."

Ruth ran her hand along the cat's spine, and the animal turned its head to lick her fingers. She scratched its cheek and smiled.

Looking up at Frank, she said, "You can't help sleeking it, can you?"

Frank frowned at her.

"Don't you like cats?"

"Yeah, I do. But what's *sleeking*?"

"Like this." Ruth ran her hand along the cat's back again.

"Oh, petting it." Frank grinned. "Let's go into the Residents' Lounge. I'm sure it'll follow us and find the fire."

Frank and Ruth went into the lounge and seated themselves opposite each other beside the fire. The cat sidled in and settled on the carpet between them. Ruth grinned at Frank. "It must have understood you, even though you're a Yank."

Frank laughed.

Matt Harper looked up from his newspaper and spoke to Frank. "Anything interesting out there?"

"A damaged plane making its way back to RAF Castle Archdale."

"Did it get there?"

"Don't know. We didn't see any sign of a crash. Weren't you curious to know what was happening?"

"Yeah, but I'm a Georgia boy. I hate this damp, cold weather. So when I get warm by the fire, I want to stay that way. I ain't movin' for nothin'."

Frank and Ruth laughed, settling back in their chairs. It was quiet outside once more. Ruth stared into the fire, unconsciously listening for any sounds that would indicate the airplane had crashed. She chatted intermittently with Frank and glanced at the cat, who seemed perfectly at ease in its new home.

As it neared nine o'clock, Frank switched on the radio that was sitting on the dresser where he had set it a couple weeks ago. Since America's entry into the war, the American technicians were keen to hear the latest news each day, so Ruth's mother had decided to leave the radio in the Residents' Lounge. Matt put down his newspaper and the trio listened in silence to the news broadcast. When the broadcast ended, Frank turned the volume down. Ruth tried to relax into her armchair again as soft music drifted from the radio.

Frank voiced Ruth's thoughts. "The one bit of news I'd really like to hear is what happened to that plane."

"Aye, exactly. I suppose if none of the neighbours find out anything first, we'll no doubt hear at church tomorrow." Ruth stopped speaking as she remembered they would be at different churches on Christmas morning.

Frank didn't seem to notice her discomfort. "Yeah, someone will know something about it by then."

They sat in silence again, watching the fire. It was comfortable like this and Ruth wished she could remain here for a very long time. The whoosh of the front door opening made her turn her head toward the doorway. A red-faced, panting Mr Booth entered the room.

"Hello, Mr Booth. Come in." Ruth rose from her chair and hurried over to the chemist. "Come and rest yourself."

"I'm fine, daughter. Just a bit winded. I don't get out on my bicycle as often as I once did. Too many hours behind the shop counter."

Frank rose and stood beside Ruth. She was sure she could feel his tension as he leaned toward Mr Booth. "I guess you didn't find the plane?"

She thought Frank might have waited a minute to give the chemist time to recover, but she was also eager to hear what had happened. She held her breath, hoping that it wouldn't be bad news. What a terrible night for it, if anything bad had happened.

"No, it was soon out of sight after it left the main street. Victor and I went in the direction it was headed, quite a distance, but we didn't see anything. There was no crash or flames. We called at a house out the road. They heard the faulty engine too and went outside to look but they didn't seen anything either. Surely we'd have seen something if it had gone down. God keep the lads, we'll pray they were spared."

"That's encouraging news, isn't it?" Frank turned to look at Ruth. His eyes seemed to twinkle as he smiled. She loved the way they did that when he was excited or happy.

She let out the breath she was holding and nodded. It was such a relief. Although they didn't know for certain, it seemed likely that the aircraft had landed safely on the lough. She said a silent prayer of thanks for the crew's safety. She knew flying accidents happened, but she didn't want it to happen here on this of all nights.

"Aye, it is that," she agreed. "Come up to the fire, Mr Booth." She motioned toward the fireplace.

"Ta, but I'd best get home. My wee woman will be wondering where I've got to."

Mr Booth had regained his breath and the redness was beginning to fade from his cheeks. He raised one hand in farewell as he left the room. "Happy Christmas to you both."

The pair returned his good wishes as they followed him into the hallway. As the front door closed behind Mr Booth, Ruth turned to Frank.

"Aye, it'll certainly be a happy Christmas for the families of those men in the plane. It looks like they had luck with them tonight."

"They sure did. I bet they'll be telling this story to their grandkids!" Frank grinned then cocked his head to one side. "But they're not the only ones who are lucky tonight."

Ruth drew her eyebrows together, puzzling over what he meant. As she watched him, Frank's twinkling blue eyes suddenly moved closer to her. Before she could react, he gently kissed her on the lips. She stood still, surprised but pleased. His lips were firm and warm. She felt her face flush but she didn't care; she wanted to shout with happiness. He had kissed her! It was wonderful, even if it was very bold.

Frank stepped back and pointed at the ceiling. Ruth looked up. A long piece of string dangled from the high ceiling. A couple of feet above their heads a sprig of mistletoe was fastened to it.

"The guys hung it up last night. They had a devil of a time climbing up there to reach the ceiling." Frank turned his attention back to her. "I was wondering when I'd get a chance to get you under it. It didn't seem right to do it when we came in earlier."

The blush that had suffused her neck and face deepened but she held his gaze. His eyes seemed to dance as he watched her. She never wanted to look away from those eyes, but she wished he would kiss her again. It had happened so unexpectedly and fast; she wanted a chance to savour it.

A tiny smile tipped up the corners of her lips as Frank leaned close to her again and gently cupped her shoulder with his hand. "I'm glad I got the chance," he whispered into her ear.

Ruth wasn't surprised this time when his warm lips met hers. It was an assured but gentle kiss, and she made no move to end it. As he drew her closer, she relaxed and rested against him. The kiss lingered but remained gentle and tender. When he pulled his lips away from hers, she looked up and gave him a dreamy smile.

His own smile matched hers. "Merry Christmas, sweetheart."

Ruth wanted to throw her arms around him and squeeze tightly, but that would be too forward. Instead, she nestled into his shoulder. She didn't know what folk would say about her walking out with him so soon after Harry's arrest. And she didn't know what her mother would say about him being a Roman Catholic. But those things could wait. It was Christmas Eve and this was magical.

Ely Lodge, near Irvinestown
Friday, 16th January, 1942

As Frank headed toward the perimeter of the construction site, checking progress on each job he passed, he noticed several men standing idle beside a partially completed ammunition storage dump set at a distance from the main structures in the compound. Not one of the men was working on the brick building. He had better find out why. It was more than a month since America had entered the war and troops would be arriving in Northern Ireland soon. There wasn't time to waste standing idle.

As Frank approached the group of men he heard Tommy Clerkin shouting, waving his arms menacingly and leaning toward Francey Byrne. The flimsy white wisps of breath spurting from his mouth belied the threat conveyed by the labourer's words. Frank knew that the situation could easily get out of hand if he didn't intervene. He increased his pace to reach the group before punches were thrown.

Francey didn't back away from Tommy but regarded him coolly. "Dev has said it over and over. It would be suicide for our country to throw itself into the war. If everyone isn't behind it, we'd never stand a chance. Our President knows what he's talking about."

Tommy glared at him. "Then what are youse doing up here earning good money, if it's not your war? Go home to your own country. They should tear up your work permits, every last one of youse."

Frank noticed that Mervyn Gormley, who was standing behind Tommy, was nodding in agreement. Just the sight of the man made Frank's muscles tense. Since that business with Harry Coalter, he didn't trust Gormley. Whenever there was any kind of trouble, the labourer was sure to be lurking though never in the forefront; he could never be blamed for anything. Frank would be willing to bet he had goaded the men involved into the present conflict.

Francey's jaw tightened but he stayed silent, turning to look at Frank as he stopped beside the group.

Tommy spit on the ground and glared at Francey. Not noticing Frank's arrival, he continued, "And youse're all likely spying for Hitler. Sure, the B-men had to shoot at spies crossing the border last week!"

"You don't believe everything you read in the papers, do you?" Francey asked.

"If it's in the *Impartial* it's true. Not like your papers."

"They never said it was spies. A lorry didn't stop – it probably had smuggled goods on it. Nothing to do with spying."

"That's just a good cover." Tommy's hard expression didn't change.

"What's going on here? Not a lot of work, by the look of it." Frank glanced around the group of men.

One of the men muttered, "Them'uns shouldn't be up here working on our airbases when their president said yesterday that he won't let anyone build airbases in the Free State. How could you trust the likes of them?"

There were murmurs of agreement from the assembled labourers. Several of them stamped their feet. Frank wasn't sure whether it was due to the cold or to scare Francey.

"It's not for you to decide who we hire, Clerkin." Frank looked at the other workers. "Or any of you. The company vets the men we hire. We need every one of you but we need you working, not threatening to throw punches at each other. Leave your politics at home and get back to work." Frank regarded them steadily, determined not to be intimidated by several of the men who were a decade older and more muscular than he was.

As the men dispersed, they avoided looking directly at Frank. Several cast glances at each other. Frank overheard one of them saying, "What would a Yank know about that lot across the border?" He decided to pretend he hadn't heard the comment.

Francey waited until the other men had left. "Ta. I do an honest day's work like any other. My country's politics are nought to do with it. I'm as good a worker as any of them."

Frank clapped him on the shoulder. "That's what we need, buddy. Keep it up."

Francey nodded and walked away.

Frank thrust his hand into his trouser pocket and clenched it into a tight ball, watching until all the men had returned to work. It was enough to deal with shortages of materials and the theft of the supplies and equipment, probably by Irish terrorists. This antagonism among the workforce was an added problem that he didn't need right now. He knew there would be conflicts and disagreements among men working together on any job, but this was much more deep-seated than that. The distrust and antagonism between the workers from Northern Ireland and the ones from the Free State was an ongoing problem, not to mention the antagonism between the Protestant and Catholic workers too. The whole situation was so complicated. It often seemed nearly impossible to walk the tightrope between the opposing factions and bring them together to get the job done.

Frank huffed out his breath to ease his frustration, watching the icy tendril swirl away from him on the cold breeze. He would not let the situation beat him. Somehow he would pull the workforce together and get the job done on time.

Presbyterian Hall, Irvinestown
Thursday, 22nd January, 1942

Ruth's eyes filled with tears of mirth. George Formby was singing the last line of "When I'm

Cleaning Windows" with feigned innocence, strumming his ukulele vigorously. Around her other audience members laughed uproariously. She glanced out of the corner of her eye to check Frank's reaction. The corners of his eyes crinkled above his wide grin. She was relieved that he didn't disapprove.

The song was quite outrageous but it was also very funny. Imagine looking in people's windows, and catching them in their bedrooms or bathrooms? It was a wonder Mr Formby was permitted to sing a song like that in the Presbyterian Hall. She was sure the minister would be shocked. But Mr Formby toured with ENSA and he did so much good for charities, as well as entertaining the troops. How could anyone object? They were so fortunate that Irvinestown was a stop on his tour of Northern Ireland. It was also very lucky that Frank was able to buy the tickets at his work. There were loads more people who wanted to come to the show than the hall would hold. When they arrived the place had been mobbed and they had had to squeeze through the crowd to get into the hall.

She felt her face heating up as Mr Formby launched into "I Did What I Could With My Gasmask". The words of his songs really were very saucy. She had often heard him on the radio, but she never thought she would ever hear him sing some of his songs in a staid place like this. If it weren't for the war, he wouldn't be performing in the Presbyterian Hall.

Frank leaned over to her and whispered, "He's a scream."

Ruth turned so she could whisper into his ear. "I'd say there's a few old biddies who'll be having fits. He's not very proper."

Frank feigned a swoon and she giggled. He was such great company.

The rest of the show passed quickly and Ruth was humming "Bless 'Em All" as they left the hall. They were buoyed along onto the street outside the church hall by the mass of concertgoers. All around her, Ruth heard people laughing and singing.

Frank smiled at her. "I know you were laughing, but I hope the show wasn't too coarse for you."

"He is quite saucy but it was very funny. And Mr Formby is so sweet. How could his concert offend anyone?" She hoped that Frank didn't think badly of her for enjoying such a saucy show. She had never been to one like it before, but she didn't see any harm in it. The whole audience had found it funny and they were respectable people, not riffraff.

Frank stared over her shoulder for several seconds then returned his gaze to her face. He paused before he spoke, as if he were distracted. "Ahh, that's true." He looked at the ground then shook his head. "What a character he is! I'll have to write and tell Nonno about the show. I think he'd have enjoyed it."

Ruth glanced over her shoulder to see what Frank had been looking at but there were so many people surging out of the hall and onto the street that she couldn't be sure what had caught his attention. "Is everything okay?"

"Yeah, I just saw someone there. From the job."

"Oh." She knew it was best not to ask too many questions about anything related to his work.

Frank sighed. "What's he doing here anyway?"

"Who? Half the town is here."

Frank lowered his voice. "Yeah, but I always wonder what he's up to – our friend Gormley."

Ruth's eyes widened. As far as she knew, the police had never proved that Harry Coalter's information about the airbase came from Mervyn Gormley. Although Gormley had always had a reputation for suspect dealings, he had never been charged with smuggling or any other type of offence either. It really was galling that he hadn't been caught with Harry. She was sure he had something to do with getting the information that Harry had been preparing to send to Germany.

Frank held out his arm and Ruth slipped her hand under his elbow, snuggling close against his side. He glanced across the road to where Mervyn Gormley was standing talking to another man then led Ruth toward the main street, walking slowly.

Ruth glanced over her shoulder at Gormley. "Has he been causing more trouble?"

"Not that I know of. But he takes a keen interest in everything that happens on the construction site, and last week he was egging on some troublemakers who were giving one of the Irish workers a hard time."

"I've seen in the paper that a couple local lads were given the sack at the airbase for slacking off. Could you not sack him too?"

"It's not that easy."

"Why? For us 'round here it'd be hard to sack someone who you've known for years and, like as not, is related to you. But you Yanks don't have the same worries. From what I hear the lads saying, youse can be sharp-enough masters. I've heard the odd fella griping that he was caught having a fag when he should've been working and soon knew about it."

"We don't have time to mess around now and men who don't pull their weight are out. But Gormley's a good-enough worker and seems to be able to pull the men together to work when he puts his mind to it. There'd be an uproar if we just let him go. For now, I'll just have to keep an eye on him. We didn't get him with Coalter, but if he steps out of line, I will get him this time."

Ruth nodded. Frank couldn't have stated her own thoughts about Mervyn Gormley any better.

They neared the corner where they would turn onto the main street and the crowd spread out, giving them space to walk comfortably. Frank looked across at the Clock Tower, which was all that remained of an eighteenth-century parish church. He loosened her grip on his arm and clasped her hand in his, pulling her across the road to the tower.

"Where're we going? Have you forgotten the hotel's up yon street?" Ruth nodded at the wide street at right angles to the tower.

"I have to stop here. It's tradition." Frank's face was serious as he gazed into her eyes.

Ruth had no idea what he was talking about; she scrunched up her face. "Tradition?"

"That's right. If a man kisses his sweetheart under the Clock Tower, they'll be true to each other for all time." Frank bent his head and gently kissed her lips.

Ruth felt the heat in her cheeks. Anyone passing by would see them. It would give the gossips even more to say about her. And was Frank worried that she might not be loyal to him after what had happened with Harry? She didn't respond to the pressure of his lips on hers as these thoughts flew through her mind.

Frank looked into her eyes. "Are you okay?"

Ruth gave him a nervous smile. "Aye. But folk'll be looking at us."

"Sorry. I don't want to give you a bad reputation. You just looked so cute walking beside me." Frank squeezed her arm. His expression showed his concern.

Ruth tried to put her worries out of her mind. "I've never heard of that tradition before."

Frank grinned. "Well, I just started it."

Despite her embarrassment and anxiety, Ruth giggled. She would try not to let her anxiety spoil their time together. Frank had never criticised her betrayal of Harry when she reported him to the authorities. He knew her loyalty to her country was more important during this war. He probably wasn't questioning her loyalty to him. She was just being too sensitive.

"Say, it's pretty dark tonight. I think we can get away with this if we keep moving."

Before Ruth could ask what he was referring to, she felt the strength of his arm as he wrapped it around her waist. He leaned in for a quick kiss before he led her across the street and kept his arm around her waist as they continued on their way to the hotel.

Main Street, Irvinestown
Thursday, 29th January, 1942

Ruth knocked on Mrs Beacom's door and waited. She noticed the lace curtains in the front window twitch. A moment later, she heard footsteps on the hall tiles and the door was flung open.

"Ach, hello. I hardly heard the door at all. I was tidying in the kitchen."

Ruth ignored the woman's falsehood. She knew that her neighbour spent much of her day at the front window so she wouldn't miss anything that happened on the street. But that wasn't Ruth's concern. She had more important things on her mind. "Hello, Mrs Beacom. Grand day, isn't it?"

"There's a bit of cloud gathering but it's a fair day, all the same."

Ruth was used to Mrs Beacom's pessimism. She looked up at the sky and was glad to see that the cloud the older woman referred to was nowhere to be seen. "I'm sure it'll stay dry for a good while yet."

"I haven't seen you about much since that awful business on Christmas Eve."

Ruth was sure her neighbour would have noticed her and Frank returning from the concert last week, huddled close together as they walked along the street. Even in the dark, the woman would have spotted them entering the hotel. It was a wonder she hadn't asked about Frank – or Harry. "At least we heard there wasn't an accident that night. They got back to the base safely."

"Indeed. God was merciful, to be sure."

Before her neighbour could turn the conversation to another topic, Ruth launched into the reason for her visit. "I'm calling for the paper drive. I wondered if you might have anything to put into it?"

"Well, I don't have much. I wouldn't be the extravagant sort, splashing out on daily papers and the like. I stick to the *Impartial* every week. I get all the news I need in there."

Ruth was inclined to think her neighbour got more news through her front window than from the weekly newspaper, but it wouldn't help her errand to say so. "Anything at all would be grand, Mrs Beacom. Old paper bags, any paper you don't need." Making an effort to be friendly, she smiled at the older woman.

"What on earth could they want with old newspapers and suchlike?"

"You'd be amazed at what they can do with the paper. They make boxes to hold ammunition cartridges and shells, and first-aid boxes, as well as all the forms that the military needs to function."

"They'd hardly want any more forms. These days there's enough paperwork about for anyone. ID cards, ration books. Stormont might collapse under the weight of all that paper."

Ruth laughed. "Well, they do need the paper for so many things. And haven't you heard about the competition? Every month the town that collects the most waste paper wins £500. There's so much Irvinestown could do with that money if we won it. You will help, won't you? It's for the war effort."

Mrs Beacom stood a little straighter. "Of course I will. Let me just go and see what I've saved up. It's as well you called for it. I've no way to take it in myself, you know."

Ruth gestured to the small wooden wagon beside her. Her father had made it for her when she was a child. They kept in it a shed behind the hotel, as it was still useful at times. "I'll have no bother getting it to the collection point at the church hall."

"Righto, I won't be a minute."

Mrs Beacom's shoes tapped across the tiles as she disappeared down the hall into the kitchen. Ruth turned her head and glanced idly up and down the street. Thursday afternoons were always quieter than other days, as the shops were shut for the half-day closing. Women hurrying from the greengrocer to the butcher to the bakery were absent, and it was too early for children to be on their way home from school. A cat stalked across the wide road, stopping to sit and lick itself midway.

A lorry drove slowly up the street and Ruth feared the driver wouldn't see the cat. She hissed and waved her arms at the animal. The cat sprang to its feet then scurried away. As the lorry approached, Ruth noticed the driver looking at her. She sucked in her breath when she recognised Mervyn Gormley. He raised his hand to acknowledge her as he drove past. She nodded in response.

Several doors past where she stood, the lorry stopped then reversed in an arc toward the pavement on the opposite side of the street. Gormley turned off the engine and got out of the cab. From the corner of her eye, Ruth watched him go to the front door of Mulligan's pub and knock loudly.

He must be getting beer for the workers at Ely Lodge. Frank had told her that they supplied drink in their canteen to the men who lived on the base. But she thought that they bought it from Reihill's at the end of the street. Well, no matter, it wasn't her business where they got their beer.

The sound of footsteps in the hall behind her made Ruth turn back to the house. Mrs Beacom handed her a stack of newspapers and several ripped paper bags. Ruth put them on top of the pile she had already collected and tied it securely.

Mrs Beacom looked past her. "Is Reihill's not supplying their drink anymore?"

Ruth glanced at Mulligan's pub. "I don't know. I wondered the same."

"Must be one of his schemes, like as not. The Yanks have an arrangement with Reihill's. But they give him cash to buy it, so he could go where he likes if he strikes his own deal. You couldn't watch him." The older woman shook her head and scowled.

"Ummm." Ruth wondered how Mrs Beacom knew what the arrangements were, but the older woman never missed anything so she was probably right. Ruth decided to say nothing, as she didn't want to speculate without any proof. Nor did she want to get a reputation for poking her nose in others' business; the whole town knew that she had reported Harry.

"He's as bold as brass, though, parking up in front of Mulligan's in the middle of the day. Not even the manners to go around to the back."

"I doubt you could get a lorry that size up the back entry, Mrs Beacom."

The older woman sniffed. "Even so, it's a slap in the face to Mr Reihill to take business elsewhere, and right under his nose."

As the women discussed the situation, Gormley and the publican rolled several metal barrels out of the door of the pub and hoisted them into the back of the lorry. The clang as each barrel hit the metal floor of the vehicle echoed up and down the empty street.

Ruth glanced over several times, being careful not to catch Gormley's eye. She wasn't sure whether he realised that she and Frank suspected him of supplying to Harry the information that her ex-boyfriend had planned to send to Germany. But she didn't want to risk a confrontation with the man, though she imagined that he would be too cagey for that. He'd not let on if he knew they had been watching him.

After a final loud bang, the street was silent. Ruth glanced at the pub. As she watched,

Gormley jumped down from the lorry then turned and reached into the back of it. He lifted out a large paper bag and held it firmly in both hands, as if it were heavy, as he followed the publican into the bar.

"It wouldn't take that much to pay the bill."

Ruth turned to Mrs Beacom, frowning. "What?"

"You'd wonder what he has in the bag. I reckon it's not the money to pay for the beer."

Ruth nodded, pursing her lips. Mrs Beacom was right. Gormley wasn't carrying the money to pay the bill. So what *was* in the bag?

"Mr Mulligan's been doing a bit of work on his place lately. Getting a few repairs done with the money he's earning from the RAF lads that come in for a drink. He'll be well fixed if he's supplying the drink to the Yankee camp too."

As she put the pieces together in her mind, Ruth only heard half of what the older woman said. So Mr Mulligan was doing some work on his premises. And Gormley had a reputation as a man about town, smuggling like so many were. Had he brought Mr Mulligan something he could use in his repair work? She would love to ask Mrs Beacom what she thought, but it would be better to keep quiet. She could discuss it with Frank later. It wasn't really her business, but she was curious now.

***

Watching the thin, goofy little man in a cop's uniform on the screen, Frank found it hard to believe that the same man had entertained them in evening dress the previous week. George Formby didn't look much like a real cop, but the actor on the screen didn't look like the comedian who had performed in Irvinestown either. He was just as funny in either role, though.

Frank glanced out of the corner of his eye to the seat beside him and he smiled as he saw Ruth's facial expressions change rapidly from disbelief to delight and back again. She laughed with gusto and joined others in the audience in spontaneous applause when it was obvious that Formby's character was going to save the day. Frank wrapped his arm around her shoulder, pulling her close to him, pleased to find that she didn't resist. He understood her desire to act modestly in public to avoid spurring more gossip about her, but she was adorable when she laughed and he couldn't help hugging her. He hadn't meant to get involved with a girl while he was here, but as he got to know her during the past few months he just couldn't resist her. Her stricken look when her boyfriend was arrested on suspicion of spying last October had just about broken his heart. He would have done anything he could to ease her pain, and he had been drawn to her ever since that terrible moment.

Loud applause filled the cinema as the film ended and Frank realised he was still staring at Ruth. She turned to him and smiled. He loved how her eyes lit up when she smiled. Without thinking, he leaned over and kissed her. He drew back from her just far enough to see her face and grinned, squeezing her shoulder with the arm that encircled it.

"You liked the movie?" He hadn't been sure whether he should bring her to a movie about espionage and saboteurs after what had happened with her ex-boyfriend. But she had been excited when she heard that one of Formby's movies was playing this week, and she didn't hesitate to accept his invitation.

"It was brilliant. The news on the radio can really get you down, but the film cheered me up. I'll be dancing home now."

"Not like that lady in the nightclub, I hope." Frank winked.

Ruth looked at him blankly for a second. "You mean Mr Formby's song 'I Wish I Was Back on the Farm'? Oh, goodness, no! I certainly won't be dancing covered only in pigeons." She giggled.

"I'm glad to hear that. I only go out with nice girls." He grinned wider as she slapped his arm in mock outrage. "You know, I'd better watch out that you don't get swept off your feet by a cop.

After that movie, I see what they can do to a gal."
Frank squeezed her shoulder again and laughed
at the expression on her face.

"You better watch your step or I might just fall
for one of the lads on the beat to spite you."

"Such threats!" He leaned over and gave her a
longer kiss than the previous ones.

"Mind!" Ruth pulled away from him and
looked around her.

"Sorry. But don't worry. No one's looking at
us." Frank tried to look apologetic. When she
relaxed, he stood up and offered his arm to her.
"Shall we go?"

Despite her pink face, she gave him a teasing
look. "Well, seeing as you're trying to mend your
ways and be a gentleman now, I might just come
with you."

Frank didn't mind that they were pushed
tightly together as they made their way up the
aisle to the exit. He tucked his elbow against his
side to pull her close to him and, when he felt her
being dragged away by the crowd, he reached out
and caught her waist, drawing her back to his
side.

The crowd spread out in the lobby. Frank let go
of her waist and clasped her hand in his. The
electric lights hanging from the high ceiling
weren't very bright but he squinted as his eyes
adjusted after emerging from the dark cinema.
"So what did you do with your time off today?"

"It wasn't really time off. Though it's half-day closing in the town, we still have work to do at the hotel. But Mum does let me go out for a while most Thursdays. I was collecting newspapers and the like for the paper drive."

He squeezed her hand. "You're a hard worker!"

"Everyone's got to do their bit." She smiled at him then her eyes flew open wide. "Oh, how could I forget? I meant to tell you – when I was at Mrs Beacom's door, I saw Mervyn Gormley. He was getting beer from Mulligan's."

"Mulligan's?"

"Aye. I thought you should know. Mrs Beacom says that the base has a standing order with Reihill's."

"Yeah, that's right. So why on earth did he go to Mulligan's?" Frank exhaled loudly. That Gormley was infuriating. What was he up to now? You just couldn't turn your back on him for a second.

"That's what we were wondering." Ruth's brow puckered. "There was another thing. Once they had loaded the barrels onto the lorry, he took a paper bag into the pub. It looked heavy."

"What do you mean it *looked* heavy?"

"He was carrying it in both hands and it seemed to be an effort."

Frank ran his hand through his thick black hair. Whatever Gormley was up to, it was probably not good. That farmer, Andy Noble, whom he had bought gravel from for the base last autumn had warned him about Gormley. The old man must know what he was talking about. "Lot of good it does knowing it," he muttered to himself. If only he could do something about the man.

He gently tugged Ruth's hand, leading her out of the door. The temperature had risen since the beginning of the month so the night was mild, but he slid his arm around her waist and pulled her to his side. He wouldn't worry about looking for an excuse to do so this time.

"What did you say?" Ruth asked.

"Just talking to myself. Andy Noble warned me about Gormley back before all that business with Coalter. I know he's trouble and I keep my eye on him, but I can never catch him in the act."

Ruth placed her hand on his where he held her waist; she squeezed his hand. "Mervyn's been doing deals of one sort or another as long as I remember. He's not easy to catch."

Frank grunted. "Yeah, don't I know it. And darn it, I wish it was only him." He was silent for a moment, considering how much he should tell her. He really shouldn't talk to her about it at all, but it had been bugging him the past few weeks and his boss was the only other person he was free to discuss it with. Before he reported the latest thefts to Mr Orchard, though, he wanted to have a way to fix the problem. He needed to think it through some more before he raised it with his boss. Ruth was a good listener and he knew he could trust her.

"We've been having big problems with materials going missing. I try to keep a tight eye on deliveries and the storage sheds but stuff still goes missing. It can't only be Gormley – it's bigger than that. They're making a fool out of me!"

He saw Ruth wince and made an effort to unclench his hand where he had pinched her waist. "Sorry."

"That's terrible, but you can't blame yourself."

"But I'm responsible. Once we receive our supplies, they should be safe on the site. I should know what's happening there. That's my job."

"I'm sure you're doing your best. There's a lot of lads working there. You couldn't watch them all. If someone has a mind to be dishonest, they'll find a way to do it."

Frank kept his voice low as they passed another couple strolling along the main street. "I know, but you'd think I could catch at least a few of them. There's always some problems with theft on a building site but I've never seen anything like this. Nails, bolts, metals and timber. There's even a couple mooring rings for seaplanes that've gone missing. Those are heavy. You don't sneak them out in your lunch box."

"You know, since the war started smuggling has gone mad here. They call the train to Bundoran in the Free State the Sugar Train because of the amount of sugar, among lots of other things, that's smuggled on it. Some people are greedy and take whatever they can get when they get the chance."

Ruth wasn't sure whether Frank knew the extent of smuggling back and forth across the border. Many people smuggled small quantities of rationed or unavailable goods from the Irish Free State into Northern Ireland. It had become almost a county pastime. And the day-excursion train trips to seaside towns such as Bundoran, just across the border in Donegal, made it easy for people to buy goods and bring them back to Northern Ireland. The Excise men were always searching people returning from day trips to Bundoran.

"There's a right lot of it about," she continued.

Yeah, if only that was all it was. "Mmm, I wish it was just some greedy people," he muttered.

"What?"

"Oh, nothing." He didn't want to tell her about Mr Orchard's warning. Irish terrorists were going to be even harder to deal with than ordinary thieves. But now that America had entered the war, he had to find a way to do it. He couldn't just submit a report and forget about it as Mr Orchard had told him they were meant to do.

"Not just greedy people? Who, then?"

Frank pursed his lips. He hadn't meant to tell her quite so much. Usually he was very careful about what he said to anyone. He was letting his guard down with her. Maybe too much, even though he did trust her. "We're not sure who's behind it yet."

"But it's more serious than just stealing?" Ruth sucked in her breath. "Oh no, is it spies? Like in the film? Have the Germans infiltrated the building site? Did we not stop Harry in time?"

Frank felt her shiver and held her tightly. "No, there's no German spies here and it's nothing to do with Harry. Don't start worrying about that."

"But someone wants to sabotage your work?"

It wasn't going to be easy to keep his guard up and also put her fears to rest. What could he tell her? "No, I don't think that's it either. They're more interested in their own ends."

Ruth looked around them then back to Frank. She lowered her voice to a whisper. "The IRA, then?"

Frank closed his eyes for a moment then opened them. He wouldn't lie to her. "You can't tell anyone what we suspect. Promise? They aren't interested in damaging our airbase. Looks like they want the materials for their own uses."

"Of course I wouldn't tell anyone. But be very careful. They're dangerous. You've no idea what they can do."

"Don't worry, I will be. But, let's not think about it anymore tonight. We should stop at the Clock Tower on our way back to the hotel. Remember that a kiss under the tower will keep your sweetheart true for all time."

Even though he couldn't see Ruth's expression in the dark, he was sure that reminding her of the story he had spun the last time they were at the tower had made her smile.

"Aye, well, as long as you behave like a gentleman. Then we'll get home to the fire. I think there's some cocoa left in the kitchen so I'll make us hot cocoa. The wee kitty will be waiting for us by the fire. We'll have to give her a name. She's been 'kitty' ever since she arrived on Christmas Eve."

"Terrific." Frank leaned over and gave her a quick kiss. He felt her lips respond to his and pushed thoughts of his job away. The problems there could wait until the morning.

Ely Lodge
Friday, 6th February, 1942

As Frank left the site office, he heard the commotion. At the main gate, a crowd had gathered and more workers were running to join them. The main gates were open and several of the men were standing on the road outside the compound. That was very dangerous, as some vehicles raced along the road without heed in the blackout. He had better get everyone inside again. Frank hurried to the gate and pushed his way through the crowd. As men turned and recognised him, they moved aside to let him pass. Frank worked his way through the crowd until he emerged on the other side of it at the road.

The men at the front of the crowd were standing in a ring, staring at the ground where a couple of workers crouched beside someone lying motionless at the edge of road. In the dusk, it was impossible to see who was lying there.

Frank bent over and peered at the prostrate man. "Who is it? What happened?"

One of the men replied. "Francey Byrne. A car hit him. Driver mustn't have seen him with the light nearly away."

The injured man groaned and tried to roll over, but a worker held him still.

"Is he badly hurt?"

"Don't rightly know but he must've got a hard knock, alright."

Frank straightened up, turned to the crowd and singled out one of the men. "Brennan, go and fetch Mr Orchard and George Watkins. Make sure Watkins brings the first-aid kit." It seemed too obvious to need to say it, but you never knew what people would do when they were under pressure. He turned to another man in the crowd.

"Nolan, get Clerkin to bring one of the trucks – lorries - up to the gate. We'll take him straight to the hospital after the first-aider has a look at him."

"Tommy's not in the yard, Mr Long."

"Gormley, then." Why had he asked for that guy as his second choice? Guess the name's stuck in my head, Frank thought.

"Not here either. We're waiting on him."

That explained why so many of the Irish workers were standing near the gate then. Gormley should have been back before quitting time to pick them up and take them to the drop-off point in County Cavan. Where had he got to?

Frank looked at Bernie Nolan, a short, worn-looking man in his forties. "Okay then, find any of the drivers and get a truck over here as quick as you can."

"Aye, will do." Nolan disappeared into the crowd.

Mr Orchard wove through the crowd to Frank; he handed a lantern to one of the workers. George Watkins hurried after him, carrying a large first-aid box and a blanket. The men in the front of the crowd pushed those behind them back to give Watkins room to examine the injured man. After Byrne's attempt to turn over a few minutes earlier, he had lain motionless. The man who held the lantern raised it above the injured man to enable Watkins to work. In its glow, Frank saw a dark wet pool on the road beside Byrne's head.

The injured man groaned when Watkins touched his left leg. There was no doubt that he had more than one injury and they were serious.

Mr Orchard pointed to two of the workers. "Get a large, flat board from the timber store. Hurry."

Behind Frank, the crowd began to shuffle apart and he heard the rumble of a truck's engine approaching. The vehicle stopped several feet behind them. Frank looked at his boss.

"When we have the board, we'll get him in the truck," the older man said.

Frank leaned backwards and flexed his shoulders to relieve the tension in his back. It felt like an hour before the men returned with the board, though it was only a couple of minutes. They placed it on the ground beside Byrne. George Watkins then rolled the injured man carefully onto it. Frank went to help him. The two men lifted the ends of the board as two other workers grasped either side. They carefully ferried Byrne to the waiting truck and laid him inside the back. George Watkins got in beside him.

Mr Orchard spoke to Frank. "I'll go with them to the hospital. Will you speak to the men and find out what happened? Why haven't they left for home yet anyway?"

"They're waiting for the truck that gives them a lift to get back to the site. I'll find out what happened." Frank watched Mr Orchard climb into the passenger seat.

The light had nearly disappeared and a half moon was faintly visible against the darkening sky as the truck drove out of the main gate. Around him, the men's faces were in shadow. Frank could just make out Nolan's features, and he beckoned the worker toward him.

"Nolan, you said Clerkin and Gormley aren't back yet. Do you know where they went?"

"Just out on messages. I don't know where."

"I reckon Gormley was gettin' in drink for the lads stopping here," another worker said.

Frank remembered that Gormley was often sent to buy beer on Friday afternoons for the workers who were billeted on site. But he was late getting back tonight. Frank pursed his lips, tapping his hand against his thigh. Was Gormley off somewhere, using the truck for his own errands? It wouldn't be surprising. You just couldn't keep up with what that man got up to. Well, he'd have a few words with Gormley when he got back.

But first, he needed the facts about the accident. With the blackout in force, pedestrians had to be very careful walking along roads, especially out in the country. Despite the fact that they could see almost nothing with their headlights covered, many drivers didn't slow down enough to compensate. Frank turned to

Nolan again. "What was Byrne doing out on the road?"

"He went to check if there was any sign of Gormley coming back."

Frank rubbed the back of his neck with his hand and grunted. "For heaven's sake, what was he thinking! He shouldn't have been standing out on the road when it was nearly dark."

"The lads were getting fed up waiting for Gormley. We thought he was late back for badness."

Inwardly, Frank groaned. If the Irish workers thought Gormley was deliberately trying to antagonise them, this accident would cause more ill feeling between the mainly Catholic workers from the Irish Free State and the Protestant workers from Northern Ireland. He would have to speak to Gormley to get to the bottom of this and then try to appease the Irish workers.

Where was Gormley anyway? Well, wherever he was, Frank would certainly deal with him when he got back. But right now he'd better arrange transport for the workers.

"I'll see about getting another truck to get you home. Tell the guys it won't be long."

Frank strode to one of the Nissan huts where American technicians bunked and asked for a volunteer. Although truck driving wasn't one of their normal duties, he was quick to get a response. He found a spare truck suitable to transport passengers and sent the Irish workers off with their new driver then he went to the site office to wait for Clerkin and Gormley to return. He was going to get some answers tonight.

Half an hour passed before he heard a vehicle engine slowing outside the main gate. He stood up and went to wait outside the door of the building. A covered truck turned into the site and stopped a few yards inside the gate. Frank strode grimly toward it. As he neared the vehicle, the cab door opened and Gormley jumped to the ground. The man looked around as if searching for something.

He spotted Frank and broke into a rushed monologue. "I never thought I'd get back, sir. There were a load of Mick Hanlon's sheep on the road and I gave him a hand to shift them. Thought we'd never get them shifted. They were the devil to catch. Where're the lads?"

Despite his city upbringing, Frank was sure that he didn't smell sheep or sweat on Gormley. If he had helped a farmer, he must not have made too much of an effort.

"How long did you spend helping the farmer?"

Gormley stared at Frank for a moment. "I don't rightly know. Time gets away from you when you're busy. I'd have been back by quitting time if it weren't for yon sheep."

Frank could ask the farmer about the incident later, but the man might be friendly with Gormley and stand by him so it could be difficult to prove whether Gormley's explanation was genuine. Nevertheless, with or without corroboration, he was reluctant to believe the labourer.

"Where did the lads get to?" Gormley asked again.

"One of the technicians gave them a ride home since you weren't around." Frank kept his tone level but there was a hint of anger in it.

"Right, right. Sorry, sir. Like I said, I didn't expect to be so long. At least the lads in the camp will have their grog tonight."

Frank hated the way the man always tried to ingratiate himself with everyone. Gormley was unfailingly friendly and accommodating, but Frank mistrusted the man. It was just so darn frustrating not to be able to prove his suspicions right.

As Frank stood staring at Gormley, another vehicle pulled into the yard and parked beside the truck that Gormley had been driving. Tommy Clerkin climbed down from the cab and walked over to the other two men. Frank saw Clerkin exchange a wary look with Gormley before he turned to his superior.

"Evening, boss. I never thought I'd get back, at all. It took ages to get the rock shovelled onto the lorry."

"You were getting rock for gravel from the Henderson farm?" Frank asked.

"Aye. Didn't get much help to stow it from them."

"You and Gormley can unload it before you go. I'll get someone to weigh it in."

Gormley shuffled from one foot to the other and wouldn't meet Frank's gaze. "Now? It's Friday night. I had a mind to meet my mates for a jar," Gormley said. "Why don't we do it first thing in the morning?"

Frank fixed Gormley with a stern stare. Even in the darkness, he was sure that the other man would sense his anger. "You can do it tonight before you leave. And you can unload the beer at the canteen. You kept all the workers from across the border waiting for a ride home after their quitting time, and one of them is off to the hospital because he went out on the road to look for you. So I suggest you get to it now."

Frank heard Gormley suck in his breath, but, for once, the man said nothing. He merely nodded then glanced at Clerkin. Neither man met Frank's gaze as they turned and walked toward the vehicles. As they walked away, Frank heard Clerkin say to Gormley, "He seems right fond of those'uns."

Frank decided to ignore the comment. Tackling Clerkin about it wouldn't help to deal with the resentment the Northern Irish workers felt toward their Irish co-workers. He went to the nearest Nissan hut and asked one of the American workers to weigh the load Clerkin had brought in. He was convinced that Gormley must be up to something; Clerkin might be in on it too. It was probably a small-time smuggling deal, but he had had enough of Gormley and he wouldn't let it pass. Weighing the load tonight would hamper Gormley if he planned to make off with any of it later. Frank knew that he had a bigger problem with the rest of the stuff that was disappearing, but, even so, he wasn't going to just let this pass. He would clamp down on Gormley and his cronies while he sought a way to thwart the IRA supporters they had unwittingly hired.

Ballyconnell, County Cavan, Ireland
Saturday, 7th February, 1942

"Are you sure I should go? Shouldn't it just be his family and friends? I'll be at the funeral." Frank kept one hand on the steering wheel as he swivelled his upper body to face Ruth.

"Aye. Your boss was at the hospital with him. It would be disrespectful if you didn't go to his wake. It's expected." Ruth thought it must be confusing for Frank. Surely, many of the nuances of social etiquette here must be very different from what he was used to where he came from.

"I'm not much good at these things. I don't have a clue what to say to his family."

"Don't worry. You'll be fine." Ruth gave Frank what she hoped was a reassuring smile.

"I still can't believe it. The man was just waiting for Gormley to get back to the base to give him a ride home, and now he's dead."

"It's terrible, altogether." Ruth shook her head. A worrying thought made her turn to Frank, her brow creased. "You won't get in any trouble going over the border, will you?"

"No. There's no restrictions on American civilian workers. It's just military personnel that they're banning from crossing the border." Frank slowed the vehicle as they drove onto the main street of a small town.

"Good. I wouldn't want you to get in any trouble. We've not far to go now. This is Ballyconnell. I'll show you where to turn just out the road."

Frank nodded. "It sure is easier getting around in the South – signposts on the roads really help."

Ruth glared in mock annoyance. "Well, they're not at war and don't have to worry about protecting themselves from spies infiltrating their country. And is that all that got you here?"

Frank pretended to think as he watched the road. "Your precise directions must have helped too." He chuckled.

Ruth dipped her head to acknowledge his praise. "Thanks. There –" She pointed at a narrow road off to the right. "Take that one. His family live a couple miles down the road."

They sat in silence as Frank drove along the new road. She wondered what he was thinking. It was such a shock last night when he'd returned from work much later than usual and told her about the accident. It must have been terrible for him to be there when it happened. Late in the evening, Mr Orchard had come to the hotel to tell him that the man had died at the hospital. Frank had looked shaken. She knew he was especially upset about it as the accident wouldn't have happened if Mervyn Gormley had collected the Irish workers when he was supposed to. Why did that man have to cause Frank so many headaches?

Ahead, on the left side of the road, stood a two-storey farmhouse, crumbling white paint flaking off the walls around the battered red door. The curtains were drawn though it was only mid-afternoon. A motor car was parked in front of the house, and carts and traps had been left along the road. Several horses were tied up in the yard behind. This must be the house.

"That's it there. You can stop along the side of the road here." Ruth pointed to a vacant spot.

Frank parked the Morris Minor van. When they got out, she waited for him to walk around to the passenger side. He offered her his arm and she slipped her hand under his elbow and let him lead her.

As they approached the house, she dropped her hand from his arm. Frank adjusted his tie at the front door. Usually she only saw him in his good suit on Sundays when they went to their churches. Sunday mornings he looked dashing in the chocolate-brown wool garment. Today it seemed to constrict him and he looked uneasy in it. She reached out and touched his forearm as he raised his hand to knock on the door. He paused and looked at her, and she gave him a quick, reassuring smile. His lips twitched in reply; then he knocked firmly on the door.

A young man in his twenties opened it. He stepped aside to allow them to enter.

"Hello, I'm Frank Long from Francey's work."

"You're very welcome," the young man said. "I'm Sean, Francey's brother."

"I'd like to offer my condolences to you and your family." Frank extended his hand to the young man.

Ruth leaned forward, her hand also outstretched. "We're sorry for your loss. Such a terrible accident it was."

The young man shook their hands. He led them down the hall and through a door at the end that opened into a roomy kitchen. A large, black range sat at one end of the room. In the middle of the room, an open coffin rested on a large table designed to seat eight or ten. Chairs and stools were placed around the walls; men and women of all ages sat, chatting quietly. The conversation stopped as they entered the room.

Sean led Frank and Ruth to an older couple, seated at the head of the coffin. Ruth stepped forward with her hands outstretched and clasped each of them by the hand in turn.

"Mr and Mrs Byrne, I'm so sorry for your loss," she said. She heard Frank repeating her words as he spoke to Francey Byrne's parents.

Mr Byrne stood up and shook their hands. He stepped to the coffin and the pair followed him.

"He was a good lad while God spared him," the older man said. He looked into the coffin, smiling sadly.

As Ruth respectfully gazed into the coffin, her eyes widened and she had to hold back a gasp when she noticed the clear signs of a head wound just behind the corpse's ear. What a terrible way for a young man to die. She suppressed a shudder and turned her attention to Mr Byrne again. The older man was laboriously bending down to kneel on the stone floor beside the coffin. Frank followed his example. Ruth felt a stab of panic. She didn't know any Catholic prayers, but she didn't want to offend the family either. She knelt beside the two men.

Mr Byrne took his rosary beads from his pocket and began to pray. Along with the mourners seated around the room, Frank joined in the responses to the older man's prayers. Ruth bowed her head and closed her eyes until they finished, hoping no one would notice her silence. She knew the mourners' eyes would be on the couple. That was the way with folk when strangers arrived. But she doubted that they would be too concerned about what religion she was; it wouldn't matter to them, not like at home. Her difference wouldn't provoke suspicion or animosity toward her. Nevertheless, when Mr Byrne finished praying and rose, Ruth quickly got back on her feet, trying to avoid drawing further attention to herself.

Francey's father led them to two empty chairs, and a teenage girl brought them each a cup of tea. After the girl walked away, Frank leaned toward Ruth and whispered, "His brother and sister look so much like him."

Ruth nodded, idly surveying the room. As she did so, she noticed more than one head quickly turn away from her gaze. She imagined that it was the same anywhere you went. If you were a stranger, people were curious, but she was glad they meant no harm. It was a different curiosity than you might meet as a stranger in the North. She spotted a couple young people who resembled the young man who had opened the door and the girl who had served them the tea. They must all be brothers and sisters, she concluded. She noticed Frank was looking around too. She saw him nod to a couple men seated on the far side of the room.

"Are they from the site?"

"Yeah, that's Bernie Nolan." Frank nodded toward a short man in his forties. "There's Brennan too." Frank glanced around the room then said quietly, "I thought Watkins would be here today. He was the first-aider that treated Byrne last night."

Ruth hesitated then reluctantly said, "Maybe he'll come later." She knew that probably wasn't true. Pressure from his fellow Northern Irish Protestant workmates would keep him away, but she didn't want to say so where others could overhear. The deep-seated antipathy was never discussed openly.

Frank's eyebrows drew together. "I hadn't expected to see Clerkin or Gormley, but I thought Watkins would be here. And some of the other men. Come to think of it, I don't see any of the men from around Irvinestown, just the ones from this side of the border." Frank sighed. "The accident did happen after most of the men finished last night. Maybe they haven't heard about it."

Ruth took a deep breath. She would have to try to set him straight, without saying too much. Not in public. "I think most'll have heard about it by now." She looked at Frank, hoping he would catch her meaning. How she could remind him how deep the antagonism between the Northern Irish Protestant workers and Irish Catholic ones ran? She knew he had encountered problems

203

between the men at the site but she didn't think he understood how deep their feelings ran. She held his gaze.

Frank tilted his head as he looked at her. His lips parted as if he were about to say something then he stopped. She thought she saw comprehension in his eyes.

"They aren't coming, then?" he asked.

Ruth shook her head. "I wouldn't think so."

"For crying out loud – I would have expected better of them."

"It's not easy to change some things."

An elderly woman seated on Ruth's right side began speaking to her. As she turned to reply to the woman, she was aware that Frank was leaning across her, listening to the conversation. She hoped his close proximity wouldn't make her face flush. She often couldn't think straight when he was close to her.

"Are you a friend of young Francey?" the older woman asked.

Ruth shook her head. "I never had the pleasure of meeting him. Frank is the gaffer where he worked." She turned her head to indicate the man who so easily flustered her.

The older woman turned her attention to Frank. "I live up the road from here. Francey was a good lad."

"I'm sure he was. He was a good worker too. It's terrible about the accident," he replied.

The woman continued to chat with the couple, telling them about Francey as a child, and what a wonderful Gaelic footballer he was. Ruth didn't know much about the sport and was sure that Frank knew even less, but she listened politely. Half an hour passed before the woman turned to reply to a question from the woman on her other side.

"How long should we stay?" Frank spoke quietly so only Ruth could hear him.

"We can leave whenever you'd like."

"It'll be coming up to dusk soon. I guess we should head back."

Ruth leaned over to say goodbye to the woman they had been speaking to then turned back to Frank. "Are you ready?"

"Before we go, I should speak to the workers who are here." Frank stood up and walked across the room to Bernie Nolan.

Ruth followed him and listened as the two men chatted briefly. Frank moved on to speak to several other men who were sitting together then held out his arm to Ruth. She linked her hand under his elbow and led him to Francey's parents to bid them farewell.

Once they were back in the van, Ruth said, "You did very well."

"Thanks to your guidance. It's not like when someone dies at home. Everyone is very quiet and formal. They seemed sad here but more relaxed and inclined to chat."

"Aye, that's the way of it. The funeral is a more solemn occasion."

Frank nodded as he started the van. Neither one spoke again until they entered Ballyconnell.

"Oh boy, there's another thing here that makes it easier to find your way around," Frank said as they drove slowly along the main street.

Ruth turned her head to look at him, her eyebrows raised.

Frank nodded his head in the direction of the shop windows. "Lights everywhere."

Ruth followed his gaze. "Oh, of course. How could I have missed it?"

She felt heat rising to her face. She must look silly not to even notice that there was no blackout here. The street and the shops were lit. It had been ages since she could go anywhere at home in the evening without stumbling her way along in the dark.

It wasn't completely dark yet, but dusk was falling and there were lights in several windows along the street. Looking through a window, she saw the butcher standing behind his counter, chatting to an elderly woman. Light streamed from the front window in the greengrocer's next door, spotlighting heaps of potatoes, carrots and turnips, which lay in boxes outside under the window.

Ruth stole a glance at Frank. He wasn't laughing at her silly error. His attention was on the street as he slowly manoeuvred the vehicle around a horse and cart that had been left beside the curb while its owner chatted on the footpath with another man dressed the same as himself, in a worn jacket and flat cap. A third man passed behind the two who were chatting, heading in the same direction as the couple were driving. There was something familiar about him. Ruth turned her attention to the man. She sucked in her breath when she got a clear look at his face.

"Oh, look there, Frank." She pointed at the man. "It's Mervyn Gormley."

Frank braked to slow the vehicle as he looked where she was pointing. "It sure is. How can that louse show his face so close to Byrne's house when he won't go to the wake? Wonder what he's up to here?"

"I guess he could be here for any reason. Maybe he's got friends in town." Although she disliked the man and, despite his reputation, she tried to be fair. Maybe he had a legitimate reason for being here today.

"I doubt that. He isn't very friendly with the Irish workers on our site. If he's here, it's probably on business."

Ruth stared at Frank. She must have misunderstood him. "He was sent down here?"

"No, not by the company. I didn't mean official business."

Ruth nodded. Although she had tried to be fair, that had been her first thought too. He was here on business of his own. Something that would likely line his pockets. As they watched Gormley, he entered a tobacconists' shop.

"Wonder what he's dealing in this time?" Frank said.

"He seems to do a bit of everything, doesn't he?"

"He sure does. Everywhere I look that louse is there. I shouldn't let him bother me so much. He's small potatoes compared to other problems we've got, but I'd still really like to straighten him out."

Ruth knew Frank was referring to the thefts the IRA was suspected of committing at the construction site. Gormley wasn't in the same league at all, but she understood Frank's annoyance. Gormley angered her too. He had got away with supplying information intended to be sent to the enemy. She was sure of it, even though they had no proof. She would love to see Gormley punished for at least some of his crimes.

"I guess you need to keep your eye on the really serious crimes, but if you ever have a chance to catch Gormley red-handed, I'd do whatever I could to help," she said.

"I know you would. You're a swell girl. How lucky did I get when I met you?" Frank smiled at her then sighed. "There's nothing we can do about Gormley tonight, so let's put him out of our minds. Will we stop in Enniskillen on the way back and get something to eat?"

"Aye, that would be grand. You're always so good to me."

"You're worth it, honey. No doubt about that." He reached across and squeezed her hand.

Ruth wanted to bounce on the seat with delight; she was so glad that she had met him. He was such a grand fella. She would put Gormley out of her mind and enjoy the rest of their evening.

Orange Hall, Irvinestown
Saturday, 14th February, 1942

"Hey, that's the song my sister told me about in her last letter – 'Chattanooga Choo Choo'. It's all the rage in the States. I see why – you can't beat Glenn Miller." Frank cocked his ear to listen as he led Ruth into the energetic swing rhythm. "Wonder how this band knows it?"

"We're not completely cut off from the rest of the world, you know." Ruth gave him a mock scowl. "Even during a war, records can be posted from America. Lots of us have family over there."

"Yeah, you lot are resourceful. That's for sure." He gave her a cheeky grin. "Gormley's a great example."

He felt her stiffen in his arms.

"Most of us aren't like him!"

Frank laughed. "I know. I'm only teasing you. You're so cute when you're angry." His expression sobered briefly. "Darn it, we weren't going to talk about him tonight and I started it – sorry." Almost without pause, he cocked his head to one side again and gave her an impish grin. "If I'm very nice the rest of the evening, will you forgive me?"

Ruth pretended to consider his question. "Mmm, I'll try."

"That's good. If you weren't speaking to me, I wouldn't be able to give you my surprise."

"What surprise?"

"Oh, you'll see." Frank picked up the pace as he twirled her in time to the music, cutting off their conversation.

When the swing number ended, the band struck up a waltz. Frank didn't recognise it but realised it must be an Irish one, as many of the dancers seemed to know it. Ruth rested her cheek against his for a moment as they slowed their pace then straightened up and pulled away from him slightly. Frank stifled a sigh. It irked him that they always had to be so careful not to do anything that would impinge on Ruth's reputation. Nothing passed the notice of the residents of a small town like Irvinestown. He really liked Ruth and wished he could show it without restraint. But then, if he were at home, he knew his grandfather would have something to say if he didn't treat a girl with respect. Maybe things weren't so different than at home. It was only in the big ballrooms in New York, away from his neighbourhood, where no one noticed or cared how you behaved.

The next set was a trio of waltzes and they stayed on the dance floor. Frank enjoyed the comfortable feeling of Ruth in his arms, even if he couldn't hold her as close as he wanted to. When other dancers jostled them, he pulled her up tight against him for fleeting moments. He was sure he wasn't the only guy who took the opportunity to get close to his girl in the crush on the dance floor.

He really hoped Ruth would like his surprise. It was a stroke of luck that he and Mr Orchard had had to attend a meeting with the contracting firm's executive and the military brass in Belfast a couple days after Francey Byrne's funeral. The trip to the city gave him a chance to get a special Valentine's gift for her. Even if it was the largest town in the county, Enniskillen's jewellers' shops didn't have nearly as much choice as the city stores. He reached into his pocket to reassure himself that the small box was still there.

The band finished the third waltz and the dancers turned toward the platform as the singer stepped up to the microphone. "That's all for now, folks. We'll take a short break for supper."

Frank frowned as he looked at Ruth. "Supper? We ate before we came out. I didn't know this was a dinner dance."

Ruth giggled. "Not dinner. Supper."

Frank thought she must expect him to understand what she meant from the way she was looking at him, but he didn't have a clue. He raised his eyebrows.

"Supper – like what you have to eat before you go to bed."

They certainly had some strange expressions over here, he thought. "Oh, is the dance over, then?" He didn't really want it to end yet as he was enjoying the evening immensely. The more time he spent with Ruth, the more he realised how special she was to him. She was fun and kind, and he hadn't met anyone else as game to try anything as she was. She really was amazing.

Ruth smiled. "No. We'll have supper then there'll be more dancing. We'll have to make the most of this last dance."

"Last dance?"

"Aye, the last one before Lent. There's no dances during Lent."

Frank felt a pang of disappointment. It was so much fun taking Ruth out dancing. He loved going for walks or to the cinema with her or just sitting in the hotel lounge together, but they could be really carefree for a little while on the dance floor.

The crowd was streaming from the dance floor to the end of the hall where the refreshment tables had been set up. Frank took advantage of the opportunity to slip his arm around Ruth's waist, unnoticed by anyone. "Will we go and join the line?"

"Aye, if you unhand me and behave like a gentleman." Ruth gave him a mock scowl. "We wouldn't want to miss the supper. They always lay on a good spread at these dances. Some of the men just come for the feed."

"Not me. I'm well cared for by you and your mother. I'm here for the dancing – it's a great excuse to get you in my arms."

Frank grinned as the blush spread up her neck to her face. It was endearing that she was so outgoing and confident yet she embarrassed so easily. He let his arm slip from her waist and took her hand as they joined the snaking line heading toward the refreshments table.

When they reached the long table heaped with sandwich platters and tarts made by the members of the Women's Institute, they selected an assortment of egg and salad sandwiches and one piece of apple tart each then went to find chairs along the wall.

As they ate their food and chatted, Frank looked around the room, noticing that many of the local men had gone back to stand on one side of the room and the women were gathered in groups on the opposite side as they had been at the beginning of the evening. It seemed to be the way they did things here. They certainly had some strange customs and that was one he had no intention of adopting. He had brought Ruth to the dance and he was staying with her, no matter what anyone said about it.

The heat in the crowded room was stifling. Frank noticed Ruth raise her hand to fan her face. She was obviously feeling it too. Hot dog, this was the excuse he had been looking for to get some time alone with her to give her the gift. The streets between the hall and the hotel would be thronged with people as they walked home later, and they might not be alone in the hotel lounge either.

"It's sweltering in here, isn't it? Like summer in New York without the flies."

Ruth laughed and nodded her agreement. "Guess we should be thankful we're warm in the middle of the winter, but it is terribly hot."

"Why don't we step outside for a few minutes and cool off?" Frank half rose from his seat as he spoke.

"Aye, that's a good idea." Ruth also rose and followed him. They returned their empty plates to the refreshment table then stopped at the door to let the attendant stamp their hands with heavy black ink before they left the building.

Once they were outside, Frank slid his arm around Ruth's waist and carefully led her along the path and through the gate to the sidewalk, letting his eyes adjust to the darkness as they walked. Across the street, he could distinguish the shadowy form of Sacred Heart Church. He guided Ruth to the curb then stopped and listened. He didn't hear any cars so, mindful of Francey Byrne's accident, he didn't dawdle as he led her across the street and through the gate into the church grounds.

Ruth stiffened as they entered the grounds. "Won't the priest be annoyed if he finds us in here?"

"He won't be here at this time of night. He's probably overseeing the dance at St Molaise's Hall." Frank leaned closer to her. "And I won't do anything that you would object to, so don't worry."

He felt Ruth relax. He led her to a large oak tree beside the church. It was even darker here underneath its sprawling branches. As he turned to face her, wrapping both arms around her waist, he caught a whiff of her Lily of the Valley scent. He snuggled against her and inhaled.

"You smell lovely," he said. "Just one more thing I like about you."

"You're always so sweet to me."

"How could I not be? You're such a swell girl. And it's Valentine's Day. I have to treat my girl right."

"Do they make a fuss about Valentine's Day in America?"

"They sure do. So it's the perfect evening to show my sweetheart how special she is."

Frank couldn't see her face in the dark, but he was sure that Ruth's eyes were shining as she looked up at him. He loved the warm way she had been looking at him during the past few weeks. She seemed to be losing the uncertainty she had had about their courtship. He thought she must be coming to terms with her previous sweetheart's betrayal of her and her country, and trying to put it behind her. He hadn't meant to find a sweetheart when he came to Northern Ireland. Lots of the workers on the airbase had local girlfriends, but he was the boss's assistant. He should keep his mind on his work but, as he got to know Ruth, he couldn't resist her.

Still holding her, Frank reached into his pocket and drew out the small box. He stifled a grunt of annoyance as he realised that she wouldn't be able to see his gift in the dark. What a numbskull he was! He hadn't thought of that when he chose this private location to give it to her. Oh well, he couldn't do anything about it. She would have to wait until they returned to the hall to get a proper look at it. He set the box in Ruth's hands and wrapped his arm around her waist again. "Happy Valentine's Day, honey."

"This is the surprise you mentioned earlier? Thank you so much."

"You haven't even opened it yet."

He heard the box snap open and Ruth bent to peer at its contents.

Frank laughed. "Guess I didn't pick the best place to give it to you."

"I can feel that it has a chain. Is it a necklace?" Ruth laughed. "And I come prepared." She reached into her handbag, pulled out her flashlight and shone it into the box. He heard her draw in her breath.

"That's lovely! Oh my goodness! Thank you!"

Ruth threw her right arm around his neck, holding the box in her other hand, and gave him a quick kiss on his cheek. He squeezed her and turned his head to kiss her on the lips, relieved that she liked it. He wanted this gift to be special and had been worried that he might not get it right. He wasn't used to buying jewellery for a girl. If he had been at home, he would have asked one of his sisters to help him choose it.

Frank released her from his embrace. "Let me put it on for you."

Ruth shone the torch on the box again and he looked at the delicate chain as he lifted it. The single loose pearl, encased inside gracefully curved silver strands that formed a teardrop-shaped cage less than half an inch long, hung from a sterling silver chain. The silver glinted in the torchlight as he felt for the clasp and unfastened it. He put the necklace around Ruth's neck and closed the clasp, and was pleased to see her hand immediately go to her neck to caress the chain.

"I'm glad you like it. I wanted to get something special for you."

"I do, but you shouldn't be spending your money on me."

"Why not? I want to." Frank wrapped his arms around her again. "A pearl grows from a grain of sand and gradually develops into something beautiful. It's rare and special, like you. I want you to remember our first Valentine's Day together." He was surprised that he could express what he wanted to say. He hadn't been sure he would be able to tell her how special she had become to him. He was also surprised that he had said their *first* Valentine's Day together. But he wasn't sorry he had said it. Now that the words were out, he knew that he wanted many more Valentine's Days with her.

"Oh, that's so sweet. I've never seen anything like it in the shops round here. Where ever did you find it?"

"I have my sources." He tapped his nose.

Ruth made a noise in her throat that might be a question or possibly an expression of disapproval.

"Don't worry. Not like our friend Gormley." Frank laughed.

"Oh, I never thought that!"

In the torchlight, he saw the look of horror on her face.

"It's okay. I know you didn't. Actually, I bought it when I was in Belfast earlier this week. Gosh, I've got to stop thinking about Gormley. Especially when I'm with you. He never seems to be far from my mind, though. I have to get to the bottom of what he's up to one way or another."

"Couldn't you stop him and search the vehicle?"

"If we search him at the site he'll probably have a story concocted about where the materials are going or that there was an error when they were loaded or something. We have to catch him actually disposing of what he's stealing."

"I think I know someone who might be able to help you. I'll have a word with Robbie Hetherington, the fella I know in the Ulster Home Guard."

"Don't be getting too involved in this. It's not your worry."

"I'll just have a word with him for you."

"Thanks. You really are such a swell girl. Now, we'll put Gormley out of our minds for the rest of this evening. Let's head back in a few minutes so we don't miss the rest of the dance. But first –"

Frank reached for the flashlight and switched it off then leaned close to Ruth and brushed his lips against hers. They were so soft, and he felt her tentatively responding to the pressure of his own. They would go back to the dance soon, but he didn't want to spoil this moment. He let the kiss linger.

***

"Stay well back, Robbie. We don't want him to see us." Ruth whispered, even though there was no need to do so.

"We've managed to follow him this far without a hitch. We don't want to mess it up now." Frank also spoke quietly, the tension evident in his voice.

Robbie's work-roughened hands were relaxed on the steering wheel. "Don't worry. He won't get wind we're on to him. With the cattle trailer hitched to the van, he'll never suspect I'm anything but a farmer behind him."

"You are a farmer, Robbie." Ruth laughed nervously.

"Aye, and I'm not in uniform, but my identity card in my pocket says I'm on official Ulster Home Guard business."

Seated between the two men, Ruth looked from one to the other. Frank's jaw was rigid and she felt embarrassed that she had attempted to make a joke. Frank was too keyed up for jokes. They had devised this plan to send Mervyn Gormley on an errand then follow him, hoping they would catch him taking the opportunity to dispose of goods stolen from the airbase while he was away from the site. Despite Frank's reluctance to involve her in this, Ruth had worked with him to devise the plan and she wanted to see it through. They had worked together to stop Harry and she knew they made a good team. So she was pleased when Frank had returned to the hotel to collect her after Gormley left the base this afternoon. They hadn't wasted any time and went straight to find Robbie to help them put their plan into action.

She was glad that they had discussed Frank's suspicions about Gormley with Robbie. Her friend took his work as an Ulster Home Guard very seriously and he was keen to help them. Ever since they had voiced their suspicions to him, Robbie had been watching for the labourer when he was out on patrols and reported to them where he had spotted him. Frank matched this information to Gormley's work assignments, so he knew when the labourer was somewhere he shouldn't have been, and therefore possibly on some crooked business of his own.

"What we need to do today is find out who he's meeting and where." Ruth kept her voice low and even, hoping to help calm Frank's nerves.

Her sweetheart's mouth was set in a hard, determined line and his eyes were ice blue as he watched the Morris Minor van on the road in front of them. He appeared calm and purposeful, but a muscle twitching in his cheek revealed his tension. She squeezed his hand briefly where it lay on his knee then released it.

Despite her optimistic tone of voice, there were butterflies in her stomach. She wanted this to work as much as Frank did. They had spent most evenings during the past couple of weeks beside the fire in the Residents' Lounge, discussing how they could catch Gormley. There hadn't been any solid evidence to prove that he was the person who had leaked information about the construction of the airbase to Harry Coalter. Although Harry had been arrested for his attempt to pass military secrets to Germany, Gormley couldn't be tied to the crime. His theft and smuggling activities were another matter, though. They could get solid evidence about this. Enough to bring him to justice. It wouldn't make up for his escape from the treason charge, but it was better than nothing.

"We're in with a good chance of catching him at it. I've spotted him a few places he probably shouldn't have been since you first mentioned it to me," Robbie said. "Today likely won't be any different."

"Yeah, and I'm pretty sure he has something he shouldn't stashed in the van," Frank said.

Earlier Frank had told Ruth and Robbie that he had spotted the labourer loitering near the supplies store this afternoon when the storeman had left it unattended for a few minutes. Frank had watched him through the window in the site office, and had seen him carry several small boxes from the supplies store and set them in the vehicle.

Robbie's confidence reassured Ruth. There was every reason to hope their plan would work.

Thursdays were now Gormley's usual day to collect the standing order for beer from Reihill's pub. After Francey Byrne died, the collection day had been changed so that there would be no reason for Gormley to be late to meet the Irish workers to give them a lift home on Fridays. Frank had sent the labourer to Enniskillen, earlier than he usually left to collect the beer, on the pretext that the kitchen needed more bread and the bakery in Irvinestown was closed for the town's half-day closing. Gormley could collect the beer in Irvinestown on his way back. The extra errand in Enniskillen gave Frank time to get to Irvinestown before Gormley. When the labourer arrived at the pub, Robbie's vehicle was parked halfway down the street where the trio could watch Gormley load the beer into the van and follow him when he left.

"Hopefully he didn't do his business before we first clocked him in Irvinestown," Robbie said.

"Probably not. I reminded him after lunch to go to Reihill's before the shift ended to pick up the beer. I didn't mention the errand in Enniskillen until just before he left the base. If he's arranged a meeting with anyone, it'll likely be out here somewhere," Frank said.

"As long as the trip to Enniskillen didn't upset his plans," Ruth said. "He'll be headed straight back to the base if he keeps on this road."

"Darn it. I hope I didn't mess up his plans, trying to buy me time to get into Irvinestown to get the pair of you so we could tail him," Frank said.

"Gormley's always been a sleekit one. He'll get time for his own business, never fret," Robbie said.

Ruth felt a little better. Today they wanted to find out who Gormley's contact was and where they met. Once they knew this, Robbie would be able to keep an eye on both men. Frank could also watch them. Hopefully it wouldn't take too long to gather enough information to go to the authorities with it. Discovering at least one of Gormley's contacts would be a step closer to prosecuting him.

"What's this, then?" Robbie tapped his hand on the steering wheel.

Gormley's van was slowing down.

"Is he stopping? What'll we do if he sees us?" Ruth felt sick. Gormley was going to spot them, she was sure of it. She felt like they were the quarry now instead of him.

Robbie took off his flat cap and handed it to Frank. "Put that on and pull it well down over your face. Ruth, tip up the collar of your coat and keep your head bent. He'll not know either of you."

Both of them did as Robbie instructed. Ruth reached out and squeezed Frank's hand again.

They could pull this off. They had to. She didn't want Gormley to keep getting away with crimes that were hurting the war effort. He might be a petty crook, but it was worse than that. His wrongdoing was unpatriotic and what he had done for Harry was treasonous.

Frank groaned. "Heck, no, he's turning off onto that small road. We'll lose him."

"Not a bother. We'll go that way," Robbie said.

"But then he'll know we're following him," Frank said.

"He won't. I've a cousin who has a farm up that road. Bert Gilroy. I'll head there. As long as he doesn't recognise either of you, he'll not suspect a thing."

Ruth kept her head bent as Robbie turned onto the smaller road. She wanted to look up to see how far ahead Gormley was, but she was afraid that he would spot her in his rear-view mirror. She clenched her hands in her lap as they drove for several minutes along the small road. No one spoke.

Ruth felt their vehicle slow down but kept her head bent.

"Ah, and what's this now?" Robbie said.

"Don't stop, Robbie, we don't want him to get a good look at us." As Ruth spoke, she took a quick peek at the road ahead and saw why Robbie had slowed down. The vehicle in front of them had stopped and was turning into a farmyard on

225

the left side of the road. Once it had disappeared into the yard Robbie drove slowly past.

Robbie glanced into the yard then back to the road as they drove past the farmyard. "The old Lawlor place."

"Old?" Frank said.

"Aye, it belonged to Jimmy Lawlor. He died last autumn. A bachelor. Lived alone."

"Who'd he be meeting there, I wonder?" Frank said.

"I don't know who it could be. The house is empty. There was no one belonging to Mr Lawlor left to run the farm," Ruth said.

"A couple neighbouring farmers have been tending the cattle in the byre over the winter," Robbie added.

"So no one lives there but the neighbours look after the place? Doesn't it have to be sold?" Frank asked.

"The government isn't bothered as long as it's being farmed. They'll likely grow potatoes there in summer to meet the quotas so they can carry on as they are. Tommy Clerkin and Ned Latimer are doing a grand job of running it," Robbie said.

"Tommy Clerkin? If he's the same guy, he works at the airbase." Frank looked at Ruth. "He's the one who I told you caused an argument with some of the Irish workers a few weeks ago. Gormley was right behind him." Frank shook his head. "I think Latimer's one of our workers too. So why is Gormley meeting them here?"

"Could they be storing whatever they've stolen at the farm?" Ruth asked.

Frank's eyes lit up and she could feel his body tense. "Yeah, that could just be it. And finding their hiding spot would be nearly as good as finding his sales contacts."

They drove slowly along the road, discussing what they had learned until Robbie slowed the vehicle almost to a stop and turned onto a long lane on the right hand side of the road. The vehicle picked up speed as he climbed the hill to the two-storey farmhouse at the end of the lane. He spun into the yard behind the house and parked. Frank and Ruth climbed out of the passenger side and followed Robbie to the back door of the house.

The Ulster Home Guard tapped twice on the door and entered the kitchen. "Hello, Auntie Betty."

"Ach, hello, Robbie." A plump woman greeted Robbie warmly, glancing over his shoulder at the couple standing behind him.

Robbie introduced his aunt to Frank and Ruth. Ruth tried to hide her impatience as they spent the next few minutes chatting about the weather. Gormley was only a couple miles away, but he seemed to have been forgotten.

The back door opened again and Ruth turned to see a young man who resembled Robbie enter the room.

"Hiya, Bert," Robbie greeted him.

After the introductions had been made, Ruth could contain her impatience no longer. "So, what're we going to do?"

Bert gave her a quizzical look and Robbie filled him in on the reason for their visit.

Betty turned from the range where she was brewing tea for the visitors and tutted. "Mind you don't get mixed up in anything dangerous."

Her son threw her an irritated glance. "This is Home Guard business, Ma."

"That may be, but just mind yourselves, lads," she replied. "Alright so, I'll make us a cuppa and say no more. Sit yourselves down."

Ruth glanced impatiently at the back door. She wanted to get back to the Lawlor farm and search for the stolen goods, but no one else seemed inclined to move.

Robbie looked at her. "Settle yourself, lass. We wanted to see who Gormley was doing business with, but we've got more than that. Looks like we've found where he's storing the stuff he steals. So we'll give them time to do their business and leave. Then we'll have a look around the place."

Frank smiled at her. "Things couldn't be going better – we'll get the evidence we need."

Ruth let out the breath she was holding. What they were saying made sense. This discovery would make a great case against Gormley. A farm full of stolen goods would be irrefutable evidence. Now they had him.

The trio sat at the kitchen table with Bert and Betty, chatting as they drank tea and ate boiled eggs accompanied by generous slices of bread that Robbie's aunt had prepared for them. Despite rationing, farm wives were always hospitable.

An hour passed before Robbie finally stood up. "Thanks for the tea, Aunt Betty. It's grand chatting with you, but I think we'd better get on now."

Frank and Ruth also thanked Robbie's aunt as they prepared to leave.

Robbie looked at his cousin; the other man nodded and stood up.

"Let's take my van. Two can sit on the chest in the back. Or maybe it would be best if Ruth waits here until we get back?" Bert said.

Ruth started to protest but Frank spoke first. "She helped me come up with the plan so I don't think she'd miss this for anything."

"No, I certainly wouldn't," Ruth echoed. She was glad he had confidence in her as part of the team. She didn't want to be left behind now that they were so close to getting the evidence they needed to have Gormley arrested.

"You sure about taking your van, Bert?" Robbie asked. "Frank arranged extra petrol for me."

"They've seen yours already. Best to take mine in case anyone's still about."

"Don't worry. The company can afford extra petrol for Bert too," Frank said.

It was completely dark as they stepped outside. Robbie went to his van and returned carrying two torches in one hand. He gave one to Frank. With his other hand, he balanced a long, solid-looking object against his shoulder. Ruth was sure it was a gun.

Robbie's murmured comment to Bert confirmed it. "Don't forget your gun."

Bert nodded and motioned his head toward the van. "I've got it."

"And your ID card."

"Got that too. We're not likely to run into anyone now but if I see anyone about the yard when we get there, I'll just drive on."

Bert opened the back doors of the van and shone his torch inside for Frank and Ruth to climb inside. "There's another torch lying on the chest that one of you can use."

Frank helped Ruth into the van. Even wearing flat shoes, it wasn't easy to accomplish this in a ladylike manner. Ruth lifted the torch and settled herself, leaving room for Frank to sit beside her on the chest.

As Bert closed the doors he said, "I won't drive too fast. You'll be grand in here."

Ruth slipped her hand under Frank's arm and snuggled close to him as the van's engine started. She felt the vehicle roll a short distance before the clutch engaged. They moved off slowly and steadily. In other circumstances, it would be very romantic, alone in the darkness with Frank.

She felt Frank shift, turning towards her. He kissed her cheek, a couple inches from her lips. "It's hard to find you in the dark," he whispered. With one hand, he cupped her face and turned it toward him then lowered his lips to hers and, as he kissed her, she forgot why they were there.

After several minutes, the vehicle slowed down and Ruth was startled back to the present. She felt the van turn as the couple pulled apart. They must be at the Lawlor farm. They bumped across uneven ground, turned in an arc and stopped. Her muscles tensed as she watched the back doors swing open.

"Alright in there?" Robbie asked.

The couple murmured that they were fine. Frank took Ruth's hand as he rose. Bent double, he made his way to the door. He jumped out and turned to help her to the ground.

Once they were outside the van Ruth looked around. They were standing behind a small shed. She noticed that Robbie and Bert were both carrying their Lee-Enfield rifles. The rifles had been standard issue in the British military since the First World War and were also used by the Ulster Home Guard.

Robbie spoke quietly. "We'll just have a wee look around the byre and the other sheds. Let's start with the milking parlour." His nod indicated the building they were standing behind. "Go careful. We'll keep the torches off until we're inside."

The group moved in single file around to the front of the building. Inside the milking parlour, they turned on their torches and the beams danced around the empty space. There was little in the building, but they opened the few creamery cans to peer inside them and lifted an upturned bucket. Their search yielded nothing.

"Will we split up to search the other buildings?" Frank asked.

"I'd rather we stay together since only Bert and I can claim official business if anyone finds us here," Robbie replied.

Frank nodded acquiescence.

"We'll take a look in the hay shed next," Robbie said.

Ruth felt Frank's big, warm hand envelop hers as the torches were switched off. The group left the building and walked across the yard. They repeated the same procedure in the hay shed as they had followed in the milking parlour, fanning out to search the building, checking behind bales of hay and pushing several aside to look under them. Again, they found nothing.

"I'm sure there's something here," Frank said. "I'd lay a bet that Gormley had stolen goods in his van when he left the camp today." Frank sighed loudly.

"If it's here, we'll find it," Bert said.

Ruth gave Frank an encouraging smile. She was sure they must find something here tonight.

"Let's keep at it, then." Frank's voice sounded more positive and determined than it had a moment earlier.

"The byre next," Robbie said. They switched off their torches and left the building.

Ruth felt Frank grasp her hand; she huddled close to him as they walked across the yard. The waxing moon partially illuminated the three sides of a square formed by the milking parlour, hay shed and byre. The farmhouse in front of them completed the square. Each of the whitewashed buildings stood silvery grey in the moon's glow.

There was a strong smell of animals as they entered the byre. A loud snort beside her made Ruth jump and squeak, clinging tightly to Frank's hand. She giggled when Robbie and Bert switched on their torches and she saw a restless cow tied a few feet from where she stood. It shook its head and snorted again as the torch beams shone around the building. Several other animals were tied in identical stalls along one side of the building, a water bucket and small hay rack in each stall.

Robbie looked at Frank and Ruth. "Wait by the door. Too much commotion will unsettle the animals." He and Bert made a quick search of each stall then returned to the couple.

"Nothing," Robbie said.

"Jeepers, where on earth have they stashed it?" Frank dug his hand into his thick hair.

"That's all the farm buildings," Bert said. "There's just the house left."

"I hope it's not locked. We don't want to damage the door and alert them that we were here," Frank said.

"We're not likely to need to worry about that. But it's not a bother if we do." Robbie grinned before he and Bert switched off their torches. The foursome trooped out of the shed.

At the front door of the house, the other three stood behind Robbie as he shone his torch on the handle and tried to turn it. It didn't budge. Ruth's heart thumped with excitement. Country people rarely locked their doors and there shouldn't be anything worth stealing in a small cottage like this. This must be where Gormley was hiding the stolen goods. She said a silent prayer as Robbie took a small piece of metal, much like the end of a clothes hanger, out of his pocket, slipped it into the lock and jiggled it. After a few seconds, she heard a click. Robbie tried the handle again and the door creaked open.

They stepped inside and Bert closed the door behind them. Torch beams danced around the room and crossed each other in a haphazard pattern as they inspected the cottage. It was as basic as Ruth had expected Mr Lawlor's cottage to be. Bachelor farmers cared little about their living quarters. The cottage consisted of a single large room with an open fireplace at one end. Two wooden chairs were set either side of the fireplace; a wicker basket sat beside one of them. At the other end of the room, there was a battered table and two chairs that didn't match. Bert peered into the basket beside the fireplace, rattling the sticks lying in the bottom of it; the others fanned out around the room. It didn't take long to conclude that there was nothing there.

"Darn it! I don't believe it!" Frank thumped his fist on the battered table.

"Where's the bed?" Ruth spun around, surveying the room, then blushed. What would Frank think of her asking a question like that?

Torch beams fanned the room again and as one of them illuminated the corner behind the table, Ruth spied a ladder fixed to the wall. There was a collective exclamation as the others saw it too.

"A loft, of course." Ruth forgot her embarrassment.

As she spoke, Frank crossed the room in a couple strides. She saw his torch beam rising up the wall and heard the rungs of the ladder creak under his weight.

"Eureka!" Frank yelled from the loft.

"Shh! What've you found?" Ruth whispered.

"You could open a hardware store up here," Frank crowed.

Ruth heard thuds as Robbie and Bert hurried to mount the ladder. She followed them, climbing far enough up the ladder to peer into the loft. She didn't need her torch as Frank had his trained on a spot on the floor beside the bed. There were boxes piled up and hand tools lying loose beside them. As the men opened several of the boxes, she saw nails and screws of various sizes. An electric drill lay beside the other goods. Robbie shone his torch around the corners of the loft, and Ruth saw that there were boxes and other goods stacked everywhere. There was very little empty space.

"Oh, my goodness! We've found it," she said.

The three men murmured agreement as they sifted through the items. Their conversation turned to how they could set a trap to catch Gormley and his accomplice delivering or collecting goods from this cottage. Ruth's toes began to cramp, balancing on the narrow rungs of the ladder. Scrambling into the loft would be awkward in her skirt, so Ruth returned to the ground floor. As she stepped off the last rung of the ladder, the sound of an engine turning into the property made her jump. She hurried to the window and peeked around the edge of the curtain. A large, dark shape passed the house and continued into the farmyard behind it.

Ruth ran the few steps back to the ladder and spoke in a fierce whisper. "A lorry's just come into the yard."

"Looks like we'll catch them in the act tonight, lads." Robbie sounded gleeful as he swung his leg onto the top rung of the ladder and climbed down, gripping his rifle in one hand. The other two men hurried after him.

As the men walked past her, she felt Frank's hand grip her wrist. "Stay behind us." He gently nudged her behind him, away from the door.

She saw Robbie and Bert position their rifles in readiness as the three men clustered around the window. Robbie shifted the edge of the curtain to peer out. At the same time, the engine sound got louder as the vehicle came back toward the cottage. Robbie dropped the curtain. For a moment, Ruth thought the vehicle might leave again but it stopped beside the cottage.

"Let's go and get them," Bert said.

"No, wait. We don't want to scare them away," Frank said. "Let them get out of the truck."

"He's right," Robbie said. "We'll wait here for them to bring in whatever they've got on that lorry or come in and collect some of this stuff. Then we'll have proof that can't be contested."

The other two men murmured their agreement. Ruth could see the sense of the plan, though she didn't like the idea of standing here waiting for Gormley and whoever was with him to come to them. She felt trapped and glanced anxiously at Frank. He held himself still and rigid, leaning toward the door. His composed determination steadied her. And she knew that Robbie knew what he was doing. She would have to trust them.

Robbie motioned for the men to flatten themselves against the walls on either side of the door. He waved Ruth along the front wall away from the door. Frank gently manoeuvred her into the corner then flattened himself against the wall several feet in front of her. She felt safer with him shielding her, but the waiting was still nerve-wracking.

"Hold steady until they're inside," Robbie said.

Tension forced out Ruth's breath in ragged gasps and she tried to slow her breathing to quieten it. She was afraid that the noise she was making would alert Gormley as he opened the door. She didn't think she had ever felt as tense in her life. What would happen when Gormley entered the room? She hoped she wouldn't find herself in the middle of a brawl, but she had no control over the situation. If it happened, she would stand out of the way and watch for any chance to help the lads. Though surely the three of them should be able to overpower the new arrivals without a fight, especially as Robbie and Bert had their rifles.

It seemed like hours as they waited. The vehicle's engine idled for several minutes and

Ruth wondered what on earth they were doing. How could they afford to waste the petrol with rationing? Then she remembered that the vehicle was probably from the American airbase; Gormley wasn't worried about using the Yanks' fuel.

When the engine was finally switched off, the night was still except for the sound of the vehicle's doors opening and closing. Ruth put her hand over her mouth to muffle the sound of her breathing. Footsteps moved around in the yard and she heard the odd mumbled comment. One set of footsteps walked toward the back of the yard and she wondered where the person had gone. Maybe they wouldn't come into the cottage? Maybe whoever was there had only come to check the cows. But no, they would have come during daylight if they were here to tend the animals. It had to be something to do with the stolen goods.

The person who had walked across the yard returned and another set of footsteps joined the first ones. Their steady clomping on the hard ground was getting closer to the cottage. Ruth saw the three men with her each shift slightly. Robbie and Bert pointed their rifles at the door, and Frank leaned toward the door while remaining flat against the wall. She heard a key turn in the lock and a mumbled exclamation outside at how easily it had turned; then the door swung open. She held her breath.

"No hanging about. We need to be smart about getting out of here. I need to get the vehicle back to the base. I'm right late already. It would've been better to leave it until tomorrow." It was Gormley's voice.

"Aye, but I needed to shift this stuff out of my place. Rather it here than there if anyone's looking. The fines are getting heavier if you're caught." Ruth didn't recognise the voice of the second man.

In the dim light, she could see that each of the men was carrying a stack of boxes. They headed straight across the room toward the ladder to the loft. When they reached the centre of the room Robbie stepped away from the wall, his rifle trained on the pair. Bert stepped into the open doorway, raising his rifle, and Frank moved to stand beside him.

"Right lads, Ulster Home Guard. Stop there," Robbie said.

The two men spun around and Gormley cursed when he saw the dark shapes blocking his access to the door. In the next second, he threw his boxes at Robbie and bolted toward the door. The second man dropped his boxes and ran after him. Frank and Bert braced themselves to block the thieves.

Robbie staggered as the first box hit him then regained his balance. "Ulster Home Guard. I said, stop now!"

Ruth winced when she saw, as well as heard the crunch of, Gormley barrelling into Frank. Her fella threw his arms around his attacker, trying to tackle him to the ground, but Gormley bit Frank's hand and pulled free. Frank cursed, reaching out to try to grab the labourer, but Gormley disappeared through the door. The second man tried to slip between Frank and Bert, but Frank shoved him back into the room. Bert shouted at the man to get down on the floor. Their captive eyed Bert's rifle then sank to his knees.

Outside they heard the vehicle's engine start. Everyone turned to look out of the door.

"Keep him there," Robbie shouted to Bert. He and Frank ran outside. Ruth moved to the window to look out.

"Oh cripes, he's gonna get away!" Frank yelled as the vehicle started to move.

"Not a chance," Robbie replied.

The vehicle lunged forward, gaining speed, and Ruth was sure that Frank was right. Despite Robbie's confidence, Gormley would escape. How could they stop him now he was in the lorry? And since they had only seen him in the dark, how could they prove in court that he had been here? He would get away with this crime too. They had caught one of the criminals but not the one they really wanted. She glanced over her shoulder at the other man. He was lying flat on the floor as Bert had instructed him to do.

Ruth jumped as she heard two shots fired outside. Another loud bang immediately followed the second shot. She squeezed her eyes shut and prayed that Frank was okay then strained to see what was happening through the window. What had Robbie fired at? As she focussed on the dark space behind the vehicle, she saw two figures standing there. They must be Robbie and Frank. Thank goodness, Frank was alright.

As she watched, one of the figures ran to the driver's side of the vehicle and she heard Robbie's voice. "Get round to the other side so he can't get away."

The one she assumed was Frank disappeared behind the far side of the vehicle. Robbie marched up to the driver's door, his rifle trained on it.

"Right, let's be having you then," Robbie shouted up at the cab of the vehicle.

Ruth held her breath, staring at the lorry's door. For the next minute or more, there wasn't a sound.

Frank's shout from the other side of the vehicle made her jump. "You heard him. We know who you are. Out, Gormley! Now!"

The driver's door opened a crack. "What're you pointing that thing at me for? I've not done nothing." Gormley raised his voice to reply to Frank. "Boss, I'm late back with the lorry 'cause I said I'd help me mate, Ned, shift a few things. His horse is lame. I was taking the lorry back right after this."

"Never mind the yarn. Get out and into the cottage. Now." Robbie shook the rifle at the man as he spoke.

Gormley reluctantly climbed out of the cab and shuffled toward the cottage. Robbie kept the rifle trained on him, following several steps behind. As they reached the end of the lorry, Frank emerged from the other side of the vehicle. Gormley glanced at Frank, then lunged toward him, veering away to run past him before they collided, but the labourer wasn't fast enough. Frank tackled him and the two bodies merged into one as they thudded to the ground. Robbie swung to face them, keeping his rifle trained on the pair.

Ruth clenched her hands, praying that Robbie wouldn't try to shoot Gormley while the two men were entangled. She heard several punches as the pair scuffled, then one man gained control and lay on top of the other. She thought the silhouette was Frank; she sighed with relief.

"Don't try anything again. Get up and into the house," Robbie said to the man lying on the ground.

The man on top got up and hauled the other man to his feet. Ruth was relieved to hear Frank's voice. "Glad I haven't lost my knack for football tackles." He shoved Gormley toward the cottage door; Robbie fell in beside Frank, his rifle still trained on their captive. Gormley walked into the house without any attempt at further struggle.

Once the trio were inside Ruth ran to stand behind Frank. She reached out and grasped his arm. He placed his hand on top of hers and squeezed firmly then let go of it.

"I'm glad we've finally got you, Gormley. I knew you were up to no good for a long time. Now we've got the proof." Frank's voice had a grim but satisfied tone to it.

"Sure, I haven't done anything to speak of – just a little bit of trading, cross the border, like. Not many who aren't doin' that these days." Gormley's voice was wheedling. "You never been to Bundoran for the day? On the Sugar Train? You'll know I'm not the only one."

"I don't think we'll find much about here that you've brought across the border," Robbie said. "Not from what I've seen."

"Smuggling's illegal too, in case no one told you," Frank said. "But, give them credit – at least they bought the stuff they bring across the border. You didn't buy what you've got here – you just took it from the airbase. That's stealing. It's also obstructing a military operation. During wartime that's even more serious than smuggling. Let's see what the police have to say about it."

Irvinestown Court House
Wednesday, 25th March, 1942

"You may not consider your crime a serious offence, Mr Gormley, but I assure you, it is. After the constabulary searched the Lawlor farm and other locations they were informed of, they found enough goods to more than adequately stock a hardware shop. Building materials, nails, screws, hand and electrical tools. They recovered all of that and more. Do you not realise that sailors risked their lives to transport many of these items through the U-boat infested waters of the Atlantic Ocean? Their efforts were in vain if the goods are not used for their intended purpose. These goods and tools are needed to construct a military base and other facilities for troops from our ally nation. American troops have already arrived in our country and are waiting to take possession of the base. What you have done is not mere theft. You have hampered American military personnel in performing their duties. That is an act of sabotage, a very serious transgression when our nation is at war." Major Dunn coldly regarded Mervyn Gormley standing in the prisoner's dock.

In the public gallery of the courtroom, Frank listened intently to the Resident Magistrate. He was aware of the warmth of Ruth's body sitting next to him, but he kept his gaze trained on the magistrate. The retired military officer presiding over the case was preparing to sentence Gormley, and he wanted to hear every word.

After the magistrate finished his address to the prisoner, he read out the sentence. Frank held his breath until Major Dunn finished speaking then let his shoulders slump as he exhaled. The sentence wasn't as stringent as he wished it to be, but at least it reflected that the magistrate considered the crime a serious one. Frank reached across and clasped Ruth's hand briefly, but he kept his gaze fixed on Gormley. The man was standing hunched and sullen in the prisoner's dock, without any sign of his usual eager, smarmy manner.

Frank watched until Gormley was led out of the court and people around him began to converse in low tones then he looked from Mr Orchard to Ruth, seated on either side of him. Ruth's face was tense and serious. He was sure she was also disappointed by the length of the sentence that Gormley had received. The trio silently stood up and filed out of the courtroom.

Once they were outside, Mr Orchard was the first to speak. "I'm glad to see this whole thing wrapped up, and it's the result we wanted. Good work getting to the bottom of this, Frank. Excellent job. And credit goes to this young lady too. Thank you very much for your help." Mr Orchard smiled at Ruth then turned to Frank. "Since you're only down the road from your hotel, there's no need to come back to the base. I'll take a run out there and see everything is okay. I'll see you in the morning. Good night, young lady." Mr Orchard smiled at Ruth again then walked away.

"That was very kind of him," Ruth said after Mr Orchard had left.

"I couldn't have a better boss. Especially with the problems we've had. He always had good advice to offer and faith in my ability to deal with whatever happened. And he didn't flip his wig when we went snooping around at the farm instead of just reporting it to the police." Frank shrugged his shoulders, unable to express how much he appreciated his boss's quiet, steady leadership. There had been times when Frank had been at his wits' end trying to get to the bottom of the thefts and didn't think there was any hope that they would get the job done on schedule. But they had finally put an end to the thefts and completion of the work would no longer be impeded. Today's trial result was a cause for celebration.

Frank touched Ruth's arm. "Do you have to help serve dinner tonight?"

"Not really. Mum said not to worry what time I got back. She'll get the extra girl, Myrtle, to give her a hand if I'm not there."

"Good. Let's celebrate with a steak at Ma Bothwell's Eating House. The guys say it's great – not that the food at the hotel isn't just as good." He gave her an apologetic grin, hoping he hadn't said the wrong thing. He just wanted to celebrate this with her on their own.

Ruth grinned back at him. "Don't worry – I'm not offended. And yes, I'd love to go."

This day just seemed to get better. Frank tried to be on his best behaviour and suppress his huge grin as they walked along the street together, but he couldn't hide it. He loved the feel of Ruth's small hand fitted under his elbow as they walked the short distance to the restaurant. He laid his hand on hers and squeezed it gently. He wanted her to know how much he enjoyed every minute he spent with her.

When they arrived at the restaurant, he was surprised to find that most of the tables were already occupied, but he spotted an empty one in the corner and began weaving across the room toward it, loosely holding Ruth's hand. Several American technicians whistled and praised the court's verdict as he passed them but he kept his replies subdued. He didn't want the restaurant staff who might overhear the conversations to think the Americans were gloating about the punishment received by Gormley and the other Northern Irish workers who had been caught and charged. He didn't want to spoil the community goodwill they had enjoyed throughout the construction project.

Once the couple were seated opposite each other at the table, all Frank could do was grin at Ruth, wordlessly holding her gaze. There was so much he wanted to say but he didn't even know where to start.

"Well, that's a worry off your shoulders," Ruth said.

"You can sure say that again!" Frank struggled to keep his voice low.

Without any further preamble, Ruth said, "But six months isn't that long. Since Mervyn wasn't arrested with Harry, I had hoped he would get a longer sentence for this."

Frank had already been thinking about it too. "I think Gormley got as harsh a sentence as the court could give him. He was tried for theft, not treason. I think we'll have to just accept that he won't ever face charges for passing information to Coalter meant for the Germans. But he'll be locked up for a little while and he won't get any work with the military in future."

"That's something, anyway."

Ruth seemed to be struggling to wipe the frown from her face, and he felt his heart tug. She had had a difficult few months. Hopefully Gormley's conviction would put an end to that chapter of her life. He reached across the table to squeeze her hand and was rewarded with a slightly teary smile. His breath caught. She looked so vulnerable; if it were possible, he would have done anything he could to protect her from the upsets she had endured.

"And the other one that we caught at the farm only got a fine." Ruth quickly wiped her eyes.

"Yeah, but Clerkin and Latimer are also out of their jobs. We won't have them back at the base. The two of them did spill the beans about who else was involved in the thefts and where they sold the stuff. So the rest of the workers who were in on it have been charged too. And there'll likely be court cases brought against some of those who bought our tools and materials, as they must have known where they were from. The information those two gave the police stopped the whole racket. That might not have happened without their help."

He watched Ruth nod her head slowly, seeming to consider and accept his explanation.

"It's a good thing it's been stopped anyway," she said.

Frank lowered his voice to a whisper. "Yeah. It's also a good thing to know that it was just a bunch of small-time crooks we were dealing with. The boss and I thought it was the IRA. I'm sure glad we were able to lay that theory to rest." He looked around the room, but no one appeared to be listening to their conversation.

"Aye, you wouldn't have wanted to run into them. Investigating Harry's involvement in spying was nerve-wracking enough; you wouldn't have wanted to tackle terrorists."

"We've sure had our share of trouble this winter, haven't we?" Frank leaned back on his chair and shook his head slowly.

Ruth smiled at him then glanced down at the table. When she looked up her eyes were troubled. "I was wondering –"

He gave her an encouraging smile. "What's going on in that head of yours?"

She drew an unsteady breath. "Have you heard anything about what's happening with Harry?"

He paused to collect his thoughts before he answered her. Even the mention of Coalter's name angered him. Last autumn the man could so easily have destroyed America's neutrality before the country was ready to enter the war. He was a selfish opportunist. But, even though they were no longer together, he had also been Ruth's beau. Of course, she would want to know his fate. He took a deep breath to rein in his anger and compose himself.

"As far as I know, he's still in Crumlin Road Gaol in Belfast."

"Did they charge him with – treason?" She stumbled over the last word.

"I don't know anything for sure, but my boss has heard rumours back through the military brass that he'll probably be charged with Treachery."

Ruth's eyes widened and her eyebrows rose. "Oh, that doesn't sound as bad as treason."

Frank stroked her forearm then grasped her hand firmly. "I don't know about that, honey. I heard it was a new law they passed to make it easier to bring spies to justice."

He saw Ruth swallow hard and he gripped her hand tighter.

"When will the trial be?"

"I don't know. We haven't heard anything about him being sent for trial yet. But, if I do hear anything, I'll let you know." He paused and swallowed. "You must be worried about him." He hated to think that she might still harbour feelings for that chump, but she had been Coalter's sweetheart for more than two years so he couldn't expect her not to care at all about what happened to him.

Ruth's face screwed up into a frown. "It's not that I still have feelings for him. But, even though I want nothing more to do with him, I can't just forget he exists. It's terrible to think he could be hung if he's convicted. How could that happen to someone I know?" Tears shimmered in her eyes as she spoke.

Frank rubbed her hand with his thumb as he gazed at her. She was so lovely. How could Coalter have done something so stupid and caused her so much upset and pain? "I know it's awful. But it would have been even worse if he hadn't been caught and the information he gathered had got to Germany."

"Aye, I know. It just makes me really sad to think he did such a stupid thing and threw away everything."

"Greed – wanting more than you have, seems to make some people do that. Look at Gormley and his little operation."

"Aye, Harry wanted to be important – move into a grand job where he'd be noticed." Ruth shook her head then stared down at the table.

Frank rubbed her hand again and waited until she looked up at him. "We can't change what either of them did. They made their own choices. So let's put them out of our minds for now. Why don't we go for a stroll around the town after dinner? I never tire of being seen with a beauty like you on my arm, honey."

His sincere flattery was rewarded with a tremulous smile from Ruth.

Main Street, Irvinestown
Later the same evening

Ruth glanced up at the face of the clock on the tall Clock Tower as they approached it. It was almost eight thirty and darkness was creeping in. After they left the restaurant, she and Frank had strolled up and down the wide main street, stopping to talk to a few acquaintances they met. She felt as if she were floating above the footpath as she walked and held her head high. She was happy to be seen with Frank now and was determined not to wonder what anyone thought of her walking out with him. While she was sad that Harry had messed up his life, she didn't owe him any loyalty after what he had done. He had made it plain when he was arrested that she didn't matter to him at all. At that moment she had realised he always thought of himself first. But that was the past. Harry wasn't part of her life now, and she couldn't be happier that she was with Frank. She was growing fonder of him every day and never wanted their time together to end.

This last thought made her frown, but she raised her eyebrows to smooth her creased forehead and forced the thought away, taking a deep breath as she did so. They would enjoy this evening. She wouldn't let the worry she felt intrude on it.

The couple continued past the Clock Tower onto a quiet side street dotted with modest houses. A pair of large gateposts stood at the far end of the street. Between them, a burly man stood, blocking the entrance to the estate grounds. When the couple reached the gates, Frank spoke briefly to the guard then led Ruth into the wooded grounds. Although Necarne Castle was a private estate, Frank was well known to the guard as the construction company he worked for was building an American station hospital in the grounds.

They strolled along a narrow, tree-lined lane. A stream gurgling somewhere to their right was a soothing sound in the near darkness. As they continued along the lane, the trees enveloped them, hiding them from the guard at the gate and the grand estate house ahead.

Frank wrapped his arm around her waist and pulled her closer to him. "You couldn't beat an evening like this – much better company than I have here during the day."

Ruth laughed. "I'm not sure that's true, but thanks. How're things going with the work, if you don't mind me asking?"

"You can ask me anything, honey." Frank grinned. "And it couldn't be better. We've got most of the building work finished at the other sites around the county. The hospital here is the last project left to do, and now that we don't have to contend with materials going missing, it's barrelling along."

"That's grand," Ruth said softly. "Getting rid of Mervyn Gormley turned everything around."

"You can say that again! Once that crooked gang was rooted out, morale improved and everyone started working harder. We're on schedule to have this hospital ready for occupancy by the end of April."

"Oh – good." Ruth tried to keep her voice from faltering, but it wobbled noticeably. A month wasn't very long and that was all they had left. She had known that Frank's work in the county would finish one day but it had always seemed far in the future. But not anymore.

"What is it, honey?"

She heard the concern in Frank's voice.

"Nothing. Everything's grand." She tried to make her voice sound cheerful but even to her ear it sounded strained.

"Something's wrong. I know it. Tell me."

"It's just that you'll soon be away. America's a very long way from here."

She heard Frank chuckle and she frowned. Didn't he care that they would be parted in little more than a month from now?

Frank hugged her tighter against his side. "Hey, don't worry. I'm not going home."

"But you said the job's almost done. What else would you do? Oh!" Ruth sucked in a loud breath. "Are you enlisting?" Her heart pounded as she thought about this.

"I might, but not yet. If I enlist, it'll be in the Engineering Corps. I'd be building, not fighting. But, right now I'm staying here – well, not exactly here."

Ruth frowned. "What do you mean?"

"This isn't the only building work that Fuller-Merritt Chapman is doing for the military in Northern Ireland. I can't tell you much, but there's still a lot of work to do at the naval base in Derry. That's where I'll be going when this job is done."

"So you're not going back to America, then?" She just couldn't believe it. She wanted to hear him say it again.

Frank turned her to face him and kissed her gently on the lips. "No, honey. I'm not going back yet. And it's not that far to Derry. I'll be able to get a lift so I can come to see you on the weekends. There's always vehicles running between the bases. Will you keep a room at Corey's for me?"

Ruth squeezed him as tightly as she could. "Of course I will!"

Frank laughed and kissed her again. "You won't find another guy to take my place while I'm away, then?"

Ruth made an irritated sound deep in her throat and Frank laughed harder.

"As long as you don't forget me."

"You'll just have to visit me often so I won't." Ruth felt the grin spread across her face as she teased him.

"Oh, I think I can do that. And you'll have to look after the castle for me."

"Eh?"

"Yeah, after all the work we're putting into kitting out Necarne Castle as a hospital, you can keep an eye on it when you're volunteering there."

"Will they be looking for volunteers, then?"

"Well, we're only building it. We don't have any say in how it's run, but I've heard rumours they'll be recruiting local people to work there. You've been looking for an opportunity like this. And since you've always looked after me so well,

I can put in a good word for you." He chuckled as he leaned down to kiss her again.

Ruth shivered as a chilly breeze slipped between the buttons on her coat and she snuggled closer to Frank, responding to his kiss. The last few months had taken some unexpected twists and turns but she had survived them. Now with Frank beside her, she would embrace whatever the future might bring.

BOOK 3

Keeping Her Pledge

In the countryside near Lough Erne, County Fermanagh, Northern Ireland
June 1942
Late afternoon

"This won't work, Davy." Pearl Grainger twisted a strand of her long auburn hair around her finger as she regarded her brother sitting in the driver's seat of the black Morris Z van. "What if we're stopped?"

"Don't worry. If we are, I'll do the talking. Odds are it'll be Constable Craig and not the excise men. He likes a quiet life." Davy gave her an easy smile.

"I hope you're right. My stomach's in knots. If we get caught, Mum'll be mortified. It would be in the papers and all."

"We won't. And sure, everyone's doing it. We'd be mad not to earn a few bob too while we can. This War won't go on forever."

"I don't know how you can be so calm." Pearl tugged at the lock of hair twisted around her finger.

"You're worse than an old hen. We never had such sport till this War started. If we weren't nipping back and forth across the border with a few things folk want, we'd be the only ones in the county who weren't."

Pearl knew that was true. Since the War started, rationing and the dearth of imported goods meant that a thriving illicit trade in scarce or expensive items had sprung up, going both ways across the border between Northern Ireland and the Irish Free State.

The van bumped along the rough, unpaved road as they made their way home from the Free State, and Pearl gripped the dashboard to steady herself. She groaned when she saw a green-uniformed figure step onto the road a few yards ahead. The Royal Ulster Constabulary officer raised his arm to flag them down.

Davy turned to her and winked. "Whisht now. Constable Craig is no match for your big brother."

The van slowed down and rolled to a stop several feet from the police officer.

"Hello, Davy, Pearl." The officer walked the few steps to the van and leaned down to peer at them through the open window on the driver's side. The pair returned his greeting.

"Where are you coming from?"

"Blacklion." Davy looked directly at the officer.

"You'd want to mind your petrol, spinning about like that. What takes you to the Free State?"

"We went to see our cousin. She's been very poorly," Davy lied.

"Ach now, that's a shame. Is she one of Rose's girls?"

"No, Mildred's."

"Your Da's sister?"

"No, Mum's."

"I don't remember a Mildred in your mother's family."

"There is, surely. She was away in Sligo a right while till she was widowed."

"Hmm, I mind all the girls in your mother's family. But I can't recollect a Mildred." Constable Craig gave Davy a long look.

The younger man rested his arm on the window frame, returning the police officer's stare, his eyes open wide like an innocent child.

The officer suddenly straightened up. "Ach now, Davy, what are you up to? It's not often I hear tell of you visiting the sick." He frowned and shifted his gaze to the van. "What have you in there?"

Without hesitation Davy replied, "Alright, you've got me. I've a hundredweight of sugar and a wee chest of tea."

Constable Craig's eyes widened then he snorted and threw his head back, laughing. "Oh, go to hell, Davy! Stop your messing." He looked across at the young woman sitting in the passenger seat. "Beg your pardon for the language, Pearl. Now, Davy, if you had a chest of tea and a hundredweight of sugar, you wouldn't be so quick to tell me."

"I have, honestly, Constable. You can see for yourself."

"Mind now, lad. Spinning tales like that could get you into trouble. Someone else might not appreciate the joke."

"There's no harm meant. I'm sorry, Constable." Davy gave the officer a conciliatory smile.

"That's alright, son. But now I'd better have a wee look inside the van. Would you open it, please?"

"Not a bother."

Davy stepped out of the van, and Constable Craig followed him to the rear of the vehicle. The younger man threw open the double doors. Inside the van, torn, paint-splattered cotton sheets covered two small mounds near the door, concealing the items beneath them. The police officer leaned into the vehicle and lifted the edge of the nearest sheet, revealing a wooden egg crate. He grasped the metal handle on top and pulled it open. The crate was empty.

"We called into Enniskillen and collected our returned crates from the train station before we went to Blacklion," Davy said.

Constable Craig nodded. The officer lifted the other sheet and found an identical egg crate. He opened it and peered into the empty container. A rectangular toolbox, tied shut with a length of rope, lay against the sidewall. A hammer protruded through a broken slat in the wooden box. The officer glanced past the toolbox to several uncovered egg crates stacked behind it.

"Will I pull out these so you can check the others?" Davy indicated the crates lying closest to the door.

Constable Craig pulled his head out of the van and straightened up. "Ach, there's no need. It seemed a bit odd to hear tell of you visiting the sick, but everything seems in order. Just watch what you say in future. Your jokes could land you in bother."

"I will, surely, Constable," Davy agreed as he closed the rear doors.

The two men walked to the front of the van, and Constable Craig leaned in the window. "Are you going to the Riding Club dance tonight, Pearl?" the officer asked.

The young woman nodded. She suddenly felt as if she had stepped into an oven and prayed that the heat inside her wouldn't suffuse her face and give them away.

"I don't know how you young ones do it – hooleys nearly every night of the week since this War started. Well, mind yourself with those Yanks and don't be stopping out too late. Give my regards to your mother."

Pearl gave the officer a tight smile as her brother got into the van and started the engine. Constable Craig rapped the roof with his hand then stepped back. As they drove away, Pearl sighed and slumped in her seat.

"How do you have the nerve, Davy? I thought my heart would stop when he asked to look inside the van."

"You worry too much."

"If he'd checked the rest of the crates, he'd have found exactly what you told him was there!"

"Well, not exactly. The tea's in egg crates too, not a chest. Amazing how much you can get into them when you take out the egg racks." Davy chuckled.

"It's no joke! We had a lucky escape this time."

"There was never anything to worry about. He wasn't really looking. Sometimes the truth is harder to believe than a lie."

"I'll never get used to this smuggling. It wrecks my nerves." Pearl shook her head and reached for a strand of her hair.

"It's hardly smuggling. We're just running a few goods that are in short supply to where they're wanted and we make a few bob. Haven't you seen the poster, 'Do Your Bit, Save Food'? We're doing our bit bringing it in."

Pearl glared at her brother. "That's not what it means."

"Don't be such a whinge. You're only out on

the odd run over the border but you're out to the dances with all those airmen several times a week. You'd half of England, the Canadians and the Yanks to choose a sweetheart from. Before this War you never had it so good."

Pearl tried to push her misgivings out of her mind. *Maybe he's right. Perhaps I take it all too seriously.* She loved the dances with the servicemen from nearby RAF Castle Archdale and the other military camps around the county. There were never as many dances before the troops came to County Fermanagh. The airmen flew long missions out over the Atlantic Ocean, providing defensive escorts for convoys of ships and hunting German U-boats, but they still had the energy to meet the local women and dance any evening they weren't flying.

Dances were so different now, less formal. With the influx of military personnel, they were livelier and more exciting. She was even learning some new dances, not just the standard sets: foxtrot, quickstep and waltz, or an Irish set dance. The British, Canadian and American airmen and soldiers were less shy than the local lads. They didn't hesitate to ask the girls to dance and loved to be on the dance floor. The confident American fliers flustered her when they flirted with her in their booming voices. She knew that her friends and neighbours were listening to every word they said to her, and Davy often mimicked them on the way home. But they were very friendly, so it was hard not to like them.

The pair drove on in silence and Pearl thought about the dance tonight. She hoped that the Canadian navigator she had met recently would be there. On Sunday night, he had told her that he was flying today but had promised that he would come to the dance if he were back in time. His name was the same as her youngest brother, Charles, but he said everyone called him Chuck not Charlie. He spoke louder than most of the lads she knew but didn't seem as brash as some of the American airmen. He wasn't at all forward and, from the first time she met him, she had immediately felt at ease with him. She had turned down his request to see her home last Sunday as she had to go home with her brother, but Chuck wasn't annoyed. He had said he'd be counting the days until he saw her again, and gave her a bar of chocolate for her younger brothers. He was so kind and thoughtful. She was still thinking about his lovely hazel eyes and his soft accent as they drove into the farmyard.

"There now – you're home safe. You'd a bit of sport and you've plenty of time to ready yourself for the dance." Davy parked the van beside the byre.

Pearl sighed. "Ach, I suppose you're right. Life's been more exciting since the War started. Maybe I just worry too much."

"You do, surely. Remember, we're just doing

our bit." Her brother grinned and winked at her.

"Alright, I'll try. Now I'd best get in and help Mummy with the tea." Pearl hopped out of the van, walked across the farmyard and went into the house.

***

Standing at the upstairs hall window in the early evening, her wet hair resting on the towel she had thrown across her shoulders, Pearl looked across the single field that separated the farmhouse from Lough Erne. She watched as a large lumbering Sunderland seaplane sliced through the water, gathering speed until it launched itself into the air. As it lifted off, a torrent of water sprayed out from it and she heard the roar of its engines.

Chuck had said that he wasn't supposed to tell her but he was on an anti-submarine patrol today. He would have left the base at RAF Castle Archdale, on the opposite side of the lough, soon after first light this morning. There were patrols around the clock, and planes were taking off and landing day and night. She often heard the roars of their engines as she lay in bed, before she fell asleep and as she awoke. Sometimes she would stand at her bedroom window and gaze out at the row of navigation lights that guided the planes in to land, strung out like lanterns on a rope across the field and into the lough.

"I thought you'd be getting ready." Davy walked up behind her.

"In a wee minute. Isn't it a lovely night? I was just watching the planes."

"Looking for your sweetheart, are you?"

"Don't be daft. And he's not my sweetheart." Pearl smiled to herself. Although she had only recently met Chuck, neither of them was seeing anyone else. They were as good as walking out together. No doubt, she would soon be able to tell the world that he was her sweetheart.

"Well, if you're standing here daydreaming, I'll wash and shave. Race you to the mirror."

Davy walked down the hall to the bedroom he shared with their two younger brothers, Charlie and Ian. Pearl hugged herself and sighed as she turned back to the window. The flying boats looked so graceful gliding through the sky, not at all cumbersome as they were in the water. Chuck had told her about the view up there. He said everything on the ground below looked tiny. It was like looking at a miniature picture with new images constantly spinning past inside the frame. She would love to see her house and Lough Erne from the sky. It was such a perfect evening. Chuck just *had* to return in time to meet her at the dance. She squeezed her eyes shut and wished.

Half an hour later Pearl stood in front of the large walnut mirror in the downstairs hallway. As she ran the brush through her hair, teasing and shaking the tangles out of it, she heard the drone of an aircraft approaching. With RAF Castle Archdale so close, she had become accustomed to the hum of the steady stream of aircraft flying overhead.

She twisted the brush sharply and tugged at a knot as Davy sidled up beside her. Without pausing, she stepped sideways to share the mirror. From this angle, she saw the landscape outside reflected in the glass: peaceful rolling hills divided by rough stone walls and thick hedges. A dark shadow moving rapidly in the top corner of the glass drew her attention. She turned away from the mirror to look through the small window in the front door. The flying boat she had heard was approaching the lough much closer to the ground than they usually flew at this distance from the water.

Davy followed her gaze. When he spotted the aircraft he ran to the door. "That plane won't make the lough," he shouted as he jerked the door open and rushed outside.

Pearl followed him. As she stepped outside the door, she heard a high-pitched whine before the seaplane's engines cut out. The aircraft plunged steeply towards the ground and crashed in the field beside the water. Flames shot up from the wreckage and crackled like a huge bonfire. Davy, her father and two neighbours who had called in for a chat, Tommy Boyd and Dick Morton, were already running toward the aircraft.

Pearl hurried across their farmyard and crossed the road but stopped at the gate to the field. The smoke billowing from the plane nearly choked her. Her stomach clenched as she gawked at the debris strewn across the charred grass and she had to grip the top rail of the gate to keep her knees from buckling. Something gleamed dully under the hedge beside where the aircraft lay. She squinted through the smoke at the seaplane's massive engine lying there intact and focused on its unsullied bulk, unwilling to look at the carnage surrounding it.

The screams of an airman lying near the wreckage prised her attention away from the engine. Davy and her father were with him. The two men grabbed his arms and dragged him several yards away from the aircraft. Another crew member lay unmoving amidst pieces of the left wing. As their neighbours ran to help the second man, there was a loud explosion. Flames shot out from the wreckage, engulfing the flier's inert form and driving them back from the heat. She gagged as the smell of burning flesh mingled with the thick, acrid smoke.

Where are the rest of the crew? There should be ten or eleven men. Pearl shook violently and tears streamed down her cheeks as she realised they must still be in the aircraft.

I'm so useless. I should be doing something. She bit her lip, drawing blood, as she watched the scene in the field but she was unable to move. She still held tightly to the gate. Tommy and Dick ran back and forth at the edge of the blaze, searching for other crew members who might have escaped from the aircraft. Her father and brother lifted the airman they had rescued and carried him towards the gate where she was standing.

"Pearl, run and tell your Mum I need her help," her father ordered as he reached to open the gate. The two men moved with urgency, and even Davy wasn't joking for once. His face was ashen and his usually twinkling eyes were clouded. Pearl took a shuddering breath and forced herself to let go of the gate and do as she was bid. Her legs felt weak as she half-staggered to the house.

As she ran, the image of a poster she had seen in town filled her thoughts: 'Women, You Are Needed in the National Fire Service: telephonists, drivers, canteen workers'. Those women would have known what to do and wouldn't have just stood there slack jawed. Not like her.

At the farmhouse, Pearl grabbed the door handle and flung it open, shouting as she ran, "Mum!" She called her mother repeatedly as she ran from the hall to the kitchen. Her mother was hurrying toward her as she entered the kitchen. Pearl gasped, "Da's coming. You've to help him."

"I've all ready." Her mother quickly dried her hands on the dish towel she was holding.

Pearl noticed her mother's first aid supplies

had been set out on the dresser. The front door clattered open and the sound of feet tramping and heavy breathing came from the hallway. Her father and Davy entered the room, carrying the airman.

"Put him here." Pulling a chair away from the long wooden table, her mother pointed to the table's surface. Pearl hung back, her hands clasped against her chest. A sharp look from her mother roused her to help move the rest of the chairs.

Mr Grainger and Davy laid the man on the table then stepped back to allow her mother to get closer to him. She gently touched the airman's shoulder. He winced and turned his head toward her.

"Hello, son. What's your name?" Mrs Grainger asked.

"Mark. Mark Hardy." His voice was hoarse and he clenched his jaw as he spoke.

"Can you tell me where you're hurt, lad?" She leaned over the airman, inspecting him for signs of obvious injuries. There were several cuts on his face and a burn on his right cheek.

"Not sure, ma'am. Leg hurts most." Mark panted as he spoke. His face was pale.

Pearl looked at his left leg. For the first time she noticed it was lying at a strange angle, jutting away from his other leg. She shuddered. She had seen a calf once that had its leg broken during its birth. She had run from the byre, unable to watch its suffering. Her father had shot it the same evening.

Tommy Boyd and Dick Morton entered the kitchen. Pearl saw the enquiring look her father gave Dick. Their neighbour shook his head and her father frowned. The men must not have found any other survivors.

"Tommy, would you fetch me a couple straight sticks from the byre?" Mrs Grainger went to the dresser and lifted a pair of scissors as she spoke to their neighbour. She disappeared down the hall and returned with a pillowcase which she began cutting into strips.

"I'll strap the leg, Andy, then you'll need to get him to Necarne." Mrs Grainger glanced at her husband as she spoke.

Mr Grainger nodded acknowledgement and turned to his son. "Clear out the back of the van, lad."

"There's, ah, quite a bit in it, Da. I'll have to think where to put it."

Mr Grainger shot an impatient look at Davy. "Don't be fretting about that. Just get it cleared." He turned to speak to Dick. "Will you get the old door lying in the back of the byre? Davy'll show you where it is and help you put it in the van. Put a load of straw on it."

Davy turned to look at Pearl, his eyes open wide and eyebrows raised. Without another word, he left the kitchen. Pearl was vaguely aware that Davy was worried about where he would hide the contraband goods but she didn't know how he could even think about that right now.

She watched from several feet away as her mother wet a cloth and carefully wiped the airman's face, clearing away blood around the cuts. When Tommy brought the sticks, her father straightened the injured man's leg as gently as he could and her mother strapped the sticks to it with deft, swift movements. The airman groaned once then screwed his mouth tightly closed; agonised grunts escaped as they worked.

"Pearl, wet the cloth for me." Speaking without looking up, her mother finished strapping the airman's leg.

The young woman started but made no attempt to move. She stared at the cuts still oozing blood and the burn on the young man's face.

Her mother looked up at her and held out the cloth. "Wet it for me, please."

Pearl gingerly grasped the cloth and went to the sink to rinse and wet it, trying to ignore the thin stream of blood draining down the plughole. She hurried back and stood at arm's length from her mother as she handed her the cloth.

Mrs Grainger wiped the airman's face again with calm, sure strokes as Pearl watched her, mesmerised. Her mother always knew what to do. When they were children they had run to her with their cuts and bruises and she soothed them. But none of them had ever been injured this badly. She was glad her mother was here. She wouldn't have been able to help him.

Pearl didn't hear the front door open, but out of the corner of her eye she saw Davy and Dick enter the kitchen.

"All set?" her father asked them. The men nodded. He glanced at her mother. "We'd best get him to hospital as quick as we can."

Pearl screwed up her face and tensed her whole body as the four men lifted the injured man. He groaned when they moved his left leg and the remaining colour drained from his face. He slumped into unconsciousness.

Mrs Grainger set the cloth in the kitchen sink and followed the men. As she passed her daughter she said, "Get your cardigan. You may come along and help me."

"What about the wee lads?" Pearl's voice shook.

"Charlie's big enough to mind his brother. They'll be grand. Come you with me."

Mutely, Pearl followed her mother into the hallway. She didn't think she would be any help but she couldn't disobey. She lifted her thick, brown cardigan from the coat rack and stepped outside, pulling the door closed behind her.

The men manoeuvred the injured man onto the makeshift stretcher in the back of the van. Then

Dick helped her mother climb in beside him as her father and Davy jumped into the front seat. Pearl sidled up to the front passenger door and looked in. She was about to ask Davy to move over so she could climb in beside him when she heard her mother calling her. Reluctantly she went to the rear doors.

"Get you in here," her mother ordered.

Pearl climbed in and settled herself on a bale of straw that had been placed in the van, opposite her mother who was perched on another bale. The airman lay on the makeshift stretcher between them. When the van began to move he stirred briefly, groaning, then lapsed into semi-consciousness. Her mother clasped his shoulder and hip to steady him and motioned with her head for Pearl to do the same. Hesitantly, she touched his shoulder, expecting him to cry out in pain, but there was no reaction. She grasped it more firmly and settled her other hand on his hip, bracing her feet on the floor to keep the motion of the van from toppling her off the bale.

For several miles, they travelled without speaking, her mother watching the injured man intently, Pearl repeatedly glancing at him then away. Once again, she was glad her mother was there. She wouldn't have had a clue what to do on her own.

She couldn't stop thinking about the crash. An image of herself standing at the gate as the men tried to rescue the crew kept going through her mind. She winced as she remembered the burning smell and the screams of the flier who had died in the field, trying to push away her feelings of incompetence. Her mother would say she was handless: she hadn't been any practical help when the plane crashed and she was really no more use here. Maybe some people didn't have it in them to do these things.

Pearl jumped as the injured man began muttering. He tossed from side to side. Her mother held him firmly and nodded for her to do the same.

"Where – ?" He tried to sit up.

"It's alright, Mark. We're taking you to the hospital." Her mother spoke calmly and slowly. "You've been hurt."

He turned his head to look at her. "Plane crashed. Where's the others?"

"Shh, don't be fretting about that now." Her mother made soothing sounds.

"Shouldn't have been on it. Asked Chuck to swap." He lay back on the straw and stared at the roof of the van.

Pearl breathed in sharply, gaping at him. She felt the hairs on her neck rise. Surely, he wasn't talking about her fella? Chuck seemed to be a common name among the servicemen who had come from overseas. He couldn't be talking about the same fella.

Her anxiety galvanised her to speak. "Who's Chuck?"

Her mother frowned at her but she ignored the look.

"Swapped with him," Mark muttered.

"What's his other name?" Pearl held her breath as she waited for his reply.

"It's –" His brow furrowed as he concentrated. "It's – Walker. Know him?"

Pearl felt lightheaded as she let her breath go. Her voice shook. "Aye. He said he was flying today."

"Nah, I did. Needed the hours. Gotta get leave. Go to London. See my girl." He groaned with the effort of talking, and Pearl's mother shot her a look that meant she should not ask him any more questions. Her mother gently massaged the injured man's arm and he closed his eyes.

Pearl was relieved not to continue talking. There were so many thoughts churning in her mind. Foremost was an image of Chuck lying amidst the wreckage of that plane. He would have been on it if this man hadn't swapped shifts with him. Maybe he wouldn't have been as lucky. He might have been one of the ones who didn't get out of the aircraft. She bit her lip to stop herself from crying and stared at the floor. Her mother would scold her if she started blubbering. She was supposed to be helping, not needing someone to look after her.

Pearl looked up as Mark opened his eyes and fixed his gaze on her.

"Can you get a message to Chuck? Tell him about the crash?" he asked.

She nodded. "I'll try." She didn't know how she would contact him; she didn't want to get Chuck in bother by ringing to leave a personal message for him at the airbase. They were supposed to meet at the dance tonight, but it wasn't likely she would get there now.

"Don't worry, lad. We'll ring the airbase when we get to the hospital." Her mother spoke with quiet confidence. "We'll let them know where you are."

"Have to tell Chuck about - buddies. You'll get the message to him?" There was anxiety in Mark's eyes as he looked from mother to daughter.

"Leave it with us. We'll sort it for you." Her mother smiled at the young man.

Pearl felt the van slow down and turn sharply onto a bumpier road. She gripped Mark's shoulder to steady him on his pallet. They must be on the long driveway to the military hospital in Necarne Castle. It would be a relief to turn over the injured man's care to the nurses.

A couple minutes later the van stopped. Pearl heard the cab doors open and slam shut then the rear doors were opened and her father was peering in. Davy appeared behind him with two porters in tow. She watched silently as the porters manoeuvred Mark from his makeshift pallet onto a stretcher and carried him into the hospital.

"We'll bide awhile and see how he fares." Her father spoke to the three of them as he helped Pearl and her mother climb out of the van to stand beside the two men. He led his family into the hospital, and a nurse directed them to the Casualty department where Mark had been taken.

They sat on a hard wooden bench outside the door to the ward, watching as staff went in and out. Seeing their calm faces and purposeful movements, Pearl was relieved that Mark was in their care. It was obvious they knew what they were doing; they weren't totally inept and unable to do anything right. Not like she was. She watched them, fascinated and envious, feeling even smaller than she had when she watched the men's rescue attempts after the plane crash.

"I'd best go and see if I can get the number to ring the airbase. I don't know if anyone else will tell them what's happened." Her father stood up as he spoke.

"He asked that we get a message to another airman who was supposed to be on the flight," her mother said. "What was his name? Chuck –"

"Walker. Chuck Walker." Pearl spoke softly.

"Aye, that's it. Don't forget to ask them to pass on a message on to him," her mother said. "Poor lad, no doubt he'll be devastated to hear that his crewmates have died."

The three of them sat in silence waiting for Mr Grainger to return. Davy frequently glanced at the clock high on the white wall opposite them, shifting restlessly. Pearl knew that he was probably worrying about whether they would get to the dance tonight. No doubt he had business cronies he wanted to meet in order to sell them some of the items he had brought across the border this afternoon. How could he think of things like that after the crash? She pursed her lips and turned her face away from him.

A few minutes later Pearl looked down the hall to see her father walking toward them.

"I got through to the airbase. They appreciated being informed. They'll send personnel to sort out the aircraft and attend to the other lads." His voice trailed off.

"What about Chuck?" Pearl asked hesitantly.

Her father regarded her for a moment with a slight frown. "Oh yes, I mentioned him to the person I spoke to. He said he would pass on the message."

"That's grand. Hopefully we'll get a chance to tell Mark before we leave," her mother said.

Davy glanced at the clock again and then at Pearl. She ignored his look, keeping her eyes trained on the door to the ward. When she thought she might go cross-eyed staring at it, the door opened and a thin young woman in a white uniform and veil stepped out of the door and came to stand beside them.

"You're the family who brought in Pilot Officer Hardy?" she asked.

"Aye," Mr Grainger replied.

"How is he?" Mrs Grainger asked.

"They've set his leg and given him morphine. He's doing grand. We're taking him to the ward shortly."

"Can we have a word with him before we leave?" Mrs Grainger asked.

"Surely. We'll bring him through here so we can stop a minute. I'll let Matron know you wish to speak to him."

"Thank you, Sister," Mrs Grainger said.

The thin woman smiled. "You needn't call me Sister. I'm not a nurse. I'm a volunteer. Ruth Corey."

Pearl watched the volunteer disappear into the Casualty department. The young woman wasn't much older than she was, but she seemed so confident and at ease. *I wish I could be like her. She's not afraid of anything. Not like me. I couldn't do anything right today.*

Davy began tapping his foot impatiently and Pearl shot him an irritated look. *Can he not think of anything except his money-making schemes?*

Several minutes later, the door opened again and a stretcher was wheeled into the corridor. The volunteer they had met earlier and a porter were pushing it. They stopped and waited as Pearl's parents rose and went to speak to the patient. Standing in front of the bench, Pearl craned her neck to listen to the conversation.

"Thank you for all you've done for me." Mark spoke in a hoarse, slightly slurred voice.

"No need to thank us, lad. We did what we could," Mr Grainger said. "I rang your airbase and let them know what happened. They'll sort everything out."

"He gave them the message for your friend too," Mrs Grainger added.

"That's – good." The injured man's speech was slow and hard to understand. His eyes drooped closed and his head slumped sideways.

"Is he all right?" Mrs Grainger looked anxiously at the volunteer.

"He's fine. It's just the morphine making him groggy." Ruth smiled reassuringly. "We'd better get him settled in the ward or they'll think I've kidnapped him." She laughed softly and nodded to the porter.

As they started to wheel the airman away, on an impulse Pearl stepped forward and asked Ruth in a halting voice, "How did you become a volunteer?"

"I wanted to do my bit for the War so I came to the hospital and signed up."

"Didn't you need training?"

"No, the nurses do that in the wards."

"You must've been working here for ages."

"Ach no, I started last month. If you're interested, write to the Matron and she'll send for you."

Pearl blushed. "Oh, I was just curious. I wouldn't be able to –"

"You could, surely. They always need more volunteers. Listen, I'd better go before they come looking for me. But, think on it. Cheerio." Ruth nodded to the rest of the family and leaned forward to push the stretcher in the direction she wanted it to go.

Pearl watched them disappear into a ward several yards down the hall. She was aware of her parents standing, waiting for her. Davy was already walking toward the main entrance. She bowed her head and, avoiding her parents' curious looks, followed him.

It was kind of the volunteer to say she could help here too, but, of course, she wouldn't be able to. The girl didn't know how clumsy and dithering she was. Pearl studied the pattern on the floor tiles as she walked, avoiding meeting anyone's gaze. When they reached the main entrance, her mother stopped to button her cardigan. From habit, Pearl did the same, glancing around to admire the marvellous reddish pillars that lined the foyer and the checkerboard polished marble floor. Necarne Castle was a magnificent old building. What amazing craftsmen the men who built it must have been.

Buoyed by the beauty of the foyer, Pearl let her thoughts race. Wouldn't it be wonderful if she could come here to help the servicemen who were patients in the hospital? No more listening to Davy telling her that the War was just a lark. She knew now that it wasn't, and she wanted to do something to help win the War. But she was so inept. She sighed then stopped herself. An impossible idea was forming in her head. She drew in a breath and held it. Could she do it? That girl had only been here since last month and she was good at her job. Why couldn't she be like Ruth? There were posters everywhere saying women were needed in war work, but she was doing nothing. So why shouldn't she try?

Pearl pushed the last button through the buttonhole and straightened the bottom edge of her cardigan then glanced around her once more. If a rich man like Captain Hermon could open his castle and family home to the military for the hospital, and that young girl, Ruth, could work here, then she could do her bit too. She would sign up as a volunteer. She promised herself that she would write to the Matron when they got home this evening. Her heart thudding, she followed her family out of the hospital.

United States Army Station Hospital, Necarne Castle, Irvinestown, County Fermanagh
July 1942

Pearl followed Lieutenant Baxter, listening intently, twisting the bottom edge of her white veil with her right hand. She hadn't expected the hospital to be staffed by American army nurses, and she found Lieutenant Baxter's very pronounced New York accent difficult to understand. It was also hard to remember to call her ma'am, not Sister, as she had always addressed the nurses in the local hospital.

"There is a lot to learn to work in a hospital. The nursing staff will teach you but you must obey the instructions you're given. You are not trained to care for patients. You will only do duties assigned to you by the nursing staff. The first thing you must learn is that it is crucial to keep the ward clean. This prevents infections. This morning you'll start your duties by wiping the bed frames." Pearl watched the nurse's starched cap bob as she nodded to emphasise what she was saying.

The nurse led Pearl into the sluice room and showed her how to prepare a bucket of hot water and disinfectant. It was amazing to see hot water gushing out of the tap, and they didn't seem to worry about how much they used. It was much better than having to boil water on the range when you needed it.

Armed with the bucket and clean cloths, Pearl followed Lieutenant Baxter back to the ward. The nurse watched as she cleaned the first two bed frames then left her to continue working.

Pearl approached the next bed in the row. The patient seemed to be asleep. She tiptoed to the head of the bed and quietly began her task. She had wiped half the frame when she heard the patient speak.

"We've got a new gal, I see."

She jumped and gripped the bed frame with the cloth for a second then peered around the pillows to look at the man. When he turned his face toward her, she gasped. The man's face was bruised and covered in scrapes. His left eye was swollen shut.

"Sorry to frighten you, honey. Usually I'm uglier than this. Accident on the assault course. The evidence'll soon be gone."

"You still won't be any better looking, Johnny." The patient across the aisle laughed at his own joke.

Lieutenant Baxter walked up behind Pearl. "Remember to change the water frequently and don't let it get cold. You need lots of hot water."

Pearl nodded and finished wiping the bed frame. She smiled hesitantly at the patient and moved on to the next bed. As she worked at the foot of the bed, she looked up at the patient lying in it. His head and right arm were bandaged. His swollen lips stood out prominently on his thin face. She quickly looked away, worried he would catch her staring at him. The patient turned on to his side and she heard his sharp intact of breath and stifled groan. She glanced up anxiously at his face. His eyes were squeezed shut and his brow was drawn into a deep furrow. She wanted to do something to help him but didn't know what to do. Should she get a nurse? She stood staring at him, holding her breath, until he quieted then hurriedly finished washing the frame and scurried to the next bed.

For the rest of the morning Pearl moved up and down the aisles, washing bed frames, and trooped in and out of the sluice room, filling the bucket with fresh water and disinfectant. Whenever she passed Ruth Corey the young woman smiled silent encouragement at her. They were expected to present a quiet, professional manner on the ward, though the patients often waylaid them to chat.

By the end of the morning Pearl's mind was filled with images of the injured servicemen lying in the ward. Some had limbs in plaster, many had cuts, scrapes and bruises, and one lay shirtless with his chest swathed in bandages. She found the most distressing wounds were the burns. Two of the men had burns on their faces and hands. As she worked on one bed frame, the patient in the bed was suddenly ill and vomited across the bedclothes. She stood staring at the mess until an auxiliary nurse arrived and sent her to fetch clean sheets. The smell of carbolic soap mingled with the vomit and bedpans waiting to be emptied tugged at her stomach.

Many of the men talked and joked with each other, teasing the nursing staff who passed their beds. A few lay silent, stifling groans as they shifted restlessly. Others struggled in and out of the ward on crutches. She was startled to see that one of these men had his trouser leg pinned at the knee. There was nothing below it.

Pearl went to the canteen with Ruth on their dinner break. The 109th Medical Battalion of the United States Army ran the hospital, and ration portions were larger and more diverse than could be had at any of the hotels or restaurants in the county. She ate a few mouthfuls of potatoes then cut a piece of the thick slice of gammon on her plate. Instead of eating it, she pushed it around on the plate. She knew she should be pleased to have such good food, but she didn't have much appetite.

"That's your first morning done. I told you, you could do it," Ruth said.

"I just about managed it." Pearl listlessly forked the food into her mouth. She didn't want to admit how much it had bothered her to see the injuries some of the patients had; they were ghastly to look at. But it wasn't just that. Tears welled in her eyes when she saw the men in pain. And knowing that she couldn't do anything to alleviate it made her feel even more upset. She would love to ask Ruth how she managed to be efficient and cheery on the ward. She never seemed daunted by anything she encountered. But that would only highlight her own lack of ability. Lieutenant Baxter had reminded her twice to change the water when she was washing the bed frames, and the nurse had told her to get back to work when she forgot herself and stared at a patient's wounds.

The girls spent the rest of their dinner break talking about their families and sweethearts. Pearl learned that Ruth lived not far from the hospital in Irvinestown and her family ran a small hotel in the town.

When it was time to return to the ward, Pearl tried to hide her unease. What would she be asked to do this afternoon? Would she be able for it?

"Don't look so worried." Ruth smiled encouragement at her. "It won't be as bad as you think it will."

Pearl wasn't sure that was true, but she forced herself to smile in return and followed her new friend back to the ward.

***

Pearl wheeled the wooden cart up the aisle and stopped at the next bed. She lifted a glass from the cart and turned to hand it to the patient.

"Would you like some water?" she asked.

"I didn't expect to see you here. You must be following me."

Still holding the glass, she stared at the man in the bed.

"Hello." She didn't know what else to say.

290

After an awkward pause she said, "How are you?"

"I'm not bad at all. I've got crutches, and you should see me fly around this joint. I'll be out by the beginning of August, touch wood." Mark Hardy tapped his head.

She giggled. "That's good."

"Pearl, isn't it? Chuck told me your name. I never got a chance to properly thank you and your family for bringing me to the hospital. I owe you for it." He smiled at her.

She felt her cheeks flush and knew she must be at least a bright pink. "It's – it's all right." She felt guilty accepting his thanks, knowing she had stood by helplessly on the night of the crash while her mother cared for him. "I'll tell them what you said."

Mark's lips spread into a grin as heavy footsteps approached them. Pearl tensed but quickly realised that they were too heavy to be Lieutenant Baxter's. She turned around to see Chuck striding toward them. When he noticed her, he frowned.

"Speak of the devil. Good to see you, buddy," Mark called to his friend. He grinned broadly.

"Good to see you too. Didn't expect to see Pearl though." Chuck turned to look at her, his eyes dark.

"I told you that I'd a letter telling me to report to the hospital today," Pearl replied.

"I'm glad I've had a chance to thank her in

person for helping me after the crash," Mark said.

Pearl watched Chuck's face become a blank mask. He nodded acknowledgement of his friend's comment but did not reply. The first time she had met Chuck after the crash she had asked whether he had received the message her father had left for him when he phoned the airbase. They had talked briefly about the crash then he had avoided mentioning it ever since. As a result, she had been hesitant to ask him about Mark's progress, even though her parents pressed her to do so.

"You may give Pilot Officer Hardy's friend a glass of water too, if he would like one." Lieutenant Baxter was standing behind her. "The men may prefer something stronger, but this is what we have to offer." Despite her serious face, Pearl was sure the nurse's eyes twinkled.

Pearl felt her cheeks flush again as she lifted a glass of water and handed it to Chuck. "I'd best be off," she whispered. She pushed the cart to the next bed.

Her face burned as she worked her way along the row, though she wasn't sure whether she was most unsettled by the nurse's gentle chastisement for chatting with the patients or by Chuck's arrival. She hurriedly handed a glass of water to each patient, speaking as little as possible to the men. It was several minutes before she felt the heat begin to lessen.

She stopped at the next bed and automatically lifted a glass. "Would you like a glass of water?" she asked the patient.

When she didn't receive a reply, she looked up. The bare-chested patient was propped up against the pillows with one arm stretched out to the edge of the bed. As a nurse peeled away the gauze bandage on the patient's shoulder and upper arm, he winced. Pearl stood with her mouth hanging open, watching the nurse remove the gauze, tugging when it stuck. The nurse dropped the used bandage in a basin beside her.

The ragged wound in the patient's shoulder oozed a rivulet of blood. The nurse wet a strip of gauze, folded it into a clean pad, and used it to wipe away the fresh blood. Pearl stared at the gaping edges of flesh where a couple stitches had broken; there were uneven tears in the skin where the stitches had dragged through it. On the farm, she had always been shielded from accidents and injuries. Her mother looked after them. As she looked at the wound, her legs felt wobbly. The glass slid from her hand and she felt water splash her calf. In the distance she heard the sound of glass hitting the tile floor.

She became aware of voices and looked at the nurse who was treating the patient. She was saying something but Pearl couldn't understand her. There was a loud rushing in her ears. Without thinking, she turned and hurried down the aisle.

As she half-ran, something crunched under her sturdy black shoes. Her face burned again and tears flowed down it.

At the end of the aisle, she stretched out her arm to open the door and escape but something blocked her way. She looked down and realised that it was the cart. She must have pushed it with her. She stepped around it, pulled the door open and dragged the cart through it.

In the foyer, she dragged her arm across her face to wipe her eyes. Her breath came in shallow, quick gasps. It was several minutes before she glanced around to see if anyone was watching her. There was a soldier on duty at the reception desk, and several nurses and porters walked back and forth across the foyer. No one seemed to take any notice of her.

What had she done? Run away like a frightened hare. She couldn't even look at a patient's wound without falling to pieces. Why couldn't she have handed him the glass of water and went on to the next bed as she was supposed to do? What would they think of her running from the ward like that? She really was a hopeless case.

"Are you okay?"

Pearl jumped at the voice behind her. She nodded without turning around.

"I saw you hurrying out and I thought something must be wrong." Chuck spoke in a quiet, gentle voice.

She shook her head, keeping her back to him.

"What happened?"

"Oh, nothing really."

"There must've been something. You looked upset."

She felt sweat break out on her forehead and her face was getting hot again. If Chuck had noticed, from halfway down the aisle, then everyone must have seen what happened. She could never go back into the ward now. She gradually became aware that Chuck was silently watching her, waiting for an explanation.

"It was really silly. I – I- saw the nurse –" She stopped and gulped air. "She – she was changing a dressing. I've never seen anything like that –" Her sentence trailed off and she stared at the floor.

Chuck reached out and stroked her arm. When she looked at him, he wasn't laughing at her. His eyes were full of concern.

"It's no wonder you're upset. That's not the sort of thing you should see. I wouldn't want my kid sister working in a military hospital. She's around the same age as you." Chuck continued to stroke her arm, moving closer as he talked soothingly. "It's really no place for my girl either. Haven't you noticed that many of the volunteers are married women? You shouldn't be around all these men. It's just too rough."

Pearl thought about it. Maybe Chuck was right. Many of the volunteers were older than she was and had families that were already grown. They were more experienced in dealing with illness and injuries. And, it was embarrassing seeing men lying in bed, often bare-chested. She had seen her brothers half-dressed but this was different.

Chuck's voice broke into her thoughts. "I'm not flying today so I don't have to be back to the airbase for a few hours. I can give you a lift home."

"I – I – how can I leave?" Pearl's eyebrows drew together tightly.

"Don't you worry your head. I'll speak to the nurse in charge. It'll be alright." Chuck smiled at her reassuringly. "Maybe we could have dinner at that eating house in Irvinestown – Corey's – before I drop you home. The guys say it's got the best steaks anywhere around here."

Pearl took a deep breath and exhaled slowly, but her chest still felt tight. She couldn't face going back into the ward. And she couldn't speak to Lieutenant Baxter either. She would let Chuck take her home. That was the best thing to do. She had tried. She pursed her lips together tightly to stop herself from crying again. It was only her first day and she had failed. How could anyone be so hopeless? She was so ashamed that she just wanted to get away as quickly as possible.

Chuck was walking toward the door to the ward as it opened. Ruth hurried out and darted glances around the foyer. She smiled when she spotted Pearl.

"I couldn't get out any sooner. I'd to finish helping Lieutenant Morris change a bed. You okay, pet?"

Pearl just stared at the other young woman without replying. She remembered seeing Ruth and a nurse changing a bed with a patient lying in it as she had rushed out of the ward. Like everything else she did, Ruth had seemed at ease and competent as she worked. *Nothing like me.*

"I'm just taking Pearl home," Chuck said.

Ruth's eyes widened as she turned her head to look first at the RCAF officer then Pearl. "Are you ill?" she asked her friend.

Pearl shook her head then lowered her gaze to stare at the floor, her hands clasped together in front of her. She felt tears threatening to fall again. When she remembered Ruth working on the ward so capably, she felt like a small child beside her friend.

"Here now, don't let it get you down. Everyone's first day's a terror. It gets better." Ruth smiled at her.

"I'll never get any better at it." Pearl spoke in a whisper.

"Of course you will. You should've seen some of the silly things I did when I started. I just about strangled myself with the linen one day." Ruth laughed.

Chuck cut into the conversation. "It's no place for my girl. I've said I'll see her home."

"The War's no place for any of us but we're in it. Everyone has to pitch in." Ruth kept her tone of voice even and friendly.

Pearl felt a stab of guilt. When she had watched her family rescue Mark from the crashed seaplane, she had wanted to do something to help. Later that evening Ruth had inspired her, and she had decided that she would volunteer at the hospital. Now what both Chuck and Ruth were saying made sense. She felt torn. What should she do? She felt warm and safe when she thought about going home with Chuck. They had been walking out together for almost a month now. He'd look after her. But, at the same time, a tiny voice inside her said Ruth was right. Everyone had to pitch in. She had to try again. She couldn't give up after less than a day. She took a deep breath.

"I'd best get back in and finish the water." Pearl's eyes were anxious as she looked at Chuck.

"You don't have to if you don't want to." His expression was kind and gentle.

"Yes, I do." Pearl spoke with a little more conviction.

"It's really no place for you. Let me take you home." Chuck spoke softly and looked into her eyes.

"I – I can't. I have to do this." Pearl turned to look at Ruth for support.

"Only if you're sure –" Chuck caught her attention and held her gaze.

Pearl pursed her lips and nodded.

"Remember, you don't have to do this, if you don't want to. You can leave any time you want. I'll see you at the dance in Enniskillen on Thursday night?"

Pearl smiled. "Yes. I'll be there."

"Okay. Nine o'clock. You watch out for those guys in there. Don't let them sweet-talk you – especially Hardy." Chuck pulled his lips into a grin but there was no hint of humour in his eyes. "I'd best get going. I'll see you Thursday." He touched her arm lightly then walked toward the main entrance.

"Right – are you ready for it?" Ruth grinned at her.

"Oh, how can I go back in there when they all saw me run out?" Pearl took a shaky breath.

"It's not the first time it's happened. Just get in there and don't worry about it. The lads are nice. They won't give you a hard time. They're glad to see us there. Are you ready?"

Pearl straightened her shoulders and took a deep breath then nodded. She gripped the cart and pushed it through the door, following Ruth into the ward. Somehow, she would do this.

Enniskillen Town Hall, County Fermanagh
July 1942

On Thursday evening, Pearl scanned the crowded room in the Town Hall, searching for Chuck. It

299

was already quarter past nine. She stood on tiptoes trying to see above the mass of people on the dance floor. When the crowd parted for a moment, she spotted the airman in his greyish-blue uniform. He was also obviously looking for her. When their eyes met he grinned broadly, leaned his shoulder into the crowd and started to work his way to her.

"There you are. You haven't run away with any of the patients, then?" Chuck laughed but there was a note of tension in it.

"When would I get the chance? There's that much work to do." Pearl tried to keep her reply light.

"Well, I'm glad you're here. Shall we jump into the crush?"

Chuck guided Pearl into the middle of the dance floor. He rested his hand lightly on her back, and paused for a moment to find the beat, then led them into the foxtrot that was in progress. The fast tempo made it impossible to hold a conversation. Pearl smiled up into Chuck's face, glad to be with him again.

It was true that she was now surrounded by men every day and they did tease her, offering to take her on dates when they got out of hospital, but she didn't fancy any of them. She had been captivated by Chuck the first time she met him, not long before the plane crash on their farm, and she had never been tempted by anyone else. They had quickly progressed from casual dates to being a couple.

The next two sets passed quickly. Pearl loved being held firmly in Chuck's arms. He was a confident dancer, and she relaxed as he led them around the dance floor. As the last tune in the second set ended, she heard the singer announce that the next dance was a set of waltzes.

Chuck leaned in closer and pulled her to him. "Almost a week now and you're still at the hospital. How're you getting on?"

"Better than the first day." Pearl smiled wryly. "It seemed so overwhelming, but Lieutenant Baxter is good to the volunteers and patient with us. Ruth helps me too. There's nothing she can't do. I doubt I'll ever be as good at it as her." She sighed, her eyes fixed on Chuck's chest.

"Don't be so hard on yourself. How could anyone expect you to do that sort of thing? Working with all those men and seeing awful things. I told you, I wouldn't want my sister to do it. And the same goes for my girl." Chuck's smile had faded, replaced by a serious expression.

"I feel so sorry for the men who have arms and legs in plaster and can't do much for themselves. There are a couple really bad cases. As well as his broken leg, one man's face and hand are badly burned. I can't look at him. I always do my work and hurry away from his bed. I feel terrible treating him like that, but I just can't look at him.

Ruth is always cheery and chats with him as if there's nothing wrong. I don't know how she does it. And it's terrible seeing the wounds when the nurses are changing dressings – some of them are red and oozing. Sometimes they smell too. I try not to look at them but I can't always avoid it. At least I haven't run out of the ward again, though I wanted to more than once. The men are brilliant, though. Most of them chat to us and have a laugh. Few of them complain. They're so brave. Like Mark. He's always friendly and never complains about the pain, even after all that he's been through."

Pearl suddenly realised that she had been prattling on and on without stopping. And, she probably shouldn't have mentioned the crash. Chuck never talked about it. She looked up at his face. He was staring at her, his jaw clenched. She wasn't sure exactly what his look meant, but she knew she must have said the wrong thing, whatever it was.

"I bet. Hardy's probably the perfect patient." Chuck spat out the words.

Pearl stared at him, bewildered.

"What more could you want?" Chuck glared at her then shifted his gaze away from her, looking over her shoulder, avoiding her eyes.

"I don't want –" Pearl looked up into Chuck's face, unsure what she was responding to. Why was Chuck so annoyed?

"Forget it." The tempo quickened and Chuck led her into another foxtrot.

Pearl's heart pounded and she felt like crying. Why was he so angry with her? What had she done?

When the music stopped, she stood still, moving only her head to glance around the dance floor, trying to avoid catching Chuck's eye.

"Why don't we go and get a soda?" Chuck smiled and his tone was softer than the one he had used a few minutes earlier. He placed his hand on her back and guided her toward the refreshment table. "Two lemonades, please," he said to the woman behind the table. He turned to Pearl and waited for her to nod her head in agreement before he pulled change out of his pocket to pay for the drinks.

He handed her one of the glasses and led her away from the table. Pearl's mind was in turmoil, unsure whether she should finish what she had been saying before the last dance set. Surely Chuck couldn't think she fancied anyone else? She had never given him any reason to think that. But, she couldn't just come out and tell him how she felt about him even though they were walking out together. He would think her very forward.

"I'm not on the roster on Saturday. Will you come to the movies with me?" Chuck was still smiling.

"That would be grand – oh, I'm working. My

303

shift doesn't finish until eight o'clock. The film would be started when we'd get there." Pearl sighed. She'd have loved to go to the pictures with him.

"Would you rather be with those guys or me?" The smile had disappeared from Chuck's face.

"Don't be silly – it's not that. I have to do my shift. Else they'll be short."

"You're a volunteer. It's not like you're a nurse or a doctor. They'd get along without you." Chuck raised his voice slightly.

"Someone has to do my duties. I signed up to work at the hospital. I can't just not go in."

"Can't or won't? Maybe you'd rather be there than spend the evening with me. Better to hang around a real crash survivor. I'm sure you'll find lots to talk with Hardy about." Chuck's eyebrows were drawn together, and the intensity of his gaze forced her to stare at the floor.

"No, it's not like that. They say everyone on the home front has to do their bit too. That's why I volunteered. I'm not a nurse but I free up the nurses to do their jobs. I am needed. I'm not just there to chat to patients. I'm working for the war effort too. Just like you." Pearl was surprised to realise how strongly she felt about this.

"How many times do I have to tell you – you shouldn't be doing that sort of work. Help your family on your farm growing extra vegetables and supplying milk and food. But I don't want my girl doing all the jobs in a hospital ward that no one else would do, and mixing with all sorts of men. It's just not right."

Pearl sighed. How could she make him see that she had to do this? Her work on the farm helped but she had to do more. Ever since the night of the crash, she saw the wrecked plane and the scene in the field over and over in her head. She had to do her part for the war effort. She couldn't just quit.

"If you hand in your resignation tomorrow, you'd be free on Saturday. You don't want to be around a place like that." Chuck had lowered his voice and his tone was persuasive.

"I'd love to see you on Saturday. But I can't quit."

"Or won't. Okay, if you'd rather be with Hardy than me, that's fine. I know the score. I'd better get going. I'm on watch tonight."

"But it's not like that –"

Chuck ran his hand through his hair and avoided looking at her. "Never mind. Look, it's getting late. I've got to get going."

"I thought one of the lads was on your plane until you get back."

"Can't have that now, can we? They'll be saying Walker never does his shifts. Leaves someone else to guard his kite. Goodnight, Pearl."

Chuck walked away before she could say anything more. He hadn't even arranged when they would next meet. Pearl slipped into a corner, trying not to be noticed. She didn't want anyone to ask her to dance. It would be a while before Davy was ready to leave, but she wished she could escape this minute.

Lough Erne, County Fermanagh
In the early hours of the next morning

Pearl sat silently in the small, wooden boat as Davy rowed, the only sound a soft slapping as the oars dipped in and out of the water. Her brother had warned her that they must be quiet if they were to escape detection. She gripped the sides of the boat, willing it to get to its destination without them getting caught. She *had* to see Chuck.

As they approached the flying boat, Pearl was awed by the size of it. Its dark bulk rose out of the water above her like a whale resting on the surface of the lough. The moon disappeared as they slid under its wing, between the hull of the craft and the float attached to its wing. She hoped that Davy had found the right seaplane. They would have a lot of explaining to do if he hadn't.

As they stopped at the flying boat's forward door Davy looked back at his sister. "Are you sure you want to do this?" he whispered.

Pearl felt a huge lump in her throat. She nodded. When she had left the dance several hours earlier, all she could think about was that she couldn't leave things the way they were. She had to finish her conversation with Chuck. He was flying most days and anything could happen. She had to sort it out with him. But now that she was here, her throat felt tight and her stomach was knotted. She didn't know what she would say to him, but there was no turning back now.

Davy tapped on the seaplane's door. It was opened by a crewman she didn't recognise. Her brother stood up and braced himself against the fuselage. He and the airman held a conversation in low voices then the man disappeared inside, leaving the door open.

Her brother sat down and turned to her. "Aye, he's there. I'll keep the boat as close as I can to the door. Be careful getting aboard. I'll be back in an hour and a half. We need to be home before Da gets up."

Pearl stood in a half-crouched position, feeling the boat rocking under her. She was glad it was dark and she couldn't see the water surrounding them. They weren't far from shore, but the water was very cold and deep. She wouldn't stand much chance of being rescued if she fell in. She saw someone in shadow inside the doorway holding his arms out to her and she jumped the short space between the boat and the seaplane. Strong arms grasped her waist and pulled her safely into the seaplane. She glanced over her shoulder to see Davy raise his hand in a mock salute then disappear. When she turned around again, she was looking into Chuck's surprised face. Another crewman stood behind him.

"What're you doing here? Y'know, I'm in a lot of trouble if you're caught. Only crew are ever supposed to be on board," Chuck said.

"I'm sorry – I don't want to get you in trouble. It's just –" Pearl looked at the other man.

Chuck followed her gaze. He motioned toward the other airman. "Pearl, this is Flight Sergeant Gary Barrett." Glancing at his crewmate, he said, "This is my girl, Pearl."

She murmured hello to the other man.

"Hiya, Miss. I think I'll go and brew up some coffee." The other man walked toward the rear section of the aircraft.

Chuck turned his attention to Pearl. "It's not just that I could get in trouble. You know what the lough's like. A storm could brew up without warning and swamp this kite. That's one of the reasons crew have to be on board to keep watch on it."

Pearl felt the knot in her stomach ease. He was concerned about her. "Don't worry. It'll be calm tonight. Davy says so."

"And what does your brother know about it? He's a farmer."

"He's out on the lough right often."

"Why?"

Pearl hesitated. She didn't want to tell him about her brother's illicit activities. Smuggled goods were often moved by land or water at night when they would be harder to detect.

"He fishes."

"In the middle of the night?"

Pearl nodded. "Aye – eels." It was a plausible, though untrue, explanation.

Chuck regarded her with one eyebrow raised but didn't pursue the topic. "I still can't believe you're out here at this hour of the night. How did you know which kite it was?"

"Davy made enquiries. He knows some people."

"No one should've told him anything. And, I don't know how he managed to slip past the Navy. Your brother is quite amazing." He shook his head slowly.

Pearl blushed and avoided his gaze. She grasped a strand of loose hair and twirled it around her finger. She wouldn't tell him that Davy was used to giving the slip to the Lough Erne Navy, as the Royal Engineers' boats that patrolled the lough were known. He always stayed well clear of them whenever he was on the lough. Their job was to protect the seaplanes moored in the water from the threat of sabotage by the IRA and to keep the navigation path clear of other vessels so the flying boats could take off and land safely.

"Never mind. You didn't come out here to talk about your brother."

"No, I – I didn't want the evening to end with harsh words. I had to talk to you."

Chuck smiled. "Let's find somewhere to sit."

He led her through the upper deck of the aircraft to a ladder. They climbed down to the lower deck. She had never seen so much metal anywhere. Their farm was made of stone and wood. On the lower deck, they stepped through the raised doorways of a couple compartments until they came to one that was obviously sleeping quarters. A bunk was placed on either side of the aisle. The blankets on one were rumpled and thrown back. She must have wakened Chuck.

He motioned for her to sit down. She glanced around but saw nowhere but the bunks to sit on. What on earth would her Da say if he knew she was sitting in a man's bedroom? Well, it wasn't his bedroom exactly, but as good as. And, she wouldn't think about what her Da would say if he knew she had talked Davy into rowing her out here.

"I didn't want us to fall out, so I had to talk to you," Pearl said. "You must know there's no one else – not since we first met. I don't want to walk out with anyone else."

She felt her face burning after making this statement. It was very bold to be so honest about her feelings. Girls should wait for the fella to take the lead. But she felt so awful about the way the evening had ended.

Chuck reached for her hand and stroked it. "I didn't mean to be so sharp earlier. I want to spend as much time as I can with you. But we've had less time to be together since you started working at the hospital. And I saw you and Hardy talking on the ward. You seemed so friendly with him – too friendly. I just saw red."

"I was only talking to him. The patients like us to chat with them as we go about our work. It doesn't mean anything. It's just friendly chat – like you'd chat to anyone you met."

"Hardy was flying when I was supposed to be. I figured you thought I dodged off the rota so you'd rather be with him than me."

"I didn't think that! I was so glad you weren't on that mission. On the way to the hospital Mark told us that you were supposed to be on the plane but he had asked you to swap with him. When me Da and the others were trying to get the crew out I just stood there watching them. It suddenly occurred to me that you might be on board. I was in agony until I knew you weren't."

"I thought you'd say I was yellow."

"I never thought that. I knew it wasn't your idea to swap."

"He wanted to finish his tour faster and get over to London to see his girl. Lot of good it did him. He won't see her for a while. I thought he might be putting the moves on you now."

Pearl raised her head and looked into his eyes.

"I don't want anyone else."

She didn't know what it was about this man, but every time she saw him she wanted to run to him and curl up in his arms. His broad, quiet bulk made her feel safe and happy.

Chuck leaned close and wrapped his arms around her. Squeezing gently, he rocked her back and forth and kissed the top of her head. "That's good, honey. I wouldn't want to lose you to anyone else. I just sometimes think I wasn't pulling my weight. I should've been on that plane."

"But I'm so glad you weren't. It doesn't bear thinking about losing you. And you're doing your share. You're flying all the time. Doing your bit. You had no way to know what would happen that night. No one could say otherwise."

"No one says anything about it and my new crew are great. But I let the guys down by not being with them. We'd flown nearly every mission together since we were first stationed here. Lived in the same quarters. And now they're all gone. You can't imagine what it felt like to go back to our barracks and be the only one in the hut that night."

Pearl felt the tears welling in her eyes and tightened her arms around Chuck's waist. She couldn't imagine what it would feel like to lose so many friends and comrades at once, men he had spent his life with since he arrived here.

"I'll pray every day for the safety of you and your new crew – that your plane will be sound and you'll always get them home."

Chuck gently kissed her lips. She closed her eyes and savoured the sensation. When she made no move to pull away from him, he kissed her again, a lingering one. Joy welled up inside her. Everything was right between them again. When he finally pulled away from her, she sighed contentedly.

"Now if you didn't have to work at the hospital, everything would be perfect." He smiled kindly at her.

Pearl's chest tightened. She thought they had sorted everything out, but it seemed her hospital work was still a stumbling block between them. Da had raised some of the same arguments when she first told her parents she wanted to volunteer. But her mother had taken her side, saying she would be doing something useful. She was sure her mother was relieved she didn't want to enlist in the WAAF or sign up for any other work that would take her away from home.

"But I do have to work there. Someone has to do it."

"Why does it have to be you? I told you before, honey, you're helping the war effort by the work you do on your farm."

"Haven't you seen the posters? 'Women, We Need You'. Helping at home just isn't enough."

"Why are you so concerned? Your brother doesn't worry about it. Is he even in the Home Guard? Why should you do more than him?"

Pearl hesitated. She didn't know how to answer that. It niggled her that Davy had never even talked about enlisting. Most people were doing everything they could to help win the War, but her brother spent his time looking for ways to make money from it. She didn't understand his attitude. But farming was a reserved occupation and he was the only son old enough to help Da. Their younger brothers were still at school. Other fellas stayed home to work family farms too. What he did besides farming was beyond her control.

She sighed. "I can't answer for Davy. But I know my own conscience. Ever since I saw the plane crash I knew I had to do more."

Chuck exhaled loudly and leaned away from her. He regarded her for several seconds, a slight frown creasing his brow. "I don't like you working in the hospital. I still think you shouldn't have to see some of the things you do. Girls, especially my girl, should be protected from that."

Pearl opened her mouth to speak but he continued. "I know you want to do your bit. I understand that." He took a deep breath and exhaled slowly. "I guess I'll have to accept it. At least we're near each other and can meet as often as our rotas allow."

The tightness in her chest released, and she felt a smile forming on her lips. "I'm so glad. I don't want us to fall out over it."

"Don't worry, honey. That's never going to happen."

Chuck pulled her close again and the pair sat in contented silence.

After several minutes, he shifted to look into her face. "Well, if you don't finish your shift in time for the movie on Saturday, maybe we could go dancing instead? If you're not too tired after work?"

Pearl beamed at him. "That would be brilliant. I'd like that."

"Swell." He grinned at her. "Hey, I smell coffee brewing. Let's go to the galley and see if Barrett's made some for us too. We should have time before your brother comes back for you."

Chuck stood up and took her hand. He pulled her up, stopped and looked into her face. "You know, you're an amazing gal. I'm lucky to have you. I'll still keep hoping, though, you'll see sense one day and give up your work at the hospital."

United States Army Station Hospital, Necarne Castle, Irvinestown, County Fermanagh
August 1942

Pearl lifted a dinner tray from the cart and set it on the patient's knee. "That's one of your favourites, isn't it?" The potatoes, carrots and beef were steaming hot, and the delicious fragrance wafted into her nostrils. Despite rationing, the hospital always had the best of the food available.

"You've got a great memory. You're one of my favourite gals." The man gave her a cheeky grin.

Pearl laughed and shook her head. As she leaned against the cart to push it to the next bed, she felt a hand on her arm and turned around.

Ruth's eyes were wide and her face tense. "You've to go to Casualty."

"But I'm doing the dinners."

"Never mind about that. I'll do it."

Ruth drew her away from the patient's bed. "I was sent to Casualty with a message. While I was there, several vehicles arrived. Chuck was in one of them."

"Oh no! What's happened?"

"I heard them say something about a flying accident, but I didn't wait to get any details."

Pearl frantically scanned the room. "What will Lieutenant Baxter say when she sees I'm gone?" She bit her lip. "Oh, but I have to go."

"Don't fret. Just go." Ruth patted her arm and gave her a gentle shove toward the door.

Without looking back, Pearl hurried out of the ward. Her black lace-up shoes tapped a sharp, steady rhythm on the tile floors as she sped along the corridor. At the door to Casualty she stopped and inhaled sharply. Her hand was shaking as she grasped the door handle and pulled open the heavy door.

She stepped into the room and stood still, glancing anxiously around her. Behind the nearest screen, there was a lot of activity and noise. She crept forward and peered around the screen. A doctor and several nurses surrounded a uniformed man lying on the table. Blood covered the patient's clothes and the floor. It had spattered the doctor's white coat. He was leaning over the patient, pumping his chest. She couldn't see the patient's face but he was about the same size as Chuck. It could only be him.

Oh my goodness, he's hurt really badly. He was spared from the crash and he wasn't supposed to be flying today. We were going for a walk after I finished my shift. This can't be happening.

Pearl stood, unable to move, as she watched the staff working on the patient. The doctor pumped his chest forcefully for several minutes then stopped and straightened up. He shook his head at the nurse standing nearest to him.

Pearl moaned deep in her throat. They couldn't just stop. There must be something they could do. They couldn't just let him go. Forgetting that she shouldn't be there, she edged closer to the table. She wanted to hold Chuck's hand; maybe his spirit would know she was there. The doctor and nurses turned to look at her as she approached.

"What are you doing here?" the nurse standing nearest to her asked.

Pearl couldn't speak. She craned her neck to see Chuck's face. As she did so, she noticed that the patient had red hair, not dark like Chuck's.

She stared at the nurse blankly. "Chuck was brought in here."

"Who?"

"That's not him. Pilot Officer Walker. A flying accident."

"This serviceman was involved in a road accident with his motorbike outside the castle gates. Two other soldiers were also brought in," the doctor said.

Pearl was aware of someone approaching behind her. A hand grasped her arm firmly.

"Walker's over there," the voice behind her said.

Pearl turned to see Flight Sergeant Barrett holding her arm. She mumbled an apology to the staff and let him lead her out of the cubicle and across the room.

"I'll warn you it's not a pretty sight." He bent over and coughed for several seconds then straightened up.

"What happened? He wasn't supposed to be flying today."

"We weren't on a mission but we were doing circuits and bumps – practicing take-offs and landings. Ground crew must not have loaded the dummy depth charges properly, and they broke

318

free from their fastenings during one of our runs. We had to make a hard turn when another kite came in from the wrong direction. The smoke outta them filled the cabin. We couldn't see or barely breathe. Walker climbed up and opened a hatch to let the smoke out and he nearly got sucked out of the plane. Got really banged up."

"Oh my goodness!"

"We're all here – 'cause of the smoke. But Walker's the worst. I'm sure he cracked some ribs as well as the gash on his thigh. Rest of us just sucked in some smoke. Maybe a few bruises."

Pearl noticed that there were several men in flying gear sitting outside a cubicle. They were coughing periodically but didn't look badly injured. A couple of them raised their hands in greeting.

"How's Walker?" one of the crewmen asked Flt. Sgt Barrett. "Can't get a crew home without the navigator."

"I'll check on him," the airman replied.

He stepped behind the curtain and Pearl followed him. She had to stifle a gasp when she saw Chuck lying on the table. This time she had no doubt it was the right patient despite the cuts and bruises on his face. His jacket had been removed and his shirt was unbuttoned. Two nurses were hovering over him. His left trouser left was ripped open to the top of the leg, and one of the nurses was cutting off his trousers. His boots had been flung into the corner of the cubicle.

"Shouldn't he have a doctor fixing him up?" Flt. Sgt Barrett asked the nurses.

One of them looked up at him. "Doctor will be with him as soon as he can. There were three soldiers injured in a motor accident outside the gates. He has to tend to them first."

"Well, my buddy looks like he needs a doctor," Flt. Sgt Barrett said doggedly.

"Don't worry, he's doing fine," the nurse replied.

Flt. Sgt Barrett turned to Pearl and gave her a half smile. She appreciated his attempt to reassure her. At the same time, the nurse spotted her.

"What are you doing here?"

"He's my – my – fella. I'm walking out with him." Pearl fumbled out the words but she stood her ground. She wouldn't be chased away. She had to know that Chuck was okay. His face was grey beneath the bruises and his eyes were closed.

The nurse nodded acceptance of her explanation then looked around the cubicle. She seemed to be searching for something.

"Where's Miss Elliott?" the nurse asked.

"Helping with the motor accident patients," the second nurse replied.

The nurse who seemed to be in charge looked at Pearl. "The auxiliary nurse is busy. I need some fresh dressings. Run to Supplies and get me gauze pads and bandages and tape."

Pearl lingered for another look at Chuck. He still hadn't stirred. She didn't think he even knew she was there. Then she hurried out of the room and down the corridor to Supplies. She returned a few minutes later, laden with the items she had been instructed to get, and set them down on the counter behind the nurse.

She edged in to stand beside Chuck and refused to back away, shifting only enough to let the nurses work. The first nurse unwound the makeshift bandage that had been tied around his thigh and handed it to the second one, who discarded the soiled wrappings. Pearl winced as she saw the blood on the bandage but didn't look away. As she watched them work, she noticed the hard muscles in Chuck's thigh and remembered how it felt when his legs brushed against her as they danced and when they stole a few minutes alone at the end of an evening. She felt heat flood her face.

A nurse popped her head around the curtain. "We need some help over here with the motor accident victims."

The nurse who seemed to be in charge said to the other one, "You go on. I'll manage here." She looked at Pearl. "Come and give me a hand, honey."

"I-I'm not an auxiliary – just a volunteer," Pearl said. She realised after she spoke that her white uniform and veil would have told the nurse this.

"Can't be picky when we're short staffed. Just take these wrappings from me and discard them like Lieutenant Thompson was doing."

Pearl knew she could do that. She didn't know what Lieutenant Baxter would say if she found out. The nurse had sternly warned the volunteers that they were not to do any nursing duties. But there didn't seem to be a choice. And she wanted to help Chuck. She glanced at his face for any sign that he was coming around, but his eyes remained closed. His breathing was shallow and fast.

The nurse worked quickly, keeping Pearl busy gathering and discarding the bandages. When almost all the layers had been removed, she braced herself to see the wound. She would not faint or run from the cubicle. She'd look away if she had to, but she wouldn't show how much it upset her. She had to do this.

As the nurse prepared to remove the last layer of the bandages, an urgent voice called through the curtain, "Can you spare anyone? We need another hand."

"Sorry, I can't leave this patient." The nurse raised her head and glanced to see who had spoken as she pulled away the last layer of bandage, frowning at the curtain.

Suddenly blood started gushing from the wound.

"Oh no!" Pearl dropped the soiled bandages

she had been holding into the bag and grabbed a gauze pad from the counter. She pressed it firmly against the wound but blood continued to seep out.

Her strangled cry caught the nurse's attention. "Keep pressing. Hard as you can while I cut the dressing."

Pearl wasn't sure whether she could press hard enough to stop the bleeding, but she leaned her weight on the wound and held on tightly. She could feel blood oozing through the pad, but she held it tightly as she had been instructed to do, praying the nurse would work quickly.

"I can feel the blood coming through," she said.

"Just keep the pressure on it. I'll have this ready in a second," the nurse replied.

Although she was working quickly, the nurse appeared calm. Pearl could only trust that all would be well. She glanced up and saw Flt. Sgt Barrett standing by the curtain, his worried eyes watching her. She gave him a small smile to reassure him, as he had done for her earlier. She didn't feel the confidence she projected but she knew she mustn't show it. She glanced at Chuck's face once more. His eyes fluttered and opened for a second but closed again.

"Right. Let's get this bandaged again." The nurse was standing beside Pearl. "Let go when I tell you."

The nurse nodded and Pearl moved her hands away from the wound. She watched as the nurse deftly wound the new bandages on top of the gauze pad. After the first couple rounds Pearl stepped back and let the nurse finish the bandage. She moved to stand at Chuck's shoulder, gently stroking it, praying that he would be okay.

When the nurse had finished dressing the wound, she looked up. "Thank you for your help. I definitely needed a second pair of hands. The wound is deeper than I expected, so we'll have to ask Doctor to stitch it. You can stay with him, if you like, while we wait for Doctor."

United States Army Station Hospital, Necarne Castle, Irvinestown, County Fermanagh
The next evening

"You don't know how lucky you are to have that girl, Walker." Flt. Sgt Barrett spoke emphatically to his crewmate lying in the hospital bed. "The nurse was distracted and she jumped in and stopped you bleeding all over everything."

Pearl blushed. "I didn't do much. Just stopped the bleeding for a couple minutes. The nurse put a new dressing on until Doctor could stitch it."

"But if you hadn't noticed the bleeding and stopped it, he'd have lost a lot of blood. That couldn't be good." Flt. Sgt Barrett gave Pearl an admiring glance.

"I'm glad you were there," Chuck said.

Chuck's eyes were half-closed but they brightened as he looked at her. When he smiled, she barely noticed the bruising on the one side of his face where he had hit his cheek against the edge of the hatch. She just saw the warm grin that was meant for her.

"How is Pilot Officer Walker, Miss Grainger?"

Pearl jumped. She hadn't heard Lieutenant Baxter walk up behind her. She would really be in trouble now. She shouldn't have gone to Casualty to see Chuck yesterday, and she shouldn't be standing talking to a patient when she had work to do.

"I was just getting Pilot Officer Walker a glass of water," Pearl said hastily.

"See that you continue to look after him as well as you have been doing," Lieutenant Baxter said.

Pearl felt her cheeks burning. "I'm sorry for leaving the ward without permission, ma'am."

"You know you shouldn't have done that. But, in the circumstances, Pilot Officer Walker is fortunate that you were there when we were short staffed. You kept a level head and acted quickly. Things might not have gone so well for him otherwise. Good work."

"Thank you, ma'am."

"But, don't take this as an excuse to disobey orders in future. If you continue to do as you're told and learn, you will make a good nurse one day."

"But – I'm only a volunteer."

"Yes, but you can aspire to train as a nurse. You have the capability. With solid training, you would make a good nurse. Meanwhile, get on with your work and let Pilot Officer Walker rest." Lieutenant Baxter strode away without looking back.

Chuck smiled at her. "Looks like you are an important part of the team. Maybe I was wrong. Seems this is exactly where you should be."

Pearl felt as if a weight had been lifted from her chest. At last Chuck understood she had a job to do here and accepted it – even praised her ability. A grin spread across her face and her eyes shone as she looked at him.

Chuck gave her a mock-serious look but his eyes twinkled. "Of course it'll be good to have my own private nurse while I'm here. Between my leg and the cracked ribs, I'll be confined to bed for a few weeks and will need a lot of attention."

"Well, I can't overstep my place –"

Chuck laughed. "I'm glad you did yesterday. And I'm glad that I didn't talk you out of working here."

"But I'll be here every day and will be with you as much as I can between my other duties."

"Swell. That's my girl."

As Pearl lightly caressed his shoulder, the men in nearby beds cheered and banged cutlery against their bed frames, reminding her that she must soon collect the evening tea trays. She gave Chuck another smile and, before she pushed the cart to the next bed, she whispered to him, "Always your girl. See you later".

When she had started working here last month, she never thought she would survive the first day. Keeping her pledge to herself hadn't been easy. But, she was still here, and now she knew she could cope with whatever came her way, no matter how long this War lasted.

About the Author

Dianne Ascroft is a Torontonian who has settled in rural Northern Ireland. She and her husband live on a small farm with an assortment of strong willed animals.

The Yankee Years is her series of novels and short reads, set during World War II in County Fermanagh, Northern Ireland. Life in the county would never be the same again after the arrival of American, British and Canadian troops during the war. These books weave exciting and romantic tales of the era. She began publishing the series in June 2015.

Her previous fiction works include *An Unbidden Visitor* (a tale inspired by Fermanagh's famous Coonian ghost), *Dancing Shadows, Tramping Hooves: A Collection of Short Stories* (contemporary tales) and an historical novel, *Hitler and Mars Bars*, which explores Operation Shamrock, a little known Irish Red Cross humanitarian endeavour.

She writes both fiction and non-fiction. Her articles and short stories have been printed in Canadian and Irish magazines and newspapers. She also writes as Dianne Trimble.

For more information about the author and her books, visit
her website: www.dianneascroft.com

her Facebook page:
www.facebook.com/DianneAscroftwriter

Twitter: @DianneAscroft

Sign up for her newsletter:
http://eepurl.com/bn_Bjz

CPSIA information can be obtained
at www.ICGtesting.com
Printed in the USA
LVOW12s1906260317
528538LV00001B/283/P